FLIP.

FLY.

STICK.

Other Titles by
Ruth Anne Crews:
Roses

FLIP. FLY. STICK.

RUTH ANNE CREWS

Author Photo by Chase Parker
Cover Design by The Very Mary Designs

ISBN (Print): 9781735909226
ISBN (EPub): 9781735909233

Library of Congress Control Number: 2024915270

Published in Albany, GA

To Paw Paw, Ray Brown, who like Coach Ray always believed in me even when I didn't believe in myself

To Addi Ford, who was the tiny, fiery redhead that inspired this version of Addison. I'm so thankful to call you my sister!

To the elite gymnasts who have inspired me and the rest of the world, thank you for being brave enough to try!

And most importantly to the Author and Perfector of my faith, who put this story in my heart and gave me the desire to write it.

Dear Reader,

This book is my love letter to the sport of gymnastics and the elite world. In 2004, I fell in love with this world when I watched Carly Patterson win the all-around. That experience inspired my very first story about a gymnast named McKenzie Carver (see if you can find her in this one!). I've been a proud member of the gymnernet since early 2016. Since then, I cannot begin to tell you how many hours I have spent watching, reading, and writing about gymnastics. Before you start this book, there are a few things you need to know.

First, if you don't know all the ins and outs of elite gymnasts or are more of a college gymnastics fan, there is a glossary in the back. It explains a little and covers terms and moves that might be confusing for you. I also put the glossary online so you can see some of the moves if the descriptions aren't enough for you. You can find it at ruthannecrews.com/gymnastics.

Second, in order to tell a story that felt true to the gymnasts' world, I felt that this book needed to include an abuse storyline. While it is not front and center, it's there as emotional and verbal abuse. If that is something that is triggering for you, please take care of yourself. It is my sincere hope and prayer that abuse will no longer be the norm in the world of gymnastics, because it's never okay. I'm grateful for people like Jessica O'Beirne of the Gymcastic Podcast, who are constantly calling for change. If you are experiencing any of the things going on with Scarlett and her coaches, please tell someone.

Finally, I want you to know that I consulted with Kerry Blair (@ thegymnastrd on Instagram) to make sure the meals I mentioned for Addison were well-balanced. She is wonderful and is working hard to make sure that gymnasts are properly fueled. I know that food can be a touchy subject in the gymnastics world, and I wanted to make sure I handled it properly.

Okay, I think that's everything you need to know. Enjoy Addison's Journey!

Love,

Ruth Anne

CHAPTER ONE

"Here we go." Addison Jessup fist-bumped her best friend, Catesby Holland as they waited for the competition to start on night two of the Olympic Trials. This was the night that would determine their future—the night all their hard work would finally pay off. The Olympic team was going to be named at the end of competition, and they had set themselves up well. Catesby was in third after the first night of competition, and Addison was in first, which meant she was close to securing the only guaranteed spot on the team.

She was acutely aware of the camera trained on her even though other girls would compete before her. She hated the attention; it made her feel anxious. But she knew it was part of being at the top. She settled into a middle split, pushing her freckled face to the ground with her fiery red French braid bouncing as she did. Addison's headphones were blasting her floor music, and she was doing her best to ignore the competition going on around her. When she felt a hand on her back, she recognized the signal that her turn was getting close. She put her headphones away and pulled off her warmup. Her coach, Ray Markum, looked over at her, his clear green eyes sparkling as a smile spread behind his dark bushy mustache. Addison was starting on floor, which was by far her best event. Even though he was both her coach and uncle, Ray didn't bother to say anything to her as she mounted the podium. She knew what she was doing when it came to floor, and her touch warm up had gone well.

Once Addison saw the start signal, she saluted the judges by throwing her hands in the air and walked out to hit her opening pose. An instrumental version of Rachel Platten's "Fight Song" came through the speakers. Addison backed into the corner for her opening pass, took a deep breath, and took off running, launching into the hardest pass of her routine. Clean landing, but she saw the flag go up out of the corner of her eye. It meant she stepped out of bounds, but she was fine with the one tenth deduction that came with it. She twirled and leaped into the opposite corner and finished her routine with all the strength, grace, and power she could muster. This was her favorite event and the biggest reason she should make the team, so she was going to make it as perfect as possible.

When she finished, Addison high-fived Catesby on her way off the podium. "Good luck," she encouraged her best friend and training partner, the blonde bun on Catesby's head bobbing with every step.

"Great job; three more just like that," Ray swallowed Addison in a hug.

Turning back to the floor, Addison cheered as Catesby's floor music started. "Let's go, Cates! You got this!" Addison knew Catesby's routine almost as well as she knew her own because they trained together day in and day out. She hit her first pass well and danced across the floor for her second pass. Catesby even managed to land the double layout in the third pass properly. She finished with her signature flourish and jumped off the podium into the waiting arms of her coaches.

"Nicely done, Catesby." Ray was all smiles as Gwyn, their assistant coach, high-fived her. Ray encouraged the girls to get prepped for vault as they waited for the rotation to end.

"Flip. Fly. Stick," Ray called as Addison stood waiting on the all clear from the judges. Her warm-up vault had been great, and she knew she was capable of winning this competition just like she had won Nationals. She saw the start signal and sped off down the runway. She started her round-off in the exact right spot and pushed off the vault table with all the power she could muster. Addison flew high in the air as she yanked her arms in. She was easily able to complete the two and a half twists she needed. She landed and willed herself not to move, only needing to take a few small steps to steady herself. The crowd went nuts as she saluted the judges. She hopped off the podium, grinning as she hugged her uncle.

"That was amazing, Addi," Ray grinned. "Pure perfection."

"I took a couple steps," Addison countered, ever the gymnast with a perfectionist mindset.

"It's one tenth each; you're still going to put up a massive score," Ray couldn't seem to stop smiling.

Scarlett Peterson, the black girl who was probably Addison's biggest competition, was getting ready to start on bars; but before she could, the crowd erupted in cheers again as Addison's score was posted on the big screen.

"Fantastic job," Ray beamed.

"I'm making this team, aren't I?" Addison knew she had earned a good score, but she was hoping he wouldn't say anything that would mess with her head. She had learned over the years that she performed better when she didn't know her exact score.

"No one can touch you at this point," Ray smiled, and Addison felt herself relax ever so slightly. She still had two rotations to go.

"Wow, Addi! That was the best vault I've ever seen you do! Maybe even the best I've ever seen." Gwyn grinned from ear to ear. Addison half-smiled and did her best not to roll her eyes. While she was thankful for Gwyn, sometimes she thought the assistant coach tried too hard. No matter how hard Addison tried, she couldn't shake the idea that Gwyn was a replacement for her mom after her death a couple years earlier.

Catesby was next on vault and nailed her Amanar—the same vault as Addison. When Catesby was finished, she found Addison trying to stay warm by sitting in her middle split with her eyes closed. Catesby knew that meant Addison was visualizing her bars routine.

"Your vault was impressive," Catesby said, sliding into her own middle split across from Addison.

"Thanks." Addison looked up reluctantly, knowing Catesby had more to say.

"He seems more relaxed tonight," Catesby continued, nodding towards their coach.

"Oh, he's already thinking about training camp and the Olympics. He's not worried about us," Addison chuckled.

"Really? I just can't believe that would be true." Catesby looked nervous.

"Catesby, if he was worried about us, he would be sitting here encouraging us and going over routines with us. Plus, we're headed to bars, and you are the bars queen," Addison reminded her best friend, hoping the encouragement would be enough to end the conversation so she could get back to visualizing her own routine.

"I guess you're right. But let's not forget, I didn't get the highest score on bars on night one." Catesby flattened herself to the floor, and Addison caught a glimpse of the silver eye shadow that went with the gold on her own eyelids. Silver and gold: their goal for tonight and for the Olympic all-around.

"So do better today. I know you can." Catesby shrugged, and Addison rolled her eyes. "Tell me your routine," she insisted. The best friends fell into their normal competition habits. They spent the next few minutes going over their routines with each other, waiting on the rotation to end.

"Addi! That vault was awesome," one of the girls said as the group transitioned to the next rotation. Addison thanked her, music blaring through the one headphone she still had in her ear.

"Seriously incredible; how do you do that?" someone else said. Addison smiled and stuck her other headphone in. She needed to make sure she was in a good headspace for bars. She set her bag on a chair and pulled her grips out. She was putting them on when she felt a hand on her shoulder. She popped out one of the headphones.

"You good?" Ray asked.

"Yeah, I'm just ready for this to be over." Addison's fingers grazed the words "You can do this!" written on her grips. Her cousin, Tate, had written it in during Addison's Achilles recovery on one of those days when Addison wasn't sure she would get to Olympic Trials at all. Tate had the advantage of knowing exactly what it took to get to the Olympics because she had done it herself, eight years ago, which made her the perfect person to encourage Addison.

"Breathe. Two more rotations; just do it like you normally would," Ray encouraged her. Addison chalked up and warmed up and then stood on the edge of the podium waiting for her turn.

Scarlett started on beam first, so Addison was stuck waiting. In a normal competition, of course, she could have just done her routine at the same time, but this was Olympic Trials. The news networks were timing the routines to make sure the biggest Olympic hopefuls were being shown on the television broadcast, and the selection committee wanted to see everyone's routines to make sure they picked the right five athletes to represent America in the Rome Olympics.

As soon as Scarlett landed her beautiful double Arabian dismount, Addison saw the signal to start on bars. Ray nodded, and Addison bounced off the springboard onto the high bar. She swung around the bar and started her releases before transitioning to the low bar. Once she did her skills on the low bar, she flew back up to the high bar. She grabbed in the right spot and released a small breath; that transition was the hardest part. To finish, she hit her pirouettes and stuck her double layout dismount. She saluted the judges with a big grin on her face. As hard as recovery from her Achilles tear had been, one benefit was that she had been able to majorly upgrade her bars routine.

Addison high-fived Catesby at the chalk bowl on her way off the podium and was greeted with a hug and kiss on the cheek from Ray. She marked Catesby's routine with her, cheering loudly every time she cleared a trouble spot. When Catesby stuck her double twisting double back, Addison's cheers got lost in the roar that went up from the crowd. Addison strained to see their cheering section, which included her dad, aunt, cousin, and grandparents along with Catesby's parents and all five of her siblings. She could just barely see the purple #AddiCates shirts they were all wearing. Catesby bounded off the podium and was greeted with a hug from Ray and Gwyn before running over to Addison.

"That felt amazing! If that's anything like your vault felt, I understand why you're not worried about Coach Ray not being all over us," Catesby laughed, turning to wait for her score. Addison glanced over her shoulder and took off in a tumbling pass to keep her head clear. Her tumbling was almost a nervous habit by this point. Catesby jumped with excitement; she scored the highest she had all season. They spent the rest of the rotation chatting and cheering on their friends.

Brittnee Chase, a former Olympian trying to make the team again, started the final rotation off on floor. She was doing well until she stepped out of bounds with both feet on her third pass. Then she nearly fell out of her final pass but somehow managed to save it. After Brittnee, Catesby started the beam rotation. She had a solid night with only a couple minor bobbles in her usual trouble spots. She high-fived Gwyn, who was their beam coach, and hugged her tightly. The routine had gone the way they planned.

"I hope it's enough to keep me in second. I just want to beat Scarlett," Catesby whispered, staring at the scoreboard.

"You should definitely make the team. You've had a great night," Gwyn said confidently as Catesby's name slid into the first place spot on the big screen. Catesby hugged Gwyn again and relaxed, knowing her competition was over. She had done her job. She had no doubt her performance was good enough to put her on the team.

Meanwhile, Addison found a quiet corner to focus on her beam routine while trying to stay warm. There was so much commotion and craziness going on around her as each of the competitors finished the competition. When it got to be too much, she sank into a middle split and tuned out everything except for the normal sounds of competition—someone's floor music, the creaking of the bars, feet pounding down the vault runway, and the squeaking of the beam. It helped keep her head in a good space.

Addison was the last one going for the night, and all thirteen of the other girls were cheering her on. This moment was one she had been waiting on her entire life. This was her chance to show the world that she really was the best, and she could prove it by making the Olympic team. She flipped, leaped, and spun on the four inch wide beam. When she stuck her full twisting double back perfectly, cheers erupted from her teammates. Ray was waiting for her with a giant hug and kiss on the cheek.

"You did it," he smiled. "You're going to the Olympics." Addison turned and, for the first time all night, watched for her score. When it finally popped up, it sent her name to the top of the scoreboard. Her total score was over a point higher than Catesby's in a sport usually determined by tenths and hundredths. Several of the girls congratulated her as they were all escorted to a back room to wait for the official announcement of the Olympic team.

As the girls entered the room, silence fell. They broke into smaller groups and sat huddled together, each hoping to be one of the five names called. Addison and Catesby sat with hands clasped and their carefully curated playlist playing through the earbuds they shared. Addison couldn't help but think about their conversation at the beginning of the year.

* * * * *

Addison: Age 16 (February of Olympic Year)

"What we do this year, we do together. No matter how things shake out, right?" Addison and Catesby sat in the middle of the floor at their home gym, Elite Gymnastics Academy, stretching. It was about a week until they left for their first competition of the Olympic year.

"Addi"–

"Look, it's been a rough couple years for me okay. My mom and Davis died, and then I tore my Achilles, which meant I missed out on the all-important year before the Olympics. But this year, this Olympic year–this is what we have been working towards forever. I want to do it with you."

"And I want to do it with you. But I'm going to be honest with you, I'm still not sure I can actually do this. Last year feels like some kind of dream, and one day soon I'm going wake up and realize it never actually happened."

"Cates, you are an incredible gymnast," Addison insisted.

"Thanks. I'm excited about this year, but it's still a little crazy that we're actually in the conversation for the Olympics, right?"

"Maybe for you," Addison laughed, only half serious.

"Shut up, hotshot," Catesby shot back with a friendly nudge. "Not all of us have cousins who were Olympians. Not to mention the fact that you've been training with elites since you were in diapers and could do a back handspring at four." Catesby leaned back, taking a moment before their practice really got started.

"Dream year, what happens?" Addison slid into her middle split and looked expectantly at her best friend.

"On the podium at Nationals, make the Olympic team, team gold medal, go 1 and 2 with you in the all-around, bars champion," Catesby listed off. "You?"

"National Champion, win Olympic trials, team gold, all-around gold, make all four event finals, and floor champion," Addison grinned.

"But if I beat you in the all-around?" Catesby asked, cocking her head slyly.

"Good luck with that. But I'd be okay with it—only because it's you," Addison giggled.

"I am the reigning world silver medalist. And if any of this doesn't happen?" The question hung in the air, neither one of the girls willing to give credence to it.

"Then we'll deal with it," Addison finally said. "But it is all going to happen. This is our year—it's what Uncle Ray and Mom have been preparing us for since we became elite gymnasts."

"Strive for perfection--" Catesby started.

"Even if perfection is unattainable," they finished together and burst into laughter.

"But yes," Catesby reiterated, returning to the beginning of their conversation, "What we do this year, we do together. No matter what happens at the end. You're my best friend. There is no one else I'd rather be on this journey with. We can do this; it's what we've been working towards. We'll do it for Coach Ashley. And for Davis, who would definitely have been at every single competition this year with some embarrassing sign."

"Just to get on TV. Like they weren't going to show him," Addison rolled her eyes. "Is Columbus going to take up the job of embarrassing us, now?"

"Doubtful, just because my mother would stop him before anything could actually happen," Catesby laughed. "What does that say? No, there is no way I'm letting you hold that sign up on national television," Catesby said in her best impression of her mother.

"Momma Ginny," Addison shook with laughter. "Oh well, it's probably a good thing. And for the record, I wouldn't want to do this with anyone else either."

* * * * *

Catesby squeezed Addison's hand as the song in their ears changed to "Fighter" by Jung Youth and Sam Tinnesz, pulling Addison from the memory. She looked around, marveling at how no one talked above a whisper, as though it would somehow disrupt the sanctity of the room. Seconds felt like hours, and minutes like days as they waited for the door to open. Finally, the doorknob jiggled, and all fourteen elite gymnasts snapped to attention. Addison quickly hit pause and stuffed her phone and earbuds back into her bag as her breath caught in her throat.

CHAPTER TWO

"Your artistic gymnastics team for the Rome Olympics: Addison Jessup, Catesby Holland, Scarlett Peterson, Brittnee Chase, and Waverly Miller," the announcer called. Each name seemed to reverberate around the stadium as the girls walked out in their new Olympic warmups carrying bouquets of red, white, and blue flowers. Ray nodded as each name was called. The team was going to be well balanced. Scarlett was a great compliment to Addison's intensity as long as she didn't get too down on herself the way he'd noticed at recent competitions. Brittnee had the Olympic and international experience that the team needed and was going to be able to step fully into the leadership role she had developed. Waverly was going to be able to use her college experience to pull the team together and keep them cheering for each other. All of them had spent their lives working towards this moment. They were joined on the podium by the men's team in addition to the rhythmic gymnasts and the trampoline and tumbling team. They took photos until the happy tears were replaced with pure joy.

"Addi!" Addison spun on her heel as she walked out

of the arena, not entirely sure where she had left her bag. She was running on a full adrenaline high and still wasn't convinced that she had actually made the Olympic team after spending so long trying to.

"Daddy!" Addison ran into his waiting open arms.

"You did it! I'm so proud of you," Luke Jessup whispered in his daughter's ear. Addison relaxed into him; he was her safe place. And this moment was something they had been working towards and dreaming of for nearly her entire life. It just looked different than she thought it would without Davis to cheer her on and her mom to help coach her.

"This is real, right? I'm not going to wake up tomorrow and realize it was all an elaborate dream?" Addison looked up at him.

"It's real. Tomorrow you get to celebrate with all of us at your Olympian breakfast," Luke laughed and squeezed her tighter. Because elite gymnastics was so different from other sports, when she was at a competition, he didn't get to see much of her. But he was still her dad, and Luke knew her well enough to know that she was hungry and tired. "I'll see you tomorrow, my little Olympian," he assured her as he kissed her head and sent her on her way.

The moment with her dad grounded her, and Addison made her way back to the locker room, where she had finally realized she left all her stuff. That evening, Ray and Gwyn made sure that Addison and Catesby had a good meal before crashing in their beds for their first sleep as Olympians.

"Good Morning! Breakfast in Conference Room C in thirty minutes," someone said too cheerfully when Addison answered the phone's blaring ring the next morning. Addison groaned and hung up. She rolled over to find Catesby's bed empty; not a complete surprise. Addison found an outfit in her mess of a suitcase and put on a little makeup, somehow managing not to be late for the breakfast. The day after competition was always hard. Normally she slept until the afternoon, but there was no time for that this morning.

"There she is," her Aunt Julie exclaimed, breathing a sigh of relief as Addison sat down at the table. "I was about to go up to your room."

"Sorry," Addison muttered, still not fully awake.

"Mom was just worried because you never responded to her text, but I called up to your room earlier," Tate grinned.

"Thank you; that was what woke me up," Addison laughed. She should have known it was her cousin. Tate had been to the Olympics before and knew Addison better than almost anyone.

"I figured," Tate shrugged. "You ready for this?"

Addison simply shook her head and started looking around for some coffee. She didn't normally drink it, but this morning called for some caffeine.

"Here," Ray offered, setting a cup down in front of her. His ability to anticipate her needs was just one of the things that made him a great coach. "You're going to need it," he laughed.

Tate giggled as Addison took a huge swig and grimaced. "I remember being where you are. But it's real, Addi Anne, so get used to it. Just take it one day at time."

An American Gymnastics Federation official tapped the mic to get their attention. "To the families of our Olympians, welcome. We are thrilled to know who is going to be representing us in the Rome Olympics in just a couple weeks. We cannot wait to see how well you all do." She spent time talking about the athletes and what the team hoped to accomplish.

After the meal, the gymnasts had contracts to sign. Once the legal part was over, Addison breathed a sigh of relief. She was officially going to the Olympics. The five brand-new teammates grinned at each other; this experience was something no one could ever take from them.

"Now that you are all officially Olympians," the official said, winking, as she collected the contracts, "Your first Olympic duty is a photoshoot."

"Olympic leos," Addison said in a reverent tone as she reached out to touch them. They were full of bling in all their red, white, and blue glory.

"I'll give you a minute to look through them all," the American Gymnastics Federation official said. "These are the competition leotards, and the training tanks are on the rack in the back. Pick your favorite of each, and we'll see who gets to wear what for the photo shoot." She stepped away to take care of some business and let the girls explore on their own.

Addison, in true fashion, went straight for the leos that were mostly blue. To her surprise, there were several for her to choose from. The first one she pulled out was royal blue with sparkles placed to look like a necklace. She liked it, but she wanted to see what her other options were.

"Here, this is yours," Catesby asserted, handing her a blue ombre leo with sheer silver sleeves and red, white, and blue crystals.

"This is one of the Olympic leos?" Addison's eyebrows shot up as she marveled over the perfection of the outfit Catesby found.

"Yeah," Catesby laughed. "I'm pretty sure I've seen this exact design in your dream folder at home."

Addison shook her head, marveling at it. "You're so right."

"Now, help me find something," Catesby demanded, laughing again. The friends turned back to the racks in front of them. They looked though all eight of the long-sleeved competition leos before moving to the sleeveless practice leos on the other rack. The girls were all geeking out about them, looking at the materials, designs, and crystals. Soon enough, all five girls were holding different leos.

Addison had the one that she was sure was made for her. Catesby had a red practice leo with blue and white stars on the top part. Brittnee had also opted for a practice leo, but hers was an icy blue color with a USA written in crystals in the center of the chest, it pulled out the icy blue in her eyes and looked beautiful with her light brown hair. Waverly chose to model the competition leo the girls had agreed they would probably wear for the team final. It was a shiny blue on top with a sheer sparkly stripe starting from the v-neck and continuing down the sleeves. Under the stripe, it was shiny red with white side cut-outs. It made her look regal and ready for competition, her beachy blonde waves falling perfectly over the shoulders—her confidence easy to see, something that they would all need in the coming weeks. Following Waverly's lead, Scarlett had also opted for a competition leo. It had a sheer, skin-tone top with a metallic blue body and a red belt with plenty of sparkles. It looked great on her dark skin. Once the photographer had approved their choices, the girls went to change.

"Blue is definitely your color," Brittnee said as Addison walked out of the dressing room adjusting her leo, her fiery red hair spilling out like a lion's mane around her face, curls too unruly to be tamed.

"Thank you, it's my favorite. This leo is perfectly me," Addison said. "That's a fun training tank."

"It is, isn't it?" Brittnee traced the USA.

"Team final? Right?" Waverly said, looking over her shoulder in the mirror at her own outfit.

"I would think so. Either that one or the one with the white bottom portion," Brittnee said. Addison was struck by how much Brittnee was already acting like the leader. She was thankful for it because someone needed to fill that role.

It was going make choosing their team captain easier when the time came.

Scarlett walked out of the dressing room, and Waverly exclaimed, "Oo, I didn't notice that one!"

"I grabbed it pretty quickly because I knew I wanted it," Scarlett said, a grin spreading across her face.

"That is not the leo you picked," Addison said when Catesby walked out in a bright blue practice leo that was clearly a replica of the one with the sparkly neckline.

"I think because I was only one who opted for a red base, the photographer suggested this one instead," Catesby shrugged. "But I like this one," she added.

"It's beautiful," Waverly said. "I almost picked that competition leo."

"Me too," Scarlett admitted, and they all burst into laughter.

"Save those grins for the camera, Ladies," the photographer said, getting them back on track. "Hair and makeup is that way." He pointed them towards a row of lighted mirrors. Brittnee led the way as they got ready for the shoot. The girls talked and laughed as each of them had their hair and makeup done.

"Everyone ready?" the photographer asked when he reappeared.

"I just finished the last one," the makeup artist said, sending them on their way.

"This is supposed to be fun, so relax and be yourselves," the photographer coached them. He put Addison in the center with Catesby and Scarlett on either side of her and Brittnee and Waverly on the outsides of the group. "Let me see your best competition faces," the photographer said. The five girls looked at each other and then got serious. It only lasted a few moments before Brittnee laughed. It was infectious and soon they were all laughing.

"Why is laughter our response to awkwardness?"

Waverly asked.

"I don't know, but it works every time," Catesby said.

"Okay, I want you to walk towards me," the photographer said. The girls did what he asked.

"Who's ready for Rome?" Waverly asked.

"We gonna bring home that gold medal?" Brittnee added, and rest of them cheered.

They spent another hour or so taking photos together and laughing. "We did it," Addison reveled as they finished up. She was surprised how tiring standing and smiling for so long could be.

"That we did," Brittnee grinned. The Olympians changed and were each given the full leo collection to take home with them.

"Today was fun! I'm excited to go to Rome with you all," Waverly said.

"And bring home that gold medal," Scarlett added defiantly.

"Definitely," Catesby agreed. "Since that leo was practically made for you, I think it should be the one we wear for the Olympic celebration when we get home from the Olympics." Catesby motioned to the blue ombre leo that Addison had on.

"Look at you thinking ahead. I like that plan, but we have the sendoff first," Addison reminded her best friend.

CHAPTER THREE

"How's it going in here?" Tate poked her head into Addison's room where clothes and makeup were strewn everywhere.

"I'm overthinking everything," Addison laughed as she plopped down on the floor, managing to avoid the piles around her.

"Do you want my advice?" The strawberry blonde found an empty spot to sit.

"Always," Addison smiled.

"Take your leo collection, undergarments, pajamas, and like two outfits. You are going to get more stuff than you know what to do with, and you'll want to have room in your suitcase to bring it all home. You remember how much I came home with," Tate laughed.

"I didn't even think about that! You got a ton of stuff." Addison did remember the bags of gear Tate had come home with from the Olympics. She remembered watching in awe as her cousin modeled warmups, leos, t-shirts and showed off all the other things she had received.

"They are going to want everyone to wear the Team USA gear while you're practicing and all that. I didn't even wear half the things I packed," Tate admitted.

"What about my gym stuff?" Addison packed her new leo collection, all her underwear, pajamas, and a small stack of clothes and started to put things away that she didn't need to take.

"You know what you need for an international competition. Why are you asking me?" Tate reached for a pile of clothes to fold.

"Because I'm going to the Olympics, Tate," Addison shook her head. "I can't focus on anything other than that. I can't even handle the little things like my hair stuff, because if I pack it now then I can't use it before I leave, or maybe I can—see?"

"Breathe, Addi," Tate instructed her, rolling her eyes. "You are never going to win those six medals you're hoping for if you can't calm down."

"Who said anything about six medals?" Addison bit her lip, trying to stop a grin. She and Tate had always been competitive, and Addison was going to do her best to beat Tate's medal count—or at the very least tie it with five medals. Tate stared at her for a moment before standing up and walking over to the open closet door. The front was covered in pictures from Addison's gymnastics meets and others of friends and family. The back of the door, however, had one single piece of paper taped to it.

"Did you *really* think you were the only one who knew about this?" Tate pointed at the paper.

"Honestly? Yes," Addison said. "How did you find it?"

"I had to pack your suitcase for Classic, remember?" Tate smiled and Addison blew out a breath. She had forgotten that fact. Addison and her dad decided to add on a Red Sox baseball game before Classic and to help Addison enjoy the time with her dad, Tate had packed Addison's gymnastics things. "You've accomplished a lot of things on this list," Tate continued, raising her eyebrows.

"You gave me the idea when we added all the steps on the Road to Rome for my vision board," Addison admitted. She had created her own step-by-step plan to get to Rome for the Olympic year.

"Step one: show I am ready and capable enough to make it to the Olympics by winning Winter Cup," Tate read off. "Your senior debut was spectacular, even after the craziness of the last couple years."

"Took me long enough to have one; it should have been spectacular," Addison said dramatically as she rolled her eyes. Winter Cup had served as her first official competition as senior since she didn't make the Worlds team the year before.

"Step two: win vault at a World Cup to prove I can make the vault final," Tate read the next line on Addison's list. "Well, that didn't go according to plan." She crossed it off and wrote above it, "Have Amanar ready so I can make vault final."

"You're just going to re-write them?" Addison shook her head. She might not have been chosen to go to World Cup but it hadn't affected her year at all. It was a pipe dream after the two years she'd had.

"Why have things you didn't accomplish on your 'How to Get to Rome' list?"

Addison sighed, Tate was right. "At least I proved I could do it at Classic."

"Well, you just walked straight into step three, didn't you?" Tate laughed. "Step three: dominate at Classic to set things up for Nationals."

Addison burst into laughter. "Dominate might have been a bit of wishful thinking. Classic was so rough."

"Classic is always rough. But you overshot your Amanar for the first time ever. You managed to put up a decent bars score since you actually stayed on the bar for the whole routine."

"Step three: have routines ready so I can become National Champion," Addison said, and Tate wrote it. "Step four: become National Champion."

"You sure did," Tate grinned. "In Greensboro, just like me. Ten years apart."

"Yeah, well, next I'm coming for your medal count and that all-around gold," Addison taunted, pursing her lips.

"All-around gold you can have, but we'll see about that medal count," Tate laughed.

"My bars have come a long way," Addison added quickly.

"They have, but we'll see if you can stay on the bars long enough to pull out a medal," Tate shot back.

"You're not helping." Addison rolled her eyes.

"Of course I am! Step five: secure the only guaranteed spot on the Olympic team. Done and done," Tate said. "Even when you're all the way in Rome, though, you'd better not forget who taught you how to do a back handspring!"

"I could never," Addison smiled as she remembered the night fondly.

★ ★ ★ ★ ★

Addison: Age 4

"Go USA!" Addison slid into a split as the broadcast started on the TV.

"Go Gwyn!" Davis cheered from his spot on the couch. The family was gathered in the Jessup's living room to watch Team USA at the team final in Paris where Ray and Ashley were coaching Gwyn Sullivan. They were all hoping for a medal that night. It was a little later than her parents would normally have let Addison stay up, but Luke knew there was no way his gymnastics loving daughter was going to miss this. Besides, her own mom was there coaching!

The American team was starting on bars, and four year old Addison let out a groan.

"What's wrong?" Luke asked, suppressing a laugh.

"Bars means there's no Gwyn," Addison informed them.

"Yes, but then you get to see her twice in a row for beam and floor," Tate reminded her little cousin. Addison settled in and switched into a middle split, her normal way to watch TV these days. She was enjoying the first rotation and when they showed a floor routine, she stood up and tried to copy as much of it as possible.

"Tate? Will you teach me how to do a back handspring or maybe a back tuck?" she asked as the gymnast on screen finished her final tumbling pass.

"Addi, we're watching the team final. Can we wait until we're at the gym tomorrow?" Tate asked.

"But there are commercials! Please?" the four year old begged.

"You knew that was going to be the answer, right?" Davis looked at his older cousin, his blue eyes sparkling.

"I did, but I had to try," Tate shrugged and Davis laughed. He knew his little sister well enough to know that she was not going to take no for an answer. "Back handspring; you're not ready for a back tuck yet," Tate said to Addison.

"Granddaddy? Can you get the mat from the garage?" Addison asked.

"Sure thing, Sweetness." Franklin headed to get the mat for Addison and Tate.

"Dad, do you need some help?" Luke asked.

"I can handle a mat, Son, enjoy the final," Franklin assured him. He returned a few minutes later and helped the girls get situated in the middle of the living room.

When the competition was on, Addison watched from various positions from the mat. But when Gwyn was on the screen, she stopped everything to watch with rapt attention. During the commercials, Tate helped Addison with her back handspring.

Team USA's final rotation was on vault, which meant they finished before Team Russia who was in the lead. While they waited for Team Russia to finish on the floor, Addison landed her first back handspring. She immediately did ten more, all while venting her frustration that Team USA only won the silver medal. Through it all, Addison kept everyone entertained.

"I don't know what was more exciting, that ending or Addi getting her back handspring," Davis laughed.

"Addi getting her back handspring, for sure," Tate smiled.

"I can't wait to show Brighton tomorrow," Addison grinned.

"She's gonna be so excited," Tate agreed. She knew that the former Elite Gymnastics Academy Olympian who was currently Addison's gymnastics coach was going to be just as thrilled as they were.

"Thank you!" Addison wrapped her fourteen-year-old cousin in a hug. "When you're on the team, you can help them win gold."

"We'll see—that's still four years away," Tate said.

"Yeah, but you're the best gymnast in the world," Davis insisted for the millionth time.

"I love you," Tate answered as she ruffled the six-year-old's hair before turning back to Addison. "Well, if I help them win gold, what will be left for you to do?"

"The same thing." Addison didn't miss a beat and Davis nodded along with her.

"Alright then, that will be two more Olympians for EGA. Bedtime for everyone," Luke said with an approving nod from his sister, Julie. The families said their goodbyes, and everyone headed home. Even after all the excitement, Luke managed to bathe Addison and have her in bed in a reasonable amount of time. With all the traveling Ashley did as a gymnastics coach, Luke had become an expert at the bedtime routine.

"Daddy? Do you think I could really go the Olympics like Gwyn and Brighton?" Addison yawned.

"I think you can. I think you can do anything you set your mind to, just like you did tonight." Luke kissed her forehead, and she was asleep before he even shut the door.

* * * * *

"And look at where you are now, getting ready for the Olympics," Tate said, pulling Addison out of her memories.

"If I can ever finish packing," Addison sighed. As she looked around her room, she couldn't help but wish Davis was here to help them do this.

"You're basically done," Tate shrugged, turning back to the list on Addison's closet door, "But I want to finish this. Step six: qualify for the all-around final and all four event finals."

"That's totally possible, right?" Addison smiled, willing Tate to agree with her. Yes, she was excited and sure of herself but if there was anything on this list that wasn't going to happen, it was making all four finals. She knew that anything was possible in gymnastics.

"Right, the bars final will be a challenge, but it's not impossible," Tate assured her. Addison went back to rearranging the things in the suitcase. The list had started out as her plan for this year, and even if everything hadn't worked out exactly like she hoped it would, she still wanted to accomplish her ultimate goal—winning the all-around. "Step seven: help Team USA win team gold."

"It's going to be close with the team that China is bringing," Addison admitted, "But we can do it."

"You certainly can. Step eight: win the all-around gold medal. That one is yours to lose."

"Not a chance. If I only come home with that medal, I will call it a successful Olympic experience," Addison insisted.

"Really? Because step nine says otherwise," Tate pushed back.

"I mean, I have other plans, yes," Addison admitted, "But the one I want the most is the all-around gold."

"That's fair. Step nine: medal in all four event finals. You really are going after my medal count, aren't you?" Tate asked.

"Five medals in a single games. I want six."

"You always did know how to swing high with your goals," Tate said, shaking her head. "I know your bars routine has come a long way, but I don't know if you will pull off that medal. Are you going to be okay if that doesn't happen?"

"Yeah. I know I will be a little disappointed, but this was meant to be a 'for my eyes only,' shoot for the moon kind of list. You are the one who chose to rewrite earlier steps."

"That makes sense," Tate said, making the decision to leave it as written. "Ah, the final step. Step ten: walk in the closing ceremonies for my birthday."

"I needed a tenth one, so I figured that would work," Addison shrugged. Tate laughed and picked up a pile of things Addison would need in Rome and put them in a nearby suitcase. "So, are you going to tell me anything about this lunch thing?" Addison asked, changing the subject to the event Tate had come to pick her up for.

"It's a lunch for all the Olympians. It's a tradition Brighton started when Gwyn made the team," Tate said. "That's all I will say."

"So, Brighton and Gwyn are going to be there?" Addison asked.

"Is this about Brighton or Gwyn?" Tate knew that Addison loved Brighton but was still adjusting to her new relationship with Gwyn.

"Can we not? Today is about going to the Olympics," Addison shrugged her off.

"You're the one that brought it up!" Tate said defensively.

"Just help me pack so we can maybe leave on time," Addison said as she threw some of her gymnastics gear into the suitcase Tate had started to fill.

"Fine, but to answer your question: yes, they are both going to be at lunch."

CHAPTER FOUR

"Welcome to the Elite Gymnastics Academy Olympic send-off lunch! This is something I randomly started with Gwyn, and it stuck," Brighton Kerry said as they sat around a table at a lunch spot around the corner from the gym. "I still can't believe we have five Olympians from EGA in the last four Olympic games."

"It's certainly exciting to be adding not just one but two of you to the Olympic ranks. And having the privilege of being your coach is just icing on the cake. It has truly been incredible to see you both grow into Olympians over the course of the last year and a half," Gwyn said, beginning to tear up.

"Oh my gah, can we not?" Addison rolled her eyes, ever avoidant of things sentimental and sappy.

"Fine," Gwyn laughed at the dramatic response. "What do you want to talk about then? This is your chance to ask us whatever you want."

"What is one thing we should be sure to do?" Addison asked immediately.

"You want to go ahead and ask the rest of your

questions, too?" Tate broke into a wide grin, and Addison blushed the same color as her hair.

"Let's start with this first one," Brighton laughed. "Experience some of the culture of Italy."

"I would tell you go to an Olympic event that is not gymnastics related so you can see what the Olympics is like for other people," Gwyn said.

"I don't think I have a better answer than those," Tate agreed.

"If you could give yourself one piece of advice before your Olympic experience, what would it be?" Catesby asked, and Addison nodded enthusiastically.

"Work hard and do your best, but be sure to enjoy the experience of the Olympics itself," Gwyn said.

"Journal, take pictures—do whatever works best for you, but be sure to record your experience. You won't remember as much of it as you think you will," Brighton said.

"Truth, but also, just enjoy it. Don't spend all your time worried about competing and the outcomes. This experience is rare. You might get it two times—three, if you're lucky. But this also might be the only time you get to go to the Olympics," Tate said. Addison sighed, knowing she was right. Gymnastics wasn't a sport that had a lot of repeat athletes.

"Okay, this isn't really about the Olympics, but I'm freaking out about training camp," Catesby admitted. "Worlds camp last year was rough, and this is the Olympics, so it's bound to be even tougher, right?"

"It's like Worlds, but it's not," Tate answered unhelpfully before continuing. "Um, for me, I didn't think it was as bad as Worlds. We had spent so much energy worrying about who was going to be on the team, but the coaches trusted that the right decisions had been made. A lot of it was about team bonding and making sure we were hitting routines. They knew the rest would come," Tate explained. The other girls agreed with her.

The rest of lunch continued with talk about what the Olympics were like and what to expect. Checking her watch, Gwyn waved down their server. "I have to go, because I need to be there early. Brighton, can I just take your car to the gym? Then you can ride with Tate, Addi, and Catesby?" she asked.

"Of course. I picked Gwyn up so she didn't have to leave her car at the gym," Brighton explained, handing her keys to Gwyn. Once the check was paid, the rest of them headed to the gym, as well.

"Dang, there are a lot of people here," Catesby remarked as they pulled into the parking lot.

"The Olympics are a big deal," Brighton laughed as Tate pulled into one of the few empty spots.

"Do you think they're ready for us?" Addison asked.

"I'll go find out. Don't come in until someone comes to get you," Tate instructed Addison and Catesby as she climbed out of the car.

Addison watched as her cousin walked into the gym that was her second home. As they waited, she could hear Catesby and Brighton talking, but she wasn't paying attention. Her mind was on all things that were to come and how she wished her mom and Davis were here to experience it with her. She knew Davis would have been waiting outside the gym for her to come in, just to make sure she knew he was here. They would have spent hours talking about what signs he would make to hold up at the arena and how she was going to do everything she wanted and more. She was still staring at the entrance to the gym when Tate re-emerged a few minutes later wearing a purple #AddiCates shirt.

"This is for you, Brighton," Tate said as she threw her a shirt. "Dad said to give them five minutes and then come in." Tate threw Addison and Catesby their own purple shirts. "Five minutes," she repeated as she and Brighton headed back into the gym.

Addison looked at the shirt she was holding. On the front was the Elite Gymnastics Academy logo, and the back said, "Olympian." She pulled out her phone and set a timer to be sure that her Uncle Ray couldn't fault her for coming in too early.

"We are Olympians. And we're headed to training camp in just a few hours. Dreams do come true," Addison squealed as she pulled on the shirt. Catesby couldn't help but wonder if all the dreams they were dreaming would really become a reality, especially since they weren't even sure who was doing the all-around yet.

When the timer went off on Addison's phone, they walked into the gym together. A chorus of congratulations echoed off the walls; all their closest friends and family were there along with supporters and families from the gym. The girls spent a little time talking to various people before Coach Ray called them all together.

"I know Addison and Catesby are thrilled that you were able to be here today. We are looking forward to Rome and bringing home some hardware. At the victory party, we will unveil their official Olympic banners, but until then, this one will have to do." Ray pulled a rope, and a picture of the best friends standing together at Nationals unrolled next to Tate's Olympic banner. Now there were four banners in row. The crowd clapped and cheered with excitement. Catesby was grinning, and Addison had tears in her eyes.

"Thank you, Uncle Ray." Addison hugged him.

"It's perfect," Catesby said. The two Olympians said their good-byes to the girls at the gym and were ushered into a room where it was just family: Catesby's parents, all five of her siblings; Addison's dad, her aunt and cousin, and her grandparents. Her uncle Ray was fulfilling his hosting duties as coach by wrapping up the party for the other visitors.

"I know it's almost time for you to go, but we have a couple of things for you," Ginny, Catesby's mom, said. "First, these are not to be opened until qualifications." She handed them each a box about the size of a shoebox. "But since we won't let you open these until competition, we wanted you to have something you could open now. Here are letters. There is one starting tomorrow, and they continue all the way through competition, hopefully enough to last until we get to see you again." She handed each of them a gallon-sized plastic bag full of envelopes of various sizes and colors.

"Thank you, Momma," Catesby whispered as she hugged her tightly.

"Yes, thank you, Momma Ginny," Addison added with another hug.

"You're so welcome. We are so proud of you and can't wait to see how well you do in Rome."

Luke hugged both girls, and Catesby moved to say good-bye to her family while Addison wrapped her grandparents in their own hugs. They would not be traveling to Rome.

"We love you, and we are proud of you," Grandma Anne held Addison's gaze for a moment to let the words sink in.

"I love you too," Addison said.

"You know, I think you were about four when you decided you were going to be an Olympic gymnast. You and Tate spent so much time at our house watching the Olympics, and you work so hard at everything you do. I always knew you'd get here. It was bound to happen simply because you set your mind to it—just like your mom did," Franklin told his youngest granddaughter.

"I love you, Granddaddy." Addison snuggled into his chest. "Thank you for all your support. I wish you were going to be in Rome."

"I think I get the better end of the deal. I get to watch

from my comfy chair," he laughed.

"Don't worry, Addi, he told me the same thing eight years ago," Tate smiled.

"I can't believe it's going to be more than three weeks before I get to see you again," Addison told her dad as she turned toward him.

"I don't know what I'm going to do with myself," he admitted. "Call me as much as you can." Luke squeezed her tightly. It would be the longest they had been apart since Ashley and Davis died. While neither of them was particularly excited about the extended time apart, they knew it was necessary for Addison's dreams to come true. Luke handed Addison her gym bag to load into her Aunt Julie's car. "I'm going to miss you."

"I'm going to miss you too," Addison choked out as she hugged him one last time. He bent down and kissed the top of her head.

"No matter what, I love you. Don't ever forget that," he whispered, and she nodded. It was part of their goodbye routine. Catesby's parents walked over to tell Addison goodbye, too, once Catesby was settled in the backseat. After a quick hug from Tate, Addison climbed into the backseat next to Catesby, and Gwyn slid in on the other side. The group drove the hour to the Raleigh airport.

Once they arrived, Julie helped the girls unload their bags. She would take the car back and join them in Rome with the rest of the family. "Have fun and enjoy it," she encouraged the girls. "Do your best, and I will see you when competition is over." Julie hugged her niece.

"Thanks, Aunt Julie. I love you," Addison smiled.

"I love you too," Julie said. "Hey, Ray, don't be too hard on them. They were good enough to make it to the Olympics," she reminded him as she kissed him and she pulled away. Ray, Addison, Catesby, and Gwyn walked into the airport together.

"It's weird to think that next time we'll be in an airport, it will be when we're headed to Rome for the Olympics," Catesby said as they settled in at the gate for their flight to Indianapolis for Olympic training camp. They flipped through the cards Ginny had given them, noticing they were written by different people.

"That's a lot of cards," Gwyn commented.

"Your mom thought of everything," Addison said to Catesby.

"She's the best," Catesby smiled.

"For the record, Ashley would have done the same thing," Ray said, putting an arm around his niece. He knew Addison would be thinking of her mom every minute of this experience.

"She was one of the most thoughtful people I've ever had the privilege of knowing," Gwyn added.

"I wish she was here." Tears pooled in Addison's eyes.

"Me too, Addi, me too." Ray hugged her tightly. "You know, we dreamed about this—about going to the Olympics with you."

"And look at where we are now," Addison smiled, wiping her eyes.

"Crazy, isn't it—what you can accomplish when you set your mind to something?" Ray said.

"It definitely is," Catesby agreed, nudging her best friend.

"The vision board helped," Addison admitted, thinking back to when they made the boards at the beginning of the year.

* * * * *

Addison: Age 16 (January of Olympic Year)

"Welcome to day one of the Olympic year." Tate sat down at the kitchen table with Addison. "You ready?"

"Olympics, here I come," Addison grinned.

"So, I had a thought. What would you think about making a vision board for this year? You remember mine, right?" Tate asked her cousin.

"Of course. That would be fun! I definitely need one to help keep me focused after everything that has happened the last couple years. Can we invite Catesby too? Since we are trying to do this together."

"Absolutely. Tell her we'll pick her up on the way to the store," Tate said.

Addison ran off to get dressed and call her best friend. The girls bought supplies for their vision boards and printed out pictures. Then they raided Addison's stash of gymnastics magazines before setting up shop at the Jessup's kitchen table. Catesby and Addison flipped through magazines and pictures, looking for just the right ones. Addison chose a photo of her and Catesby and her favorite picture from Melbourne—the one with Tate hugging Addison from behind with Tate's all-around gold medal hanging around Addison's neck. She also managed to find pictures of each apparatus, and Tate printed out pictures of the medals the athletes would be competing for in Rome.

Catesby filled her board with words like "inspire" and "dream" with the Olympic Rings in the center. She added a picture of her and Addison and one from the medal stand at Worlds the year before, when their team had won the gold. She added the pictures of the medals Tate printed and a picture of the bars.

"It's amazing how different the two of you are," Tate laughed, observing the best friends at work.

"Well, it's what makes us great friends. We can appreciate our differences," Catesby said with assurance as she high-fived Addison. Next, she added some quotes from a gymnastics magazine to her board.

"Tate, will you write flip, fly, stick for me? Your handwriting is so much better than mine," Addison asked as she found some sparkly stars to add to the collage.

"Of course! Yours is really coming together."

"Thanks. This was a great idea." Addison flipped through more magazines and pictures, trying to decide what else to add. Tate wrote the words, and Addison stared at her board. "It's missing something," she said after a moment.

"What if you add the steps you'll take along the way to the Olympics? I can print out the schedule for the year, and you can add the logos of the different competitions?" Tate offered.

"Oh, I like that idea," Addison said, and Tate worked on getting a schedule and some logos printed for her. "How's it going over there, Cates?"

"It's coming together, I think. I still can't believe this is really the year everything could happen."

"I'm just ready to actually compete again," Addison sighed.

"Winter Cup is just around the corner," Catesby reminded her.

"Official senior debut, here I come. I can't wait to show off my floor routine, it's going to be awesome!" Addison cheered.

"It definitely is," Catesby laughed as Tate handed Addison the list she had printed. Addison cut out the logos of the Winter Cup, Classic, Nationals, and the Olympic Trials--all the steps on the journey the media had labeled the "Road to Rome."

"This is exactly what I needed; thank you," Addison said, holding her finished vision board for Tate and Catesby to see.

"It looks great." Catesby looked up, but she was still working on her own.

"I love it," Tate smiled.

"It reminds me so much of yours," Addison admitted, shaking her head. "I think you were in my head."

"It makes sense; you stared at mine as much as I did, if not more," Tate reminded her. Her own vision board had hung in her parents' living room for the majority of her own Olympic year. Since they lived next door to each other and both had parents working at the gym, they were always in and out of each other's houses.

"You're not wrong. I'm pretty sure I could reproduce it from memory; it's pretty burned in there." Addison rubbed her temple, smiling. Tate had been her hero her whole life, and getting to follow in her footsteps was what she had always wanted to do.

"Okay, I think I'm done too," Catesby finally said as she held hers up. Where Addison's was full of pictures of gymnasts and the steps on the Road to Rome, Catesby's was full of encouraging and inspiring words, personal photos, and Bible verses.

"It's perfectly you," Tate said.

"For sure. It's beautiful," Addison added. "Do you know where you're going to hang it?"

"Not sure yet. Probably in my room, but we'll see what Momma says—maybe the kitchen?" Catesby shrugged.

"Just make sure it's somewhere you will see it regularly," Tate said.

"How's it going in here, ladies?" Luke asked as he walked into his overrun kitchen.

"We just finished!" Addison handed him the poster board.

"It's perfect! Where should we put it?" he asked the girls. They walked around the small living space. He stopped by the kitchen table, staring at the seaside scene that currently hung there. "What about right here?" Luke gestured to the photo on the wall.

"You're sure? I know how much you love that picture," Addison said.

"It'll only be up for a few months, and this is a big deal for you. This is the Olympics we're talking about; you have been working towards this your whole life," Luke reminded her.

"Okay, let's do it!" Addison couldn't stop smiling. They worked together to take down the seaside picture and attach Addison's vision board to the wall. After dinner, Catesby's mom came to pick her up.

"Let's see these vision boards," Ginny said as she walked into the Jessup's kitchen.

"Here's mine," Catesby announced, handing her the vision board she had created.

"Cates, it's beautiful and so you." Ginny looked over the poster board.

"Thank you! I'm really happy with how it turned out," Catesby said. "And that's Addison's," she added, gesturing to the wall behind the table.

"Wow, Addi! It looks great—and in such a prominent spot," Ginny said, a little taken aback.

"Tate's hung in their living room when she was trying to make the Olympic team, and since we are at the table together for breakfast every day, we thought this would be a good spot for Addi's," Luke explained. "It's important that Addison see it daily."

"Well then, we'll have to find a special place for yours when we get home," Ginny said. "Thank you for including Catesby today."

"Of course," Tate said.

"See you at practice tomorrow, Addi." Catesby grabbed her stuff and walked out the door with her mom.

"I have one more thing for your vision board," Tate told Addison, pulling a box out of her bag.

"Tate," Addison gasped, her eyes as big as saucers as she saw the medal in Tate's hands.

"I only dug my all-around medal out of storage, and I didn't want to make Catesby feel left out, so I thought it was best to wait until she left."

"I think it was a wise decision," Luke said as Tate hung the medal from one of the nails that held the picture up.

"Thank you, Tate." Addison teared up seeing the medal next to her own vision board.

"I promise we will take great care of it," Luke said as he hugged his niece.

"Of that, I have no doubts," Tate laughed. "I just thought it might be some good motivation for you."

"It will be." Addison was totally mesmerized by the sight of the gold medal and the vision board. "Thank you for today, Tate. It was really special."

"You are going to do great things." Tate wrapped her arms around Addison's neck from behind, just as she had in the photo on the vision board. "I can't wait to see you compete in Rome."

"I'm so glad I have you in my corner," Addison said.

"No place I'd rather be," Tate said.

* * * * *

"The vision boards definitely helped," Catesby agreed, pulling Addison from the memory. "When you called me so excited to make a vision board, I thought you and Tate were a little crazy, but it was so nice to have to keep me motivated."

"Me too! I can't wait to see what we accomplish together in Rome," Addison grinned.

"But first, we have training camp, where you have work on building a team."

CHAPTER FIVE

"Nicely done! Three more just like that," Gwyn said to Catesby on day three of training camp. She had just completed a perfect beam routine, even though beam was her weakest event.

"Focus, Addi. Worry about you," Ray said, recapturing his niece's attention.

"Sorry." Addison shook it off and hopped up to latch onto the high bar. It had been a rough practice, but things finally seemed to be starting to click. Catesby finally hit her beam routine, and Addison was determined to do a full bars routine without a major error. Waverly managed to pull out a halfway decent vault, which they were pretty sure she wasn't even going to need. Brittnee had finally managed to get her double-double back into her floor routine, and Scarlett had officially landed her double Arabian dismount on beam ten times in a row.

"That was actually a good practice. Way to go, everyone. Let's have two more like this tomorrow. Until then, rest and enjoy yourselves. I will see you bright and early in the morning." The official from the American Gymnastics Federation dismissed practice, and the girls headed to their rooms to shower before dinner.

"Movie night after dinner?" Waverly asked as they went their separate ways.

"That sounds wonderful," Catesby smiled.

Later that evening, the girls settled in Brittnee and Waverly's room for the movie and were all laughing in a matter of minutes. They ended up completely ignoring the movie and instead fell into a conversation about their weird competition habits and superstitions.

"What is with the constant tumbling?" Scarlett asked Addison, a hint of annoyance in her voice.

"It keeps my head clear—part of having a strong mental game," Addison explained. She would never forget the day they put together her mental arsenal after what Addison considered to be the worst competition of her life.

* * * * *

Addison: Age 11

"Get your stuff, I'll take you to the gym." With a grunt, Addison obeyed her dad. She came back in her warmup with her gymnastics bag. "You ready?"

"No," Addison responded as she took a deep breath, her mistake-filled routines from the weekend playing through her mind. When they pulled up at the gym, she hesitated before opening the car door.

"Go have fun," Luke smiled. "I'll see you later."

Addison hopped out of the truck, walked into the gym, and begrudgingly started to warm up in the pre-elite gym. She didn't have practice that morning because of the competition over the weekend so she was in the middle of the pre-elite teams getting ready for practice. She kept looking for her coaches and Tate but couldn't find them anywhere. Her fear of how bad practice was going to be kept getting worse and worse. When she finished warmups, the pre-elite coach sent her to the elite gym.

When Addison walked in, she found only Ray, her mom, and Tate.

The weirdest part of the whole thing was the grin plastered across Ray's face. "All warmed up?" Addison nodded, unsure of what was going on. When she looked at Tate, her cousin just shrugged. They were both in the dark.

"I know that competition did not go like either of you wanted." Both girls looked at each other and then at the floor. "But it's over. We can't change anything that happened, so we are going to move forward. Today is all about having fun and remembering why you love this sport."

"What are you talking about?" Tate looked at her dad.

"I want you both to show me everything you can do. Pick an apparatus and don't hold anything back," Ray explained before adding, "But please, don't hurt yourselves. Let us know if you need help."

"Are you serious?" Addison asked, still in shock. She had expected a lecture and hard drills to improve her skills after her terrible performance.

"Yes," Ashley answered confidently. "Where are you starting?"

"Floor," Tate said without missing a beat. She looked at Addison, who nodded vigorously.

"Let's go then!" Ashley laughed and went to turn on some fun music.

Addison and Tate picked opposite corners of the floor and started tumbling. Within a few minutes, they were both throwing tricks they had never competed. For Addison, it was a chance to show just how many things she had tackled or nearly tackled. And it was a chance to remember how much tumbling calmed her down.

After they finished on floor, the cousins moved to beam. They opted for the low beams to show off—and practice—skills they had not quite mastered. Tate was able to show that she was closer to getting her harder skills back than even she realized, after the couple years she had taken off from gymnastics. On vault, Tate tried for an Amanar into the pit. It went so well she tried again and almost landed it on a mat. Addison even proved she ready for a bigger Yurchenko vault when she managed to land the one and half on her butt, showing she could get it all the way around.

Bars was the weakest event for both Addison and Tate, but they managed to have fun swinging and doing tricks. Tate had not even been training bars, but she was still able to pull out a few moves. Addison proved that with a little more work, she was going to be able to get her bars routine upgraded enough to hang with the rest of the elite girls.

Both girls were surprised to find that it was a fun afternoon spent laughing and challenging each other to do better. Once they had done everything they could think of to do, Addison and Tate lay down in the middle of the floor, exhausted but smiling. The bad competition cleared completely from Addison's mind for the first time.

"Anything you want to tell me?" Ray asked as he sat down on the floor next to Addison.

"Not anymore," she admitted, biting her lip.

"You are an incredible gymnast. You just proved that over and over again. I didn't know you could do half that stuff. But gymnastics is not just about skill; it's about mental toughness and being able to shake off a bad rotation. You have the skill; you just have to get the mental part down. Do you think you can handle that?"

"I don't know how," Addison lamented as she sat up, pulling her knees into her chest.

"That's why we're talking and why we did this," Ashley chimed in. "As your coaches, it's our job to help you to try and figure it all out." She smiled.

"I think one big thing for Addison would be not paying attention to the scoreboard," Tate said thoughtfully. "It was after your score popped up on floor that you were really unable to get yourself out of your head." Ray looked at his daughter in surprise; she was growing up on him.

"She's right," Addison sighed. "So, no scoreboard. I think I can do that. But I still have to figure out a way to get out of my head if I mess up."

"Do you know what I've noticed?" Ashley spoke up again. "Whenever you get nervous waiting, or if you do something wrong, before you do it again, you always do some tumbling trick."

"I do?" She didn't even realize she was doing it.

"You do," Ashley said with a smile. "I think tumbling clears your mind. I've even noticed that practices generally go better after floor." Addison knew her mom was right, even if she couldn't explain it.

"Tumbling, no scoreboard. Anything else we can add to her mental arsenal?" Ray asked.

"Oakleigh's coach was big on visualizing perfect routines. She taught me how to do it during the Olympics," Tate offered. "It was a bigger help than I thought it would be. It also gives you something to do while you wait your turn during competitions . . . at least, that's what Oakleigh did. And she never looked at the scoreboard until she was finished competing, either," Tate added, finishing up her explanation of her best friend's competition habits.

"You probably already do that without realizing that's what you're doing," Ashley said thoughtfully. "So making a conscious decision to visualize your routines can only help. What do you think, Addi? Can you do those things?"

"If it's going to prevent me from having another competition like the one I just had, then yes, I can, because that was awful. That cannot happen again." Addison shook her head, holding back the tears threatening to spill over.

* * * * *

"Whatever it takes, I guess. Right?" Scarlett shrugged, pulling Addison from her memories.

"We all have weird competition habits," Brittnee stepped in.

"Yeah, I have this obsessive need to check the scoreboard every chance I get," Waverly laughed.

"Oh, I don't pay attention to it," Addison said, and Scarlett sighed like it didn't surprise her in the least.

"You really don't pay attention to the scoreboard?" Waverly asked Addison.

"Nope; it's too much added pressure," Addison laughed.

"I don't know how you do it. I need the scoreboard to ground me," Brittnee said, thinking about how she checked her score after each rotation.

"I don't fully understand it, either, but Addison has this irrational need to be perfect. If she sees her score and it's not exactly what she thought it would be—higher or lower— it takes her focus off the gymnastics she's supposed to be doing," Catesby explained.

"I guess I do get that," Scarlett said, starting to

understand Addison a bit better.

"You would never survive in college gymnastics," Waverly told Addison, laughter in her voice.

"Oh, I know. Brighton and I have talked about it often." Addison had no intention of being a collegiate gymnast.

"Brighton?" Confusion colored Waverly's tanned features.

"Sorry, Brighton Kerry. She's an assistant coach at NC State. She was an EGA Olympian, too," Addison explained her connection to yet another Olympian.

"I didn't know there was another EGA Olympian besides Tate and Gwyn," Brittnee said.

"She was the first. Brighton didn't win any medals at her games, though," Catesby added, and Addison pulled out her phone to show them pictures.

"Oh, yeah, I know her! I completely forgot she was an EGA gymnast," Waverly said as soon as she saw the pictures.

Suddenly noticing the time, Brittnee stood up and waved her arm toward the door. "Well, this was more fun than movie night, but we have practice in the morning, so I'm going to have to ask you to leave our room please," Brittnee said, and the other girls burst into fits of laughter before walking out of the room.

"At some point soon, we are going to have to pick between Brittnee and Waverly for team captain," Addison noted, her hand was on their doorknob a few minutes later.

"That's tomorrow's problem; I don't know how we're going to pick," Catesby answered, shaking her head.

"Goodnight," Scarlett said, heading for her room as Addison and Catesby walked into theirs.

"Do you think she's really okay with being by herself?" Addison asked as the best friends climbed in their respective beds.

"Probably, but I would hope she would say something if she wasn't. Plus, Waverly and Brittnee are close, and so are we, so who was she going to separate?" Catesby said.

"I guess you're right. I'm just worried about her. She didn't eat much at dinner even on this two-practice day. Plus, she just feels a little standoffish," Addison noted.

"Did you ever consider that she just might not like you?" Catesby laughed.

"Shut up," Addison retorted. Then she sighed, "But you didn't notice her plate at dinner?"

"No," Catesby shrugged. "Scarlett is competitive. She is the reigning World Champion, but you have beat her at every turn this year. She's allowed to have some feelings about that. We have practice tomorrow," Catesby turned over. Addison knew that was her cue to go to bed, but she couldn't help but worry about Scarlett.

The next morning, Addison and Catesby repeated their morning routine of reading their letters together before breakfast.

Dear Addi,

I'm so proud of you. You and Catesby never cease to amaze me with your abilities and talent. All your hard work has finally paid off, and you are getting ready for the Olympics. Crazy, isn't it? The dream that you've had forever is finally coming true. I know you have big plans for the Olympics and want to bring home as much hardware as possible. There is no doubt that you can do anything you set your mind to. You continue to prove that over and over again. You are one of the strongest women I have ever had the privilege of knowing. You inspire me day after day. It is my hope and prayer that all your dreams and goals will be reached during this Olympics.

I know it doesn't need to be said, but the best place to get ready is practice. Work hard this week. Get all the falls and bouncy landings out of the way so that when you get to Rome they are out of your system.

I love you,

Momma Ginny

"Who was your letter from this morning?" Addison asked Catesby as they headed to breakfast.

"Your dad, what about you?"

"Your mom," Addison smiled.

"Nice! I should call her. Maybe tonight?"

"I'm always up for a conversation with Momma Ginny," Addison laughed. As they walked to breakfast, Addison remembered another conversation from the first night she met Catesby.

* * * * *

Addison: Age 6

"How was your first day of practice with the team?" Luke asked his daughter at dinner.

"It was good," Addison shrugged.

"What did you do?" Davis followed up.

"Floor, beam, bars, and vault." Addison looked at him like he should have already known that.

"Did you learn anything new?" Ashley tried.

"Nope." Addison took a sip of her water.

"Really, nothing new?" Luke questioned, and the rest of the family stifled a laugh.

"Not at practice. But I watched Tate and Selah practice, and Selah did her double Arabian dismount on beam," Addison said dreamy-eyed. They all knew she'd be practicing with them if she could.

"Do you know how Selah got the skill?" Ashley asked.

"She practiced. I know." The six-year-old's sassy side was showing.

"Addison Anne!" Ashley reprimanded her.

"Sorry," she muttered.

"I think Mom was just trying to remind you that if you want to be as good as Tate and Selah, then you have to work hard," Luke said.

"I know that, and practice was fine, but I already know how to do all the stuff that Jocelyn was working on tonight," Addison said.

"Coach Jocelyn," her mom corrected her gently. "And I'm sure it will get better as you go." Ashley smiled; it was something only Addison would complain about as someone who had grown up in a gym.

"Is Columbus's sister on your team?" Davis asked.

"Yes, and she didn't stop talking the whole night," Addison answered, rolling her eyes.

"Yeah, she talks a lot, but do you like her? Don't you know her from school?" Davis was excited. Columbus was his best friend from baseball, and he wanted them to have friends in the same family.

"She's not in my class, but I've seen her at recess. Today she mostly talked and I listened. I was trying to be good in practice because it was my first one," Addison told him, immediately forgetting the disdain she had felt for practice just a few minutes earlier.

"Well, Catesby's awesome. I bet you'll be best friends, just like me and Columbus," Davis grinned.

* * * * *

"Addi? What do you want for breakfast?" Catesby pulled Addison out of her thoughts as they walked into the kitchen.

"I think I'm going for an omelet today," Addison smiled. Some things never changed. Catesby still talked more than anyone she knew, and her mom was the same way. Plus, Davis had been right about them being best friends.

After their morning workout, the American Gymnastics Federation officials called them all together, and they knew what was coming. "We are going to be voting on team captain this afternoon, but we have made a decision. Ray Markum will be head coach, and Kristen Bowen will be your assistant coach." The officials had decided on who would be the main coaches at the Olympics helping the girls during the team final. The girls jumped up to hug their coaches. Addison and Catesby rushed to Ray while Brittnee ran over to Kristen.

When the group was dismissed to lunch, Scarlett caught up with Addison and Catesby. "Looks like that problem is going to have to be solved," she whispered, nodding at Brittnee and Waverly just ahead of them. The girls agreed, but it was not going to be an easy choice. Lunches in hand, the three settled at a table away from everyone else, but it backfired when Brittnee and Waverly walked over.

"We should talk this whole team captain thing," Waverly said.

"That's what we were trying to do without you," Catesby laughed.

"Oh, well, we just thought we could do it all together," Brittnee sighed. "If that's okay with you guys?"

"Fine by me," Catesby grinned, and Scarlett and Addison just nodded. "To be honest, I think we all know it's between the two of you."

"I think it should be Britt," Waverly said before anyone else could speak.

"I agree," Scarlett said. "But I think Waverly would be a great choice, too," she added quickly.

"It needs to be Brittnee," Addison chimed in. "Britt, you have the Olympic experience, and you have been so encouraging every step of the way."

"She's right; you have cheered us on at every competition and camp this year," Catesby said, and Brittnee blushed bright red.

"Agreed," Scarlett said.

"But what about Waverly?" Brittnee asked sheepishly.

"Waverly would make a wonderful team captain, but she's not you," Catesby said. "Wave, I'm so thankful for you, but Britt's done this before. I think that simple fact means we need her to be our captain."

"She's right, Britt," Waverly smiled. "It should be you."

With Waverly's insistence, Brittnee finally relented.

"Okay, we're all together on this, right?" Addison looked at her teammates.

"Right," they all agreed. Later that afternoon, when the officials from the American Gymnastics Federation asked the girls to write down their choice for team captain, all the girls wrote the same name.

Practice that afternoon was the best one they had all week. There was a lightness that had not been there before. Ray and Kristen were getting in a groove with the other coaches, and the girls felt the relief of having chosen a captain without any drama.

"This is looking like a gold medal team." The officials were grinning as practice ended. "We're thrilled to announce that, by unanimous vote, our team captain for the Rome Olympics is Brittnee Chase." Everyone clapped while the girls wrapped Brittnee in a hug.

"Thank you," she whispered to each girl. Brittnee had encouraged Addison through every competition this year, and now she was going to lead them through Olympic competition. It was coming faster than they were ready for.

CHAPTER SIX

"I can't believe this is real," Catesby exclaimed as the five teammates stood on the balcony of their suite in the Olympic Village in Rome. Here, the girls shared a suite with a living room, balcony, three bathrooms, and three bedrooms. Catesby and Addison shared a room as did Brittnee and Waverly, while Scarlett was by herself.

"Believe it! But also, it's time to go," Brittnee answered, winking as she put a hand on Catesby's shoulder. The team headed to the practice space for their first time on the official Olympic equipment. Their run-through was a little rough, which they expected with new equipment and all the travel. It was done and they knew the next one would be better.

"Why is everyone so tall?" Addison asked, looking up at the Olympians walking around them.

"I think it's just that we're short," Brittnee laughed. "Come on, let's go exploring before the media summit this evening." Together, they figured out how to get around a little better as they enjoyed seeing all the sights of the Olympic village.

Back at their suite, it was time to get ready for interviews. Addison took a shower and decided it was best to let her fiery curls do their own thing, like they clearly wanted to. She pulled on leggings, a blue polo, and the Team USA jacket that was a part of their Olympic wardrobe. She put on some makeup and was lacing up her tennis shoes when Waverly appeared in their room. "Ready?"

"Yep," Addison nodded, turning to Catesby who was pulling on her own jacket. The five girls walked out to meet the official from the American Gymnastics Federation who would escort them to the media summit.

"Holy moly," Addison muttered as they entered the media zone. It seemed to be an unending hallway of studios and cameras from every country. She took a deep breath as she tried to remember what Tate had told her: *They just want to know about you.* She swallowed and walked into the American studio behind her teammates. When they were situated, they introduced themselves to the reporter before the interview began. Thankfully, he helped them feel comfortable before the camera started rolling.

"We are here with the women's gymnastics team. Two time Olympian and team captain, Brittnee Chase; world champion and Olympic alternate, Waverly Miller; the reigning world champion, Scarlett Peterson; the reigning world silver medalist and bars champion, Catesby Holland; and national champion, Addison Jessup. Welcome to Rome! How are we feeling?" the reporter asked after introducing them all.

There was a lot of nervous laughter before Waverly spoke up. "We are very excited for the competition to start, and we're continuing to make sure that we are as ready as possible."

"We have made becoming a team our priority, and we've definitely become friends," Brittnee added.

"You had your first practice today. What was it like to practice here in Rome?" the reporter asked the group.

"I think we're all adjusting to the Olympic equipment," Scarlett said.

"Plus, we're still getting over some jet lag, but it's really cool to practice surrounded by the Olympic rings," Catesby grinned.

"It's definitely a dream-come-true moment," Addison added. The reporter asked a few more questions to the group before starting individual interviews.

"Addison, you're the youngest person on this team. Do you think that gives you a disadvantage?" the reporter asked.

"Not at all!" she answered with confidence. "I might be the youngest, but aside from maybe Brittnee, I have the most international experience of anyone on this team."

"That's right; you have been competing internationally since you were eleven," he smiled. "But you didn't compete for most of last year. Why was that?"

"I tore my Achilles tendon. It took a long time to recover and feel like I was ready to compete, but I made it."

"That couldn't have been an easy experience for you."

"Not in the least," Addison answered, remembering it all so vividly.

* * * * *

Addison: Age 15

"Time to put it all together," Ray told Addison. They had been working on a new tumbling pass for her floor routine. She had finally mastered the double double, but she had yet to do all the elements in the pass together. Addison stood in the corner of the floor, took a deep breath, and took off running. She started with a punch front and pushed through each element before the double double, which she landed with a slight stumble. "That was pretty good for your first time! Again," Ray said with a smile on his face, and Addison knew he was proud of her.

After the fifth time, she finally felt like she had a handle on it. "It's looking good. Let's see five more then we'll move onto beam," Ray told her. She nodded and backed into the corner. She took off running and launched into the punch front. She landed a little wonky but still managed to get into the back handspring. As she came down, however, she knew she was off. Then she heard a popping sound before she crash landed.

"Addi!" Ray and Gwyn, who was working with Catesby on beam, rushed over. "What happened?"

"I'm okay," Addison said, but she winced in pain, feeling like someone had kicked her as she tried to stand. "I heard something pop when I was doing my back handspring."

"That's not good," Ray sighed. "I'm going to call your dad and Dr. Swilling."

"Uncle Ray, I'm okay. Really." Addison tried to stand again only to cry out in pain.

"Yeah, you're done for the day," Ray insisted as he carried her into the office.

"What's wrong?" her Aunt Julie asked as they entered. She tried not to look too scared.

"Not sure yet. She did something to her ankle. Can you call Dr. Swilling and Luke? I need to talk to Gwyn about finishing up with Catesby."

"Are you okay?" Julie asked Addison.

"I'm fine, really. I don't understand why everyone is making such a big deal out of it," Addison said, but she couldn't help wincing again when Julie lightly turned her foot.

"Sure you are. I'm going to call Dr. Swilling and then your dad," Julie said, shaking her head.

"Aunt Julie--"

"I don't want to hear it. You can't walk," Julie admonished as she pulled out her phone and called Dr. Swilling. "Hi, this is Julie Markum. I'm calling for my niece, Addison Jessup. She injured her ankle during gymnastics practice today. No, she can't walk on it. Great; we will be there as soon as we can."

"We're going?"

"Of course we're going. As soon as Ray gets back, we'll get in the car." Julie rolled her eyes. Addison was quick to brush things off. She made her next phone call as Addison huffed in her chair. "Hey Luke. Listen, Addi's hurt, but she's sitting here with me in the office."

"What happened?" Luke asked, anxiety and relief mixing in his voice.
"She did something to her ankle."

"But she's okay?"

"You know Addi--she's insisting that everything is fine," Julie laughed.

"Of course she is. Did you already call Dr. Swilling?"

"Yes; we're about to head that way," Julie informed him.

"I will meet y'all there. Can I talk to Addi?" Luke asked, and Julie handed the phone to Addison. "Are you okay?"

"Yes, Daddy, I'm fine. Ow!" Addison looked over at her aunt, who had just moved her ankle.

"That good, huh?" Luke laughed at his daughter's stubbornness. "I will see you at Dr. Swilling's office." With Gwyn and Catesby set up for the rest of practice, Ray carried Addison to the car while Julie told the office ladies and staff what was going on before getting in the car. At Dr. Swilling's office, Ray went to get a wheelchair for his niece.

"Hey Addi," Luke smiled, walking back with Ray. "I checked you in." The quartet walked into the doctor's office and only had to wait a few minutes before being called back.

"What brings you in today?" Dr. Swilling asked as she walked into the room.

"I was doing a tumbling pass when I heard something pop in my ankle. It hurts a lot–kinda feels like someone kicked me, and I can't really walk on it," Addison admitted, refusing to see her uncle's smirk.

"That's never a good thing. Let me look at it. Can you lay down for me?" Addison did as she was told, and Dr. Swilling squeezed the calf muscle. "My guess is that your Achilles tendon is ruptured. You are going to have to have an MRI to see the extent of it."

"My Achilles?" Addison asked.

"Yes. I won't have any more information for you until we know how bad it is. I'm sorry," Dr. Swilling said with an apologetic shrug. "Let's see if we can get you in for that MRI."

"An MRI? Really?" Addison hated getting them because it meant she had to lay still for a long time. This may not have been her first gymnastics-related injury, but she was pretty sure it was going to be the worst one.

"It's the only way we're going to see the full extent of the tear, which will tell us the best way to fix it," Dr. Swilling explained as she checked her computer for the availability of the MRI machine.

"Okay, let's do this," Addison nodded. She wanted it fixed immediately so she could get back to training.

"Great. We have a spot in about fifteen minutes. Someone will escort you to the MRI soon." Dr. Swilling walked out of the exam room, and a few minutes later, a nurse came to get Addison for the scan. The MRI lasted about thirty minutes before Addison was escorted back to the exam room. She sighed, thinking about everything that was at stake. Her ankle just had to be okay.

"How did it go?" Luke asked.

"I laid still for thirty minutes, Dad. It went fine," Addison laughed dryly. "Are Uncle Ray and Aunt Julie still here?"

"Of course. You know Coach Ray isn't leaving until we have answers," Luke assured her. They talked while they waited on the results from Dr. Swilling. Addison was scared of what was going on with her ankle and what it might mean for her Olympic dreams.

"I have good news and I have bad news," Dr. Swilling announced when she walked back in.

"Before you tell us everything, can we get Uncle Ray and Aunt Julie? I think it would be better if he hears the news directly from you."

"Yes, of course." Dr. Swilling had one of the nurses bring her aunt and uncle in from the lobby. "The bad news is that your Achilles tendon is fully ruptured. But the good news is we can fix it with surgery, and I can have you back to training within a year."

"What does that mean?" Addison gulped, calculating.

"My best guess is about nine months but maybe a little longer. You're going to have to actually stay off of your ankle and do what I say. Can you handle that?" This was not Dr. Swilling's first time dealing with Addison and her injuries. She knew that Addison liked to get started as soon as possible and wasn't always the best at listening to instructions when she was trying to accomplish her goals.

"Yes. If it means going to the Olympics, I can," Addison assured everyone in the room.

"Great. I'm going to set you up in ankle splint and get you crutches while your dad gets the surgery scheduled," Dr. Swilling said, nodding to let Luke and Ray leave the room to make the arrangements with the desk staff. "Julie, how's Tate?"

"She's great," Julie answered as Dr. Swilling worked on setting Addison's ankle. "She's almost done with college. She hasn't fully decided what she wants to do but for now, she's teaching at the gym, plus she's still traveling and speaking to young gymnasts." The family loved the care Dr. Swilling had given all of their athletic children over the years.

"That's so great," the doctor responded before turning to Addison. "Addi, this is going to need to stay on except when you're in the shower."

"Thank you for everything, Dr. Swilling." Addison hugged her.

"I will see you for surgery and follow up soon," Dr. Swilling told her with a smile. A nurse brought some crutches so Addison could hop out of the office. She was careful not to put any weight on the injured foot, exaggerating her hops to prove she was going to be a good patient. Her dad had been able to schedule her surgery for the next week, which Addison was thankful for. The sooner the surgery, the sooner she could get back to training.

"Are you okay?" Luke asked as she buckled her seatbelt.

"I don't really know how to answer that question," Addison said thoughtfully. "I'm super angry my Achilles is torn. I'm scared because I have to have surgery." She started to tear up a bit. "I just want to make that Olympic team next year. I'm still in a lot of pain. And really, I just want to get in my bed and sleep for a week."

"Let's get you some food and let you sleep. It's been a long day," Luke responded with a half-smile.

"Do you think Grammy will have any of her vegetable soup?"

"There's almost always some of it in her freezer," Luke laughed, thinking of all times he had asked her to fix him some of her magical vegetable soup over the years. "Why don't you call her?"

"My phone's still at the gym. It was a whirlwind getting out of there," Addison realized. It had been a long afternoon, but she had survived.

"Use mine," Luke said, handing it to Addison so she could call his mother.

"Thanks, Dad. Hey, Grammy. This is Addi."

"Well, hey, Sweetheart. What's going on?"

"I tore my Achilles tendon at practice today, and we've been at the doctor this afternoon."

"Oh no! Are you okay?" Her grandma's concern came through the phone loud and clear.

"I will be. I'm having surgery next week, but I was hoping I could have some of your vegetable soup tonight?"

"Of course! I'll heat some up for you. Tell your dad to bring you here." Addison could hear her open the freezer and felt a bit of comfort just anticipating her grandma's special soup. "I'm sorry about the surgery. What does that mean for your training?"

"Dr. Swilling said that if I do everything she asks, then I can be back training full time within a year."

"A year? That's great! That means you can still go to the Olympics." Anne breathed a sigh of relief; she knew how important it was to her granddaughter.

"I know; I was glad to hear that, too. We're going to stop by the gym to get my stuff, and then we'll come to your house."

"See you soon." Anne reminded Addison that she loved her before hanging up.

After a quick stop at the gym, Luke and Addison pulled into his parents' driveway. Normally, Luke would have just parked at their own house across the street, but with Addison on crutches, he wanted her to have a shorter walk to the door. A dinner with her grandparents was just what Addison needed after her day.

The next week, Luke took Addison to the hospital for her surgery. It had been a rough week. Being injured meant that Addison couldn't train, and she didn't know how to handle herself with all the extra time. Addison was ready to have the surgery so she could get back to somewhat of a normal routine, and Luke was ready for her to have something to do again, even if it was just physical therapy.

"Are you nervous?" Luke asked as they waited.

"A little," Addison admitted. "I just want it over with, if I'm being completely honest." Luke hugged her. He was going to wait for her the whole time she was in surgery, so when she woke up, she was back in a room with her dad.

"Hey, Addi," he said gently. A nurse came to check on her and then the surgeon, who told them everything went great. Addison was in a cast but would transition to a boot in a couple weeks, and she would have follow-ups with Dr. Swilling.

It took a few weeks, but Addison eventually settled into a new routine. She was going to physical therapy three times a week; seeing a counselor once a week, which she had been doing she since her mom and Davis died; and getting in some light upper body workouts at the gym when she could. Yet there were still many nights when she cried herself to sleep. She missed her mom and Davis, and now she was dealing with an injury that could keep her off the Olympic team if she wasn't careful.

To keep her spirits high, she spent time cheering on her best friend as Catesby received all the opportunities that Addison had hoped to get. She continued to work out and train as much Dr. Swilling would let her. The first apparatus she was given clearance to truly work on was bars, as long as she didn't mount or dismount them. Thankful for something to get Addison working again, Ray gladly hoisted his niece onto the bars whenever she wanted to practice.

Addison was a couple weeks into bars practice when she woke up to see her grips sitting on her dresser with "You can do this" written on them in Tate's swirly handwriting. She lightly brushed the words with her fingertips and put them in her gymnastics bag. It was the perfect motivator for her to keep going. Everything was going the way that it was supposed to as she worked hard on her recovery. She did everything asked of her in exactly the way the doctor prescribed. As someone who constantly pushed boundaries as far as she could, simply obeying a strict workout regimen was a new thing for her. But doing what her therapist asked had worked for her, so she willing was to do it if it kept her Olympic dreams alive.

"I know that you've been working so hard and doing everything asked of you," Dr. Swilling said as Addison sat across from her early in August.

"And?"

"I'm clearing you to train on beam but be careful: soft standings, minimal tumbling, and don't dismount unless you absolutely have to—like competition." Dr. Swilling said. "You are still in recovery but I know how important this is to you."

"Thank you for everything!" Addison practically skipped out the doctor's office. It was the best news she had received in a long time, and she knew that doing what she was told had finally paid off.

"I can train on beam so I can try for Worlds!" Addison announced as her family sat around the dinner table that night.

"Best news I've heard in a while," Ray smiled.

The very next day, she was back in the gym, and her coaches started to work on her beam routine. "So, I have something I want to talk to you about," Ray said cautiously as he sat down across from her.

"It's about Nationals, isn't it?" Addison knew him well.

"Yes. In order to give you the best chance for Worlds and even the Olympics next year, I think it would best for you not to compete at Nationals," Ray said.

"I'm not saying no or that I don't agree with you, but can I ask why you think that?" Addison pushed back on him.

"Of course. You and Gwyn still aren't clicking—which is not that big of a deal, but still. And based on where you are currently, the only thing you would be able to compete on is bars. We could petition for beam, but I honestly don't think you would be where you want to be by Nationals."

"Where I want to be?"

"You are the most competitive person I have ever had the privilege of coaching. You know you don't like to compete if you don't think you can win, and you're not in winning shape right now."

"I don't know what you're talking about," Addison insisted, trying to contain her laughter.

"Uh huh, sure you don't," Ray said as he shook his head. "Are you okay with this decision?"

"No, but I understand," she responded honestly. "This year has been awful. I've spent so much of it waiting around. I know I'm not where I need to be or want to be. As much as I want to compete at Nationals, I guess I really have to be okay with it. I mean, Nationals are less than a month away, and after spending six months injured, I'd rather not hurt myself trying to get ready that quickly."

"There is that. But you are taking this much better than I expected," Ray sat back.

"I've matured. Plus, I've been going to therapy every week for almost a year. It's been good for me, you know."

"You have to stop growing up on me," Ray sighed.

"I will do my best," Addison smiled. "No Nationals, but do you think

I could make still make it to Worlds?"

"I do. We'll petition you to selection camp which will give you more time to get up to Addison standards on beam and see where Dr. Swilling says you are for floor and vault. There is a good possibility that you could even make the team—especially with those bars upgrades. If not, we'll work towards the Olympics next year," Ray told her.

Addison sighed, getting her to Worlds selection camp was what was important. If it took skipping Nationals and using her scores from National Team Camp in September then it would be worth it. "Worlds. Then the Olympic year." Addison smiled. It wasn't the way she had hoped things would go, but navigating the unexpected was just par for the course lately.

* * * * *

"I know you're glad to be here," the reporter said, pulling Addison out of her memories.

"I sure am," Addison grinned.

"You train at a gym that is famous for producing Olympians. One of those Olympians is your own cousin, Tate Markum, who won the all-around eight years ago in Melbourne. You are coached by Ray Markum and Olympic gold medalist Gwyn Sullivan. How do you deal with the pressure that comes from having such a legacy to contend with?"

"The pressure I feel comes from me more than anyone else. I know what I'm capable of and get frustrated when I can't live up to that. Growing up at a gym that produces Olympians has simply shown me that my dreams are attainable, because I've seen others do it. I train in the shadows of three giant Olympic banners that tell everyone their accomplishments, and I've spent my life waiting to have my own banner. I have no doubt that I can do the things that I've set out to do," Addison answered confidently.

"You have talked about being in the arena when Tate won the all-around and have said that is your own goal for these games. Do you have any other goals that you're hoping to accomplish?"

"I would love to help my team win the gold in the team final and win some individual medals," Addison said.

"Well, from what I've seen, that's definitely possible! Now, I want to transition to something that's probably a little hard for you to talk about, but your mom and brother died in a car accident a couple years ago. Your mom was your coach. What is it like to be here without her?"

"It's hard. We had talked about going to the Olympics together for as long as I can remember. Doing it without her was not something I even thought was possible, but I did it. I know she is so very proud of me," Addison said in one quick breath. She had wondered when the interview was going to go here and was ready with her answer.

"I'm sure she is, too. So, we have a picture of your brother, Davis, from Nationals a couple years ago with this sign."

Addison looked to see a picture of Davis holding up a poster that said, "If gymnastics was easy, they'd call it baseball."

"Was this something he did often?" the interviewer asked.

"All the time! I never knew what his posters were going to say. This was one of my favorites though because Davis was a baseball player," Addison laughed.

"He seems like a character! Do you have any guess as to what his Olympic signs would have said?"

"Oh gosh. I think one of them would have said something about his little sister having more gold medals than you. Davis was my biggest fan. He never had any doubts that I would get to the Olympics," Addison said. That was the part of Davis she missed most—his unwavering conviction that she would do everything she set out to do.

"He clearly loved you. Do you have some ways you will honor your mom and brother?" the interviewer asked.

"Simply being here and continuing the journey we started together. But also my floor routine is set to 'Fight Song' by Rachel Platten. It's a song that has helped me through so much over the last couple years," Addison explained.

"I look forward to seeing it. Best of luck to you as you begin your Olympic journey," the interviewer said. As soon as the interview ended, Addison was escorted to another journalist. She sighed; it was going to be a long afternoon. She just hoped there would be a chance for her to tumble at the end of it.

CHAPTER SEVEN

"You have to stop moving." Brittnee put a hand on Addison's shoulder in an attempt to get her to stop bouncing on her toes.

"Sorry, nervous energy." Addison stilled, her heels dropping to the ground.

"No one likes the cameras," Brittnee assured Addison over her shoulder as she was motioned over to start another interview. Addison knew Brittnee was right, but she couldn't seem to stay still long, so she walked over to watch Brittnee.

"Unfortunately, I am one of the gymnasts who has experienced abusive coaches. I was pushed past my limits in just about every area. I was yelled at, forced to participate in unnecessary weigh ins, and constantly told that I was a terrible gymnast. Then as I started winning, everyone was pitted against me. But I have changed gyms and coaches, and now, Kristin and Louis have been the biggest blessings. They have helped so much—in addition to the hours of therapy I've done," Brittnee told the interviewer. Addison had heard Brittnee talk about her coaching changes, but she didn't know the full story of why she changed. She was even more thankful they had chosen Brittnee as their captain with everything she had been through.

"Are you done?" Catesby found Addison.

"I guess everyone wanted to talk to me first," she shrugged. "How did it go?"

"I don't even know. I think I answered the same questions about twenty times," Catesby sighed. "Are you okay? Because I like talking, and it was a lot for me."

"I'm okay. I could use a tumbling session," Addison smiled. "But I know that's not an option until everyone is done." Catesby and Addison walked over to watch Waverly's interview.

"Competing in college taught me how to be a part of a team. I learned that even if I make a mistake, I can still help my team. Plus, things are just more fun in college. There is less pressure and more comradery," Waverly told her interviewer. Waverly's college experience was a big part of her story. Deciding to return to elite after competing at the collegiate level was not something a lot of gymnasts did.

"Have you told anyone that you want to tumble?" Catesby asked her best friend. Addison rolled her eyes as Catesby nudged her over to the officials from the American Gymnastics Federation who were with them.

"What do you need, Addison?" one of them asked her, knowing she had been anxious.

"I need to be able to get some of this energy out, and I normally do that by tumbling," Addison explained.

"Okay. We have about ten more minutes here while everyone finishes up, and then I'll get you to the gym. I'm not sure who's on the schedule, but I don't think it would be a big deal for you to throw some passes. Can you wait fifteen more minutes without going completely crazy?"

"Yes, thank you." Addison finally settled, comfortable knowing that she would be able to tumble soon. While they waited on everyone to finish, Addison sank down into a middle split and stretched.

"Time to go," Catesby told Addison a short while later. She hopped up and followed the group out.

"I called your coaches, and Gwyn is going to meet us at the bus stop to take you to tumble," the official told Addison as they walked out of the media area.

"Thank you," Addison said. True to her word, Gwyn was waiting on her.

"You ready?" Gwyn winked as they walked to get on a different bus that would take them to the practice area. "Do you want to talk about it?"

"There were just so many questions about Mom and Davis," Addison said.

"It's not that you're having to deal with the craziness of the Olympics? Because I know it can be a lot, especially when there are expectations on you," Gwyn said knowingly.

"There is that." Addison shook her head. "I wish I had thought to bring my headphones."

"You shouldn't shut the world out; you have to embrace the hard. You have worked hard to get here, and now you have to do what you know you can."

"But it's okay if I go tumble right? Because all this nervous energy has to go somewhere," Addison laughed.

"Oh, I know you. Coach Ray had things to handle tonight, so I volunteered. You, my tumbling queen, are always welcome to tumble."

"Thank you for everything," Addison said as they stepped off the bus. She and Gwyn may not have clicked initially, but Addison was thankful that Gwyn cared for her so well now. When they walked into the practice area together, Gwyn spoke to one of the coaches on the floor who nodded and moved his girls off.

Addison slipped off her tennis shoes and jacket, tucking her shirt into her leggings and walking to the corner of the floor. She closed her eyes and took a deep breath. She took off running and launched into a tumbling pass. She landed, her heart pounding, tears threatening to spill down her cheeks. She sucked in a ragged breath and threw another pass. The tears flowed when she landed. She wiped them, willing them to stop as she trotted to the opposite corner. *Breathe. It's okay to miss them. I miss them too, but they are always with you.* The words her aunt often said played through her mind as she launched into her next pass. She was starting to feel better, the blood pumping through her veins reminding her that she was alive and doing the thing she loved most in the world. She backed into the corner for her fourth tumbling pass and threw the opening pass of her floor routine. It was what she had been working up too, and she did it beautifully—allowing herself to feel every element and connection. As she landed it, a big smile spread across her face; that was just what she had needed. She thanked the coach who had let her tumble and walked over to put her tennis shoes back on.

"You all good?" Gwyn asked.

"Yeah, let's go eat," Addison answered truthfully.

"I miss you," Addison admitted when she called her dad before bed that night.

"I miss you, too. How's Rome?"

"Overwhelming. There are so many people, and everyone is so much taller than me," she giggled.

"That's not hard, Addi. You're tiny," Luke reminded her.

"I know. I just didn't expect everyone to be at least a foot taller than me," Addison laughed.

"You'll get used to it. How's practice going?"

"It's going. Today was our first practice on the new equipment. It was rough, but we'll get there," Addison explained. She caught him up on the things that happened since they talked last and told him all about the interviews she had done that afternoon. Addison hung up when

Catesby climbed into her bed on the other side of the room. They had practice in the morning, and sleep was important. She put her phone on the charger and reached for her well-worn stuffed fox, pulling it tightly to her chest. Sleep came in fits and starts, something that was normal when she was confronted again with the grief of losing her mom and Davis.

* * * * *

Addison: Age 14

"Can I help–" Luke opened the door to find two police officers standing there.

"Are you Luke Jessup?" one of them asked, and he nodded, unable to speak for the lump of fear that jumped to his throat. "Can we come in?" Luke stood to the side and let them into his house.

"Luke, what's going on?" Anne appeared in the living room.

"Ma'am," the police officer said. "Mr. Jessup?"

"This is my mother. She lives across the street," Luke said. He needed to know why they were there, so he didn't give them any further explanation.

"We have bad news. Your wife and son were involved in a car accident tonight," the police officer said. "Would you be willing to come with us?"

"Yes, of course. Mom, will you check on Addi? I'll let you know what I find out." Luke followed the police officers out of his house and to the hospital. He tried to keep himself calm as he walked into the ER, but when he was immediately pointed to a doctor, he knew something was horribly wrong.

"Mr. Jessup, I hate to have to be the one to tell you this, but your wife and son were both declared dead on the scene," the doctor explained once he had taken Luke into a nearby waiting room. Luke sank into a chair nearby, his head in his hands. "I'm so very sorry for your loss," the doctor said before handing him paperwork. Then he left the room to let Luke have some time to himself as everything he said sank in.

Luke let out a choked sigh. What was he supposed to do? He stared at the paperwork in his hands and somehow managed to get it all handled. When he saw their bodies, he nearly didn't make it out of the room himself. After a conversation with the doctors and the police, he called Ray to come pick him up. They would worry about his car later; he was in no shape to drive.

"Luke?" Ray asked as Luke climbed in the car.

"They're . . . they're gone," Luke managed, tears finally running down his cheeks. Ray sucked in a ragged breath and let it out slowly before pulling out of the parking lot. As they drove back to the house, the silence was only broken by Luke's sobs.

They pulled into Ray and Julie's driveway and looked at each other. "How do you want to do this?" Ray asked, ever the level-headed one.

"I have no idea." Luke looked at the clock on the dash. It was late; he wasn't even sure who would still be awake. In the house, they found Julie, Anne, and Franklin sitting around the kitchen table.

"Where are the girls?" Ray asked.

"Tate's at your house, Luke. Addison decided to go to bed; I think it was the only way for her deal with the unknown. My guess is that Tate's asleep on your couch," Julie shrugged. "I haven't heard from her in a while, and I think she would have come back over if she heard the car." She paused before blurting out, "Just say it, because I need to hear it."

"Ashley and Davis are dead," Luke managed to say. "All the rain knocked out the power by the practice field. They were trying to turn at a light that was out, and someone plowed straight into them. The police said there were no survivors. The other driver and both of them died on the scene." Luke let out a shaky breath. Julie gasped and turned into her husband as her own tears flowed.

"This has to be some terrible dream," Franklin insisted.

"I can't believe they're both just gone," Anne groaned, not bothering to wipe the tears spilling from her eyes. They all cried together for a while.

"I don't know how I'm supposed to go home and sleep in our bed," Luke said. "Not that I'm going to sleep much anytime soon."

"Oh, Luke! You can sleep in our guest room tonight if you want," Julie offered. "You don't have to worry about Addison, since Tate is with her. We'll tell them tomorrow."

"That would be wonderful," Luke said, and Ray wandered away to make sure that everything was ready for him in the guest room. He was halfway down the hall when it hit him; Ashley was dead. She wasn't going to be at the gym tomorrow to help him with practice. They had coached together for the last time. He knew he was never going to find someone who understood him like Ashley did. There was going to be hole at the gym that no one would ever be able to fill. Ray steadied himself against the wall and let it all wash over him. As he caught his breath, he took his time preparing the guest room before walking back to the kitchen. Once there, he sat down at the computer to type up an email. The gym would need to be closed for a few days, maybe even longer, so they could all grieve.

The next morning, Luke walked into the Markum's kitchen to find his parents cooking breakfast, just like he expected.

"Did you sleep at all, Son?" Franklin asked, handing him a cup of coffee.

"A little. What about y'all?" Luke took the coffee from him and sat down.

"Your mother tossed and turned all night," Franklin said.

"You only know that because you were up, too," Anne pointed out. "I keep waiting for Davis to walk through the door and ask for all the bacon I have. I know I made too many waffles since Ashley isn't here anymore."

"Have you seen the girls yet?" Luke didn't want to think about what breakfast should have been like that morning, and his thoughts turned to Addi.

"Not yet, but Julie was going to check on them—not tell them, just check on them," Anne assured him. As if on cue, Tate, Addison, and Julie walked through the door.

"What's going on?" Addison looked around the room. "I know something's wrong."

"Last night, there was an accident," Luke answered slowly. "Your mom and Davis died." Luke watched as Addison sank to the ground, sobs overtaking her. He sat with her on the floor and pulled her into his arms. Together, they cried on the kitchen floor until Anne made them eat some of the breakfast she had been working so hard on.

"They're just gone?" Tate said in disbelief as they sat around the table. "I can't believe this is real."

"I know. I keep waiting for Davis to walk in and crack a joke or for Ashley to come offer some words of wisdom," Julie said.

After a minute of painful silence, Tate blurted out, "Okay, I can't just sit here. Can we go to the gym?"

"Why?" Ray asked.

"Because it's better than just sitting here wanting things to go back to normal," Tate said with a tinge of anger in her voice.

"The gym . . . What are we going to do?" Julie asked, thinking for the first time about what Ashley's loss would mean to the gym.

"I drafted an email last night, but I figured we should close for at least the rest of the week," Ray answered. "Personally, I know I can't coach right now without Ashley there."

"Close the gym?" Addison asked and her uncle nodded. "But everyone there loves Mom."

"I know but"—

Sensing that everyone's heightened emotions could turn this small disagreement into hurtful words, Anne stepped in. "I think you are wise to cancel classes for the rest of the week, but what if instead of having formal practices, you keep the gym open for people to come if they want? You could basically just have open gym and let the girls be together," she suggested as Ray's phone rang.

"Speaking of the gym, this is Ginny Holland," he said when he saw the name on his phone. He walked into the living room to answer her call. "Hey Ginny. I'm so sorry I haven't communicated with you and Catesby before now. We are not having practice this morning."

"Is everything okay? I was surprised everything was locked up and dark when we got here this morning for the girls' practice," she said.

"No, it's not. Ashley and Davis were in a car accident last night. They died," he hesitated as he said the words out loud for the first time.

Ginny gasped, "Are you sure? Sorry, I know you are," she added quickly. "It's just not what I expected you to say. I'm so very sorry."

"Me too. We were just talking about what we are going do about the gym. I will let your family know as soon as we decide," Ray said.

"Thank you. I'm praying for y'all. Let me know if there is anything we can do. I can bring a meal, and I know Columbus and Catesby will want to see Addison," Ginny said.

"I appreciate that. I'll keep you updated," Ray assured her and hung up the phone. He was walking back into the kitchen when he nearly ran into Addison. "What are you doing?"

"I wanted to hear what you told Momma Ginny. This is just . . . I don't know, but I don't like it. And Granddaddy just keeps offering me more pancakes."

"We're all figuring out how to deal with this. But I think Grammy might be on to something with the open gym. Would you be up for it?"

"If it gets me out of this house, then yes," Addison said and followed him into the kitchen.

"Did you tell Ginny?" Luke asked.

"Yes. She said they are praying for us and are here for whatever we need. But I think Anne is right; I'm going to head to the gym and figure out how to get the news out. Addi is coming with me. Tate?"

"I'm in," Tate said.

"I'm going to go change," Addison said, heading to her house while Tate went to her room.

"Are you sure about this?" Luke asked Ray.

"No, but I don't know what else to do. Addison's right, though: the girls all love Ashley," Ray said. "Look, I know you're dealing with a lot, and I can't imagine how hard the last twelve hours have been for you. Can I suggest that you use the time while we are at the gym to figure out everything you need to handle? And start on funeral plans?"

"We'll help him," Anne assured Ray as the family got ready to go their separate ways.

"I love you, and I'll see you later," Addison hugged her dad extra tightly before she headed to the gym with Ray and Tate.

When Ray got the gym door unlocked, he turned toward the office. "I need to make some phone calls and send some emails. You're welcome to work out, but please warm up and be safe. Tate, you got her?" Ray asked, looking to Tate to make sure Addison didn't push herself too hard in her grief.

"I got her. Come on, Addi." Tate and Addison walked into the main part of the gym. Tate turned the lights on and plugged her phone in to play some music. They warmed up, and Addison did a few tumbling passes before she just lay down on the floor. "Are you okay?" Tate asked, concerned.

"Of course, I'm not okay. Mom and Davis are just gone," Addison sobbed.

"You're not physically hurt from gymnastics?" Tate asked, trying to correct her question.

"I'm not hurt physically," Addison answered, easing the fear on Tate's features.

"Honestly, it hasn't fully hit me that they are gone," Tate admitted, sitting down beside her cousin.

"Me either. I've gone longer without seeing them when they were at one of Davis's baseball tournaments, so I just keep assuming I'll see them in a few days. But then my mind reminds me that they are gone. Are you up for beam?" She asked, ready to stop talking and resume moving to get the thoughts out of her head.

"Let's see if I still got it," Tate laughed, and they climbed up on beams that were side by side. They did some turns and leaps. Then Addison did a back handspring and turned to her cousin, who did her own. "I did it!" Tate cheered.

"You did. It wasn't too terrible, either–especially after not training for the last couple years." Addison shook with laughter.

"Shut up," Tate giggled. "Do you think I can still do an aerial?"

"Tate, you've been doing aerials on the beam since you were like ten years old. Yes, I think you can still do it." Addison rolled her eyes as Tate did a perfect aerial. "Exactly. It's going to be a long time before you lose that skill."

"You know, Mom told me that an aerial was Aunt Ashley's signature move. She added it into every cheer routine she ever choreographed," Tate said thoughtfully.

"Why do you think I do one in every floor routine?" Addison smiled, but it slowly faded. She hopped off the beam and sank to the floor again.

"What's wrong?"

"No Mom for the Olympics," Addison said shakily before collapsing into sobs. "How am I supposed to do it without her?" The sobs continued for a while as the realization of all that was to come, all her Mom would miss, washed over her. There were so many things they had spent her life talking about: her senior debut, the Olympics and Worlds, high school graduation, and even her wedding someday. How could she plan for any of it without her mom?

CHAPTER EIGHT

"Jet lag is real," Scarlett complained as the Olympians rode the bus to the practice area the next morning. It was their first day with two practices in Rome, but everyone seemed to be dragging a little that morning.

"Or maybe it was all the interviews yesterday?" Brittnee offered. The media summit the day before had apparently taken a toll on more than just Addison, who had to keep talking about the worst two years of her life. Practice was plagued by the little things that were typical of tired gymnasts, like toes not being pointed, bent knees, or splits not hitting 180 degrees.

They were about halfway through their allotted gym time when Ray called everyone together. "I know you're tired and adjusting to the media attention that comes with being an Olympian, but you're having to learn that being here is more than just doing your routines. We have to pull it together if we want to win medals. Point your toes, hit your handstands, and focus fully. But please, also have fun. You are a much better gymnast when you actually enjoy what you're doing. Help each other; you know each other's routines well enough. That being said, let's change this up a little. Let's start on vault, we're going to go one at time and cheer each other on." This was Ray's attempt to shake things up and hopefully encourage them all to do their best.

By the end of the practice, the girls were having fun and doing better than they had been at the beginning. The little things were fixed, and they realized that working together made them not only a stronger team but stronger gymnasts.

"Great job today, Addi," Gwyn said as the team got ready to eat lunch.

"Thank you," Addison smiled. Their relationship had come a long way since Ray first told Addison that Gwyn was going to be his new assistant coach.

* * * * *

Addison: Age 15

"I have some news," Ray told Addison and Catesby as they finished their warmup. They both looked at him with anticipation. "I found a new assistant coach."

"You what?" Addison's anger flared. Her mom had been Ray's assistant coach for longer than Addison had been alive.

"Addi, you know that we have to have an assistant coach for the Olympics–especially if you are both going to make the team," Ray explained, doing his best to calm her down. He knew it was risk to tell her at practice, but he was excited and hoped she would be too.

"I can't believe you would replace Mom," Addison spat.

"No one is replacing your mom. She left a hole that no one can ever fill, but I have to have an assistant coach. I cannot take you and Catesby to the Olympics or any other competition without help. It is too much for me to do alone," Ray explained gently. "And if you will let me finish, I think you will be happy with my choice."

"Who is it?" Catesby braved asking.

"Gwyn Sullivan," Ray answered with a smile. The mouths of both girls dropped open as she came in from the office.

"Hi, girls," Gwyn said with a grin. "I know I can't replace Coach Ashley, and I won't even try. But I'm excited to be back at EGA, and I'm excited for the opportunity to be your assistant coach." Catesby smiled, but Addison walked off in the opposite direction fuming.

Ray left Catesby with Gwyn and went to talk to his niece. "Addi?"

"How could you?" she asked, tears streaming down her face.

"It's Gwyn, Addi. You've looked up to her for as long as I can remember. She's an Olympic gold medalist, and she trained with me and Ashley," Ray said. "I knew you would be upset when the time came for me to name someone, but I didn't think you would react like this."

"Of course I'm upset! Everyone is moving on with their lives like nothing happened, but everything is different! Dad is talking about redecorating the house, making Davis's room a guest room, and now you're announcing a new assistant coach." Addison sank into a ball in the middle of the floor.

"Oh, Addi, I'm sorry," Ray sighed as he sat down next to her.

"So, Gwyn's not hired?" Addi looked up hopefully, but Ray just shook his head.

"Take a few minutes to calm down." Addison stood up defiantly as he continued. "Think about Gwyn and all she might be able to offer you, me, and Catesby on this road to the Olympics. If you're ready, you can join us today. If not, I'll see you tomorrow," Ray finished as Addison walked out of the gym.

"Gwyn?" Addison said timidly as she reappeared in the gym a few hours later.

"Are you okay?" Gwyn asked, genuinely concerned.

"I'm not, but I will be. I wanted to apologize to you. I treated you unfairly and never even gave you a chance. I just don't like anyone taking my mom's place," Addison admitted.

"I get it. Coach Ashley . . . she was the best coach I could have possibly asked for, and everything I know I learned from her. I'm not her. I'm not your mom, but she did basically train me," Gwyn said, a smile spreading across her face.

"So, I should just like you because Mom trained you?" Addi's eyebrow quirked up.

"No, that's not what I mean," Gwyn tried to backtrack. "You don't have to like me. I mean, Catesby and I got along just fine. But you do have to respect me and listen to what I have to say. Remember, I have

Olympic medals, so I do know a thing or two about what you're trying to do," Gwyn finished with confidence, crossing her arms as the beginnings of a smile began to form on Addison's face.

"I can do that." Addison shook her head, fighting off laugher.

"Good. So, are you going to practice today or not?" Gwyn challenged her, and Addison slipped out of her t-shirt and shorts, revealing the leotard she was still wearing, to let Gwyn take her through a warm up. "Coach Ray told me that you do better if you start on floor, so start there?" Addison nodded, and the two worked through her normal workout before practicing a new tumbling pass a few times.

"Where to next? Beam is your specialty, right?" Addison asked Gwyn, who laughed and nodded. They worked through beam pieces together before Addison showed Gwyn her full routine.

Gwyn let out a long, low whistle. "You are freaking talented. I mean, I knew that, but to see you work up close and personal is just impressive."

"Thank you," Addison grinned. "I hate bars, so I don't like to end there. Is it cool if we do those next?"

"Hate? That's a strong word," Gwyn clarified as they walked to bars.

"I can't tumble on bars, so it's not my favorite," Addison explained with a shrug. "But I know it's necessary if I want to win the all-around gold. So maybe not hate, but it's definitely my least favorite apparatus." Addison grabbed the low bar. After the bars set, they finished on vault before Addison got ready for the cool down.

"So, was practice with me as bad as you expected?" Gwyn asked.

"I never expected it to be bad," Addison said, blushing. "I just don't like anyone–you, Uncle Ray, Dad–trying to replace Mom."

"Good to know," Gwyn said.

"Are you done? Can we go home now?" Julie stuck her head in the gym.

"That's my cue," Addison said, relieved she could stop trying to explain herself. "See you tomorrow, Coach Gwyn!"

* * * * *

"You good?" Catesby asked as the girls got on the bus to the cafeteria.

"Yeah, just hungry," Addison sighed, shaking off the memories.

The friends sat at lunch and marveled at all the other athletes who were wandering around: basketball and volleyball players who were literally twice their height, wrestlers whose plates were loaded with food, swimmers and track and field athletes who all talked and laughed together. There were conversations around them in multiple languages, and people were signing autographs and trading pins. Some athletes looked as tired as the gymnasts felt. Others looked like they were headed to practice. Addison hoped that she would be able to remember this forever—the feeling that she was a part of something so much larger than herself.

That afternoon, the Chinese team was in the practice area when the Americans walked in to the gym. Addison had been friends with Xiao Mei for a few years and was excited to see her across the gym. Addison raised her hand in a hello, and Xiao Mei returned the small gesture.

Practice fell back into normalcy. The girls had adjusted to the equipment and were working on perfecting their routines. During one of their breaks, Xiao Mei and Addison met over a chalk bowl and quickly exchanged the hellos and congratulations for their respective wins. Once the Chinese team finished their practice, the Americans were allowed to chat for a moment and snap some pictures. Xiao Mei and Addison hugged and took a couple pictures together, hopeful they would see each other again soon. Xiao Mei wished Addison luck and told her she would see her in the all-around. Addison knew she was a fierce competitor and one of the few who had scored nearly as high as she had in the all-around.

After the Chinese team left, the Americans finished practice. They had found their rhythm and were getting into the groove of Olympic practices. They were functioning like a team and settling into the Olympic madness. Thankfully, in the days before podium training and the official start of competition, there was still time to work out the little kinks. Addison knew she still had some work to do, but she was learning how to handle the mental side of gymnastics. Her routines were looking great, but in a sport where perfection is expected, there was always room to improve.

CHAPTER NINE

"Alright, ladies, this is podium training. I need you to understand that this will help determine the final all-around spot during qualifications. This is your one chance to get a feel for the equipment before competition officially begins," an American Gymnastics Federation official said as they gathered before walk-in. It was their first time in the Olympic arena, and the girls were all a little antsy.

"Do I have to do the all-around today?" Waverly asked her coach.

The official heard her question and answered, "No, it's not necessary. But you can if you just want to. Everyone else will, even though Addison and Catesby have already claimed their all-around spots for qualification."

"Thank you," Waverly nodded. She was only planning to compete on bars and beam, so she was thankful to be able to focus on them. Team USA was one of the few countries using podium training to determine which girls would compete on what apparatuses, not just for prep.

"Remember, no matter how this all shakes out, we are a

team," Brittnee said, putting her hand out. The rest of the girls quickly followed suit.

"1, 2, 3, U-S-A!" they cheered together.

The girls walked in to the huge arena with the other three countries in their sub-group, heading straight to the floor to wait impatiently for warmups to start. Waverly stood by the podium and cheered on her teammates. When warmups ended, Catesby stayed on the podium since she was going to be first one up. Addison watched Catesby and talked to Ray in hushed tones and rushed sentences before her first routine.

"On floor from the United States of America, Catesby Holland," the announcer said as Catesby walked out to hit her opening pose. Her routine was full of beautiful, artistic moves that served her well. Brittnee was next, and her routine was spot on. Addison could tell she was trying to show why she should be the other person competing in the all-around. Scarlett was next, she started strong, making only a couple minor mistakes. Addison high-fived her on her way up to the podium as she readied for her routine, which she nailed.

The team rotated to vault and seemed to remember what podium training was supposed to be for—getting used to the raised platforms and the equipment being used at the Olympics. Brittnee was up first and was the only one not doing an Amanar. She did a Yurchenko double full, landing with a giant hop. She sighed, rolling her eyes. That was not how she wanted her vault to go. Scarlett was next, and in a very uncharacteristic move, she almost sat down her landing. During Catesby's turn, Addison noticed Scarlett talking to her coaches. When Scarlett walked away from the conversation, she looked mad at the world.

"It's just one rotation. You can do better on the next one," Addison said to Scarlett. Scarlett glared and turned in the opposite direction. Addison shrugged. There was only so much she could do; she knew she needed to be prepared herself.

The girls moved to bars and did the touch warm up. Addison's warm up was off; she had more power and energy than she normally did her releases were bigger and less controlled. She nearly fell trying to catch her piked Tkathev.

"Breathe. This is just practice; treat it that way." Ray knew Addison well enough to know when she was stressing out. She already knew she was competing in the all-around in qualifications, so she truly had nothing to be worried about. "Flip. Fly. Stick," he reminded her, and Addison smiled. There was so much wrapped up in those three words.

* * * * *

Addison: Age 16 (February of Olympic Year)

"Addi…Addison!" She spun around to see her uncle calling and motioning to her. Addison was waiting on the floor judges to finish scoring the girl before her so she could start. It was the third rotation of her first official competition as a senior elite, which meant that she was eligible to go to major international competitions like the Olympics. This was first time that the world was going to get to see what she hoped would be her Olympic floor routine and she was slightly nervous. The waiting was not helping. She crossed the podium and squatted down to be able to hear her coach better. "Flip. Fly. Stick," he told her and Addison stared at him confused for a moment before she was being waved at by the judges. It was time for her routine to start. As she walked out to hit her starting pose, it dawned on her what her uncle was trying to say. She burst into a wide grin; she just needed to do what she had practiced. She had to think through the routine and breathe, the journey to the Olympics was just beginning.

The opening notes of the instrumental version of "Fight Song" played through the arena's speakers and Addison launched into her routine. She breathed and thought through each part of it. Hitting her final pose, Addison grinned. That was what she wanted the World, the gymnastics community, and the Olympic selection committee to see. She scrambled off the podium and over to her coach.

"Did you understand what I was trying to say?" Ray asked, pulling her into a hug.

"You were channeling Mom, trying to remind me to relax and do what I had practiced," Addison said, tears brimming. It was exactly what Ashley would have said if she was there.

* * * * *

"You got this," Ray said as Addison spring boarded to the high bar for her full routine, pushing the memory from her brain. She hit her releases and moved to the low bar before transitioning back to the high bar. She caught the bar but didn't have quite enough power and had to muscle her way into the giants that started her pirouettes. She landed her dismount with bent knees, but it was over. She had made it through bars.

"Let's go, Scarlett!" Brittnee called as Scarlett started her bar routine next. They all watched as her hopes for competing in the all-around crashed to the ground. Addison knew what was going to happen about a second before Scarlett slipped straight off the high bar onto the mat below. Scarlett had been doing a release move, but she did not grab the bar in the right way. She looked frustrated and annoyed as she walked over to the chalk bucket to re-chalk her grips.

"You can do this!" Waverly cheered as Scarlett was lifted to grab the high bar again. She did a couple giants and executed her release perfectly. Her teammates all cheered her on together. When she walked off the podium, her coaches only said about three words to her before letting her stew in silence.

Addison watched as Brittnee glanced at Scarlett before climbing onto the podium for her routine. Brittnee hit the scary parts and stuck her dismount perfectly. When she finished, Brittnee came to sit beside Scarlett.

"What are you doing?" Scarlett spat.

"I wanted to check on you after that fall. I know it's not easy to come back after that."

"Why do you care? It just means you get to do the all-around instead of me." Scarlett turned away from her. From where they sat, Brittnee and Addison both saw one of Scarlett's coaches give a slight smile. It didn't sit right with either of them, but Brittnee didn't push the issue any farther.

The American team would end on beam, ever the great equalizer in gymnastics. Catesby was up first; she had a couple of major bobbles and nearly came off the beam as she finished her tumbling series. But somehow, she managed to stay on. Scarlett sank farther into the hole she dug for herself, falling during her mount. She had never done that at an international meet, and she fell again on her full turn. It was hard to come back from a fall, especially when you already weren't in a good headspace. Addison knew that from experience.

During Addison's turn, she found herself next to the beam after her Arabian. This particular fall was so common for her that she didn't even think about it as she hopped up and finished the routine with her signature flare. Brittnee had a couple scary moments, but somehow managed to stay on the beam after landing her split leap on one foot. Even Waverly's routine had a few uncharacteristic bobbles and balance checks.

Ray looked at the weary girls as they marched out of the arena. "I know that didn't necessarily go the way we hoped, but it's podium training. It's a chance for you to get used to the arena before competition. Hold your heads high; you have so much to be proud of." Addison watched as Brittnee sat by Scarlett on the bus ride back to the suite, but Scarlett turned her back to Brittnee so that the two rode in silence. When they made it back, Scarlett shut herself in her bedroom for the evening.

The girls were going to let her have some space, but about an hour later, Addison thought better of it. She knew that when she was in a bad headspace, the best thing for her was a conversation. Scarlett's coaches hadn't talked to her at all after the practice; they were letting her stay upset instead of trying to help her get her mind in the right place. So Addison braved knocking on Scarlett's door.

"What do you want?" Scarlett spat when she answered the door. "Came to rub it that you had great day while I failed miserably?"

"I just wanted to check on you. I know you had a hard day, so I wanted to see if there is anything you need," Addison said, a little shocked at Scarlett's reaction.

"Not from you, Little Miss Perfect." Scarlett slammed the door, and Addison wandered back to the shared living room where she sat down on the couch in a haze.

"Scarlett's not okay, is she?" Addison turned to Brittnee.

"No, no, she's not. I'm worried about her, too," Brittnee confessed.

"Is there anything I can do?" Addison asked.

"Just keep trying to talk to her and being kind to her." Brittnee put a hand on Addison's shoulder. "Just be you."

"Thanks. Hopefully tomorrow will be a better day," Addison said, smiling timidly.

"That won't be hard; it's opening ceremonies!" Brittnee squealed.

CHAPTER TEN

"I know, I know, you're all disappointed. But we are too close to competition for you to walk in the opening ceremonies tonight. I'm so very sorry," one of the officials from the American Gymnastics Federation explained as the girls gathered for their morning workout. "However, this will be the only workout today so that you can enjoy the event from the TV in your room tonight. I know that you are still waiting to hear about the third all-around spot for qualifications, but we want you to finish practice before we announce it. Our lineups are not due for a few more hours. Make today count."

"Yes, ma'am," all five girls said in unison as their workout began. In about forty-eight hours, the Olympic competition would begin. Ray didn't have to push Addison to be perfect; she knew she had to be. If she wanted to qualify for all four event finals, she would have to be at the top of her game.

"Let's see your floor routine," Ray said after Addison fumbled on the beam for the fourth time. "Get out of your head," he whispered as she walked over to the floor. She nodded, tensing and releasing her shoulders. She tumbled until her passes were higher and tighter than they had ever been. Having the chance to tumble also cleared her head enough that she was able to land her beam Arabian perfectly. As practice came to an end, she hadn't even thought to look out for Brittnee and Scarlett because she was so busy perfecting her own routines.

"Our three all-arounders will be Addison, Catesby, and Brittnee," one of the officials announced as the team gathered to end practice. "Scarlett will be competing on vault and floor, and Waverly will be on bars and beam." The girls were dismissed to talk about the practice with their coaches.

That afternoon, Catesby and Addison were the first ones back to the suite. They didn't have a lot to talk about with Ray because practice went pretty much according to plan. Waverly was the right behind them, and Brittnee returned next. The girls all showered and changed so they'd be ready to watch the opening ceremonies that night. When Scarlett finally returned, she didn't speak to anyone and just disappeared into her room. Brittnee knocked on the door, but this time Scarlett didn't even bother to answer it.

"I got the popcorn," Waverly announced a few hours later, pouring the popped bags into five different bowls as the girls gathered in the living room of their suite to watch the opening ceremonies.

"I'll get Scarlett," Brittnee said, walking back over to Scarlett's closed door. This time, Brittnee disappeared into the room for a few minutes before both girls walked out.

"It's crazy to think that the ceremony is happening so close to us and we aren't there," Scarlett said as she got settled on the couch and tried to act as though nothing had happened.

"I'm so bummed we can't go, but I get that it's more important for us to be ready to compete," Brittnee sighed as the ceremony began. Addison couldn't help but remember being at a different opening ceremony eight years earlier.

* * * * *

Addison: Age 8

"I'm so excited to be here," Addison said as she, her dad, Davis, and Aunt Julie settled in their seats for the opening ceremonies at the Melbourne Olympics.

"Crazy, isn't it? And tomorrow we get to watch Tate compete," Julie smiled.

"And see your mom coach in person at the Olympics for the first time," Luke reminded his kids. They had been in Australia for three days and were looking forward to competition beginning.

"This is so cool!" Davis said as the lights dimmed. The siblings both sat with rapt attention through the main part of the opening ceremony.

"Dad, Addi's asleep," Davis whispered, pointing to his little sister a short half hour later.

"She's out," Luke nudged Julie as the parade of nations started.

"To be fair, this is not the most exciting part. We'll wake her up when they light the flame," Julie laughed.

"I can't believe Tate is actually an Olympian," Davis said.

"Me neither. What's that like?" Luke asked his sister.

"It's incredible to see her dreams come true—all the things she worked so hard for. It's like all those long practices, crazy competitions, and money was worth it. I have a feeling you'll get to experience it for yourself. We both know Addison already planning her own Olympic experience," Julie retorted.

"You're right. Do you think she can do it?" Luke asked.

"Of course she can!" Davis exclaimed. "She's Addi, and she knows more about gymnastics than almost anyone. Honestly, she's probably even better than Tate, but don't tell them I said that. It would just go to Addi's head and fuel the competitiveness between those two."

"He has a point," Julie smiled.

"Looks like we're going to be doing this again in eight years," Luke said, thoughtfully stroking Addison's hair. The family talked and laughed, enjoying seeing all the nations that were competing in the

Olympics. They woke up Addison for Team USA's entrance and the lighting of the Olympic flame.

"That was so fun! Thank you, Daddy," Addison bubbled, hugging Luke as they stepped on the bus back to their hotel.

"You're so welcome. I'm glad you had fun," Luke said.

"Tomorrow Tate competes, and it's going to be awesome," Addison yawned; she was fading again.

"Yes, it is," Davis agreed with his little sister.

* * * * *

"What it in the world is that?" Catesby laughed, pulling Addison from the memory. While opening ceremonies are impressive, they often had strange elements in them, like the blobs of color that were currently dancing around the arena. The blobs eventually came together to form the Italian flag and the Olympic rings. The girls enjoyed the spectacle of it all, but they were all waiting for the parade of nations.

"It does seem strange that is happening across town and we're not walking in it," Waverly reiterated as the other athletes started walking in.

"True, but we can walk in the closing ceremonies," Addison reminded them.

"Yes, they are on Addison's birthday after all," Catesby added.

"Well, that's a must then," Brittnee laughed. "Happy birthday to Addison."

"Thanks, guys, truly," Addison grinned. They waited for Team USA and tried to see if they recognized anyone in the delegation. Everyone except for Scarlett ate lots of popcorn, but they all enjoyed the opening ceremonies from afar.

"The Olympic Games have officially begun," a reporter said as the Olympic flame was lit. The girls hurried to the balcony to see if they could spot the fireworks, but didn't have any luck.

It was a night Addison knew she would remember forever, even though she didn't get to walk. As she headed to bed, Addison noticed Brittnee and Scarlett talking to each other. Addison guessed that Brittnee was trying to comfort her about the all-around decision, and she hoped Scarlett would listen.

The next morning, the atmosphere had shifted. Things were truly beginning. The team's practice was full of energy that hadn't been there the last few days, and the girls were hitting their routines consistently. They were actually starting to look like a gold medal team, even if they didn't have one yet.

CHAPTER ELEVEN

"You might want to open those boxes tonight," Ray reminded Addison and Catesby unnecessarily. The unopened boxes had been taunting them from their suitcases for the last week. The team had just finished their last practice before qualifications. The American gymnastics federation officials had given everyone a big speech about being prepared and reminded them of how important it was—not that any of them needed that reminder, either.

"Thanks, we will." Addison hugged him. These were rare moments during the biggest competition of her life: times when she saw the difference between her coach and her uncle.

"I'll give you a minute," Catesby said, noting the moment. She scurried off after Brittnee and Waverly.

"No matter what happens tomorrow, you have so much to be proud of," Ray smiled. "Everyone loves you no matter what—me, your dad, Aunt Julie, Tate, Grammy and Grandaddy, and especially your mom and Davis." Unshed tears filled his eyes.

"I wish they were here," Addison sighed as her own tears spilled over. "Davis was just as excited about all this as I am."

"Oh I know. Don't you remember our Montreal wrap up?" Ray's face cracked into a wide grin.

"How could I forget?"

* * * * *

Addison: Age 12

"Last night. Time for our wrap up, right?" Tate looked at her parents as they all sat around the living room of their hotel suite.

"Of course," Julie answered, turning to her husband. "Do you want to lead this charge?"

"That is my job," Ray laughed. "First question: What has been your favorite part of this Olympic experience?"

"Not having to compete and just getting to enjoy it," Tate said without hesitation. "I know, I know," she added, holding her hands up defensively as she felt both of her cousins' eyes on her. "I'm probably not the person you think would say that after the hell of a year I've had trying to come back, but yeah," she finished with a shrug.

"There is nothing wrong with that," Ashley assured her. "You worked so hard this year, and it didn't happen. But you've had such a great attitude about the whole thing." Ashley reached over and rubbed her niece's back lightly as she continued thoughtfully, "I think for me, it was about getting to see Addison and Tate interact. It was the first time they watched a major competition together live."

"No one warned me how intense you are, Addi!" Tate grinned.

"I tried; you didn't listen," Davis shrugged. "I loved getting to see Addi get excited about her own Olympic experience in four years."

"Aw, Buddy, that's so sweet," Ashley said, pulling him in for quick hug.

"Mom!" Davis rolled his eyes.

"That was my favorite part too," Luke admitted. "I just kept picturing you down there, Addi Anne."

"Because it's going to be true," Addison insisted, pursing her lips. "I loved getting to see Team USA win that gold medal!"

"That was definitely cool," Julie said. "Um, I think I have to go with

Ashley. I loved seeing Tate and Addison interact, just because it was so funny."

"I know I'm a lot, but gymnastics is my favorite. And I know who I want to win," Addison said defiantly.

"Never apologize for being you, Addi–ever," Tate said, looking her straight in the eyes. Addison nodded. "That just leaves you, Dad."

"I'm going with Addi: seeing Team USA win that gold medal after all the close calls," Ray answered. "Next question: what is one routine you'll remember forever?"

"Arabella Saunders' gold medal bar routine." Addison couldn't get her answer out fast enough.

"I thought you'd go with Camryn Harper's floor routine," Davis admitted.

"It's second," Addison said.

"Okay then, I'm going with Camryn's floor routine," Davis said.

"That's a good one! For me, it's Oakleigh's floor routine during the all-around final," Tate said.

"Oh, we know," Ashley rolled her eyes. "I thought you were going to have to leave the arena during that final."

"I was so close to sending you to the lobby before you embarrassed yourself on international television," Ray laughed.

"It was stressful! And she's my best friend," Tate defended herself.

"It's okay, Tate. We all have those moments, your mom has certainly had a few," Luke smiled at his niece before catching Julie's eye roll. "Mine was the beam routine that won the gold medal–the German girl."

"It was so pretty!" Julie said. "I think mine is going have to be Rosa's bar routine."

"Oh, that's a good one. I'm going with the Chinese beam routine– the one that got the bronze. That acro series into the leap series was incredible," Ray marveled.

"Her coach knows how to work that code," Ashley agreed. "Um, I know Davis already said Camryn's floor, but that one. During the team final when she knew they had the gold medal, it was just so cool."

"Question number three: what is your favorite thing you did, saw, or ate while you were here?" Ray asked. "I loved getting to go to the opening ceremonies because that's something we gymnasts never get to do."

"That's what I was going to say!" Ashley playfully slapped him.

"You can say the same thing," Addison reminded her before adding her answer. "Getting to go to all the gymnastics events."

"Definitely. That's not something a lot of people get to do!" Luke reminded them. "I think my favorite was that meal we had after the all-around. That steak was incredible."

"That restaurant was so good! Um, my favorite was getting to see Team USA receive their gold medals," Julie said. "Your turn, Davis."

"Easy. Getting to listen to Addi talk about what she is going to do when she makes the Olympic team," Davis smiled.

"It's going to be great, isn't it?" Ray smiled. "Question number four: what is something that you think you'll tell your kids or grandkids about this trip?"

"I was there when Camryn Harper won the all-around," Tate laughed.

"That I saw Team USA win a gold medal," Addison added and Ray, Ashley, and Julie agreed with her.

"I got to see Camryn Harper and Arabella Saunders inspire Addison's Olympic routines," Davis said.

"Is everything you say going to be about me?" Addison looked at her brother.

"Probably," Davis shrugged, "But that's what this trip is about, right? Getting you ready for the Olympics? I'm glad it was close enough that we could go even though Tate didn't make the team. Sorry Tate." She nodded in understanding. "But I can't be at the Olympics and not think about you. You've wanted to go to the Olympics your whole life. You're my little sister, and now we are only four years away from it being your turn. Of course I'm excited!"

"Thank you, Davis." Addison hopped up from her spot beside Tate and hugged her brother. "I love you."

"I love you, too," Davis said as Addison settled in next to him.

"Well, I think Davis already answered our final question: what about this trip has changed or challenged you?" Ray smiled.

"I have a whole list of things I want to learn as we prepare for what's next," Addison said.

"I would expect nothing less," Tate said approvingly. "I think for me, I learned that I could be okay without competing and still enjoy myself," she added.

"That's a big one, Tate," Ashley said. "I saw how the coaches reacted from afar, and it was good for me to remember that when I'm at a big competition like this, everyone is watching."

"Wow, Ash," Julie said. "I personally was challenged in my belief that there is one way to do things. Clearly things are changing, though, because Team USA won gold, and the athletes actually seemed to be enjoying themselves."

"Took the words right out of my mouth," Ray said. "Both the Julie and Ashley."

"I'm with Davis, actually," Luke said. "It was so special to get to spend this time with Addison before she competes for herself. It was good to see how she wants to prepare for it."

"See, Addi? I'm not the only one," Davis laughed, hugging his sister tightly.

* * * * *

"Davis always knew you'd get here," Ray smiled, pulling Addison out of the memory.

"He did. He was so proud of me."

"He still is," Ray assured her. "Go enjoy your night with Catesby. Open the box and relax before tomorrow."

"Thanks, Uncle Ray. For everything. I'm really glad you're my coach." Addison hugged him one last time before running off to meet up with her teammates.

Dinner in the dining hall was always an adventure, because the girls never knew who they were going to run into. But after eating their fill, Catesby and Addison sat on the floor in their room with the boxes they had been given before they left.

"Ready?" Catesby asked Addison. When she nodded, they unwrapped the boxes at the same time. Addison opened hers to a find a photo album full of pictures. There were ones of her early gymnastics days, ones with her family, and ones with her and Catesby. She cried and laughed, showing Catesby some of her favorites. Once she had looked at all the pictures, Addison dug through the rest of the box. She found a pair of American Flag sweatbands she could wear over her grips, some new bobby pins, and an eye-shadow palette. There were a few pieces of dark chocolate, her favorite candy, and a few of the sparkly stars that had adorned her vision board for the last year floated around the bottom of the box.

The last thing she pulled out was a small box with a note attached. "These were Mom's. I think it's time you had them. I love you, Dad. P.S. They are real." Addison carefully opened the box to find a pair of small diamond studs. She gasped, and Catesby looked up from the letter she was reading to see what Addison had found. She admired the earrings and showed Addison the Olympic ring necklace her parents had given her. Once both boxes were empty and they had shown each other everything. they enjoyed a couple pieces of Addison's chocolate, finished getting ready, and climbed into bed, ready for whatever the next day would bring.

CHAPTER TWELVE

"Let's see that opening tumbling pass," Ray instructed Addison as they started warmups for qualifications. Addison nodded, took off running, and launched into it. She flipped and tumbled through the air, clearing her mind. She landed and took a few deep breaths. This was it. Olympic competition was about to begin. The leos the girls picked for today had a skin tone sheer part on the top. The bodice was half red and half blue with the opposite color sparkles and a sheer belt. The white bottom had both red and blue sparkles.

Brittnee called the team together for a quick pep talk before walk in. "Today everything counts. This is what sets us up for the rest of the Olympics. Do your best, encourage each other, and no matter what happens—"

"We are a team," they all said together. They had been ingraining that reassurance into each other since this whole thing started. The girls lined up to be escorted into the arena, each one in her Team USA warm-up with her bag on her back. The Olympic officials made sure they were in order for entering the arena: the French team who was starting on floor, the Canadians who were starting on beam, the Americans who were starting on bars, and the Italians who were starting on vault.

Once the American team was settled in the bars area, they immediately went to work getting their grips on. The two-minute touch warm up started, and the girls took turns warming up handstands and releases. The bell dinged, and they cleared off the podium, leaving Brittnee, who was up first, alone.

"Let's go, Britt!" Scarlett cheered. They all echoed her as Brittnee received the green light to start the routine. She grabbed the low bar, and her routine started. She pirouetted and released, soaring over the bar and looking great. She did the giants that lead into her dismount but landed weird, taking multiple steps to try and keep from falling. She saluted the judges and hopped off the podium, bee-lining it for her coach.

Next, Waverly was cleared to go, and she spring-boarded to the high bar to start her routine. It was a beautiful, clean routine that put up the score they were hoping for. She had helped set them up for the team final.

"You got this, Addi," Catesby called as Addison re-chalked and waited for the green light. It popped up, and Addison spring boarded to the high bar. Her routine was a blur, but she hit her double layout dismount perfectly and saluted the judges. It was exactly how she wanted to start her Olympic competition. She hopped off the podium and hugged her coach before getting her grips off and finding a line to tumble on until the cameras disappeared. She hated when they focused on her. It threw her off, but she knew they were waiting on her score for the broadcast. When there were so many gymnasts competing, it baffled her that they would spend time waiting for one person's score.

Meanwhile, Catesby's routine proved why she was the

reigning world bars champion and why she was anchoring the Americans. She flew high above the bar and hit all her releases. She put up a massive score that would easily land her in the bars final, no matter how the rest of the day shook out. Addison, on the other hand, would have to wait to see if her score—which she still refused to know—was good enough to make it in.

With the first rotation of qualifications over, they were escorted to the beam by the Olympic volunteer. "You can do this," Addison whispered to Catesby as she walked to the podium, and Catesby smiled. She looked at her coach, who offered a few words of wisdom before she received the green light. With one last deep breath, Catesby saluted the judges and started her mount. She managed to make it through the routine without any major mistakes and stuck her dismount.

Addison was up next. She closed her eyes, picturing the perfect routine in her mind one last time. Then she rushed up the steps of the podium, re-chalked, and waited. As she did, she took a moment to take stock of everything. She heard the Canadian gymnast's floor music, the familiar sounds of the bars creaking with use from the Italians, and the sounds of French feet pounding down the vault runway. Just before the green light popped up, she wondered what kind of story the media was crafting, but thankfully she didn't have time to think about it. She saluted the judges and turned to face the beam, her hands hovering above it for a slight second before she started her squat through mount. She only had one major balance check after landing her Arabian, and her dismount was perfect. She hopped off the podium and was given a big hug and kiss on the cheek from her uncle.

Brittnee was up next. Her beam skills had improved dramatically since her last Olympic appearance. She had multiple Worlds medals on beam and even managed to get a dismount named after her by being the first one to do it in international competition. Addison watched as one of the steadiest beam workers in the world was shaky from the start. She had to fight to stay on the beam at the end of her acro series and even bent at the waist doing her full turn. It was very uncharacteristic for Brittnee, but she managed to pull off her dismount without major errors.

Addison looked at Catesby. Catesby's chances of being in the all-around final had all but solidified since only two athletes per country were allowed in each final. Brittnee was the other person doing the all-around for the Americans and that routine was not going to get the score Brittnee needed. It also meant that Addison would probably make the beam final because there was no way Brittnee was after that shaky routine—as long as she ended up in the top eight gymnasts on beam.

Waverly was the last one up, and she hit everything exactly like she needed too. She was as calm as Addison had ever seen her. At the end of her routine, Waverly's qualification round was done—the advantage of not competing in the all-around. Waverly hopped off the podium and pulled on her warm-up, glancing up at the scoreboard when her score popped up a couple minutes later.

"Halfway," Catesby whispered as she and Addison walked arm-in-arm to the floor holding area. Waverly, after a short conversation and hug from one of the Canadian gymnasts, came running up behind them.

"Who was that?" Scarlett asked, pulling off her warmup.

"Mia Maloney. We competed together in college," Waverly smiled. "She's one of my best friends, but we've been on opposite training schedules here, so we haven't been able to see much of each other."

Addison thought back to the few interactions she'd had with Xiao Mei and how she was looking forward to spending more time with her soon. She was hopeful that Xiao Mei would make it into the all-around final. She knew Mia Maloney had a shot, as well.

They started their warmup on floor, and Addison was tempted to sneak a peek at the scoreboard, but she knew it wouldn't give her all the information she wanted. They were in the second of five subgroups competing, so the final lists wouldn't be out for a while. Several of the big countries, including China, had yet to compete. Shaking herself out her mental lapse, Addison let her worries of qualifications slip away as she tumbled during her warmup.

"Go, Catesby, go!" Waverly cheered as Catesby prepped for her floor routine. At the green light, she sailed through the routine with her signature style, looking beautiful doing it. Her last major hurdle to get into the all-around was to just hit her Amanar on vault.

"Nicely done!" Addison high-fived her when she finished.

"Thanks. You're gonna kill it," Catesby laughed.

"That's the plan," Addison smiled before turning to cheer for Scarlett. The music for Scarlett's floor routine started in the wrong place, and she had to wait to restart her routine, which threw her off slightly. She seemed to pull herself together enough to be ready when it re-started, though. But it did affect her because her first tumbling pass was off. She didn't do one of the elements she had been struggling with which dropped her difficulty score and then she landed out of bounds on her final pass. It was not her best performance, but she got through it with grace.

Brittnee was up after Scarlett. She squeezed Scarlett's hand as they passed on the stairs. Addison watched as Brittnee stepped in the chalk, rubbing it up her legs and getting it on her palms. She stretched, her hands over her head, and then bent down to touch her palms to the floor. Brittnee paced, waiting on the green light. When she saw the signal, she threw her arms in the air to salute the judges and walked out to her opening position. Her routine was flawless and beautiful. Addison could see why so many people loved Brittnee's floor routines, and it was clear why she had made the floor final four years earlier in Montreal.

When Brittnee finished, Addison looked at Ray, who gave her a thumbs up. They weren't worried about this one. She saw the green light and lost herself in the routine, allowing herself to feel each element individually, landing her passes with confidence. She was grinning as she hopped off the podium. The whole routine felt great.

The only thing left was vault. Brittnee was up first with her double twisting Yurchenko, which looked great. Scarlett's Amanar was good, but she had two big steps on the landing. Catesby hit her Amanar with just a small hop on the landing. Addison's first vault was the Amanar, which she executed perfectly, and her Cheng was just as beautiful. To top it off, she stuck the landing on them both. For the first time that day, she turned to the scoreboard and waited. When her total score flashed onto the board, it was in her normal range. She was confident the top spot for the all-around was hers. Catesby had finished second, pretty much guaranteeing herself a spot in the all-around final, as well. In doing so, she knocked Brittnee out of the running. Since only two gymnasts per country could compete in the all-around final, Brittnee would not be competing in the final yet again.

* * * * *

Addison: Age 12

"Do you know who is competing in the all-around today?" Addison asked Tate. Qualifications were only the beginning, but Addison wanted to make sure she knew who she needed to be looking for as they began the hunt for the all-around gold.

Tate pulled out her phone and checked the texts from Oakleigh.

The friends had been communicating nonstop for the last few weeks. "Oakleigh, Camryn, and Brittnee," she read off.

"Brittnee, really? That's impressive," Ashley commented, ever the gymnastics coach.

"She's really talented and trains at the same gym that Brianne did. Remember Brianne? She was on the Olympic team with me," Tate reminded her, and Ashley nodded.

"She beat Oakleigh at Nationals, so it's going to be close." Addison's eyes were glued to the floor as the teams marched in with a blur of colors and flags. She was in awe.

"It's as amazing as you think it is," Tate laughed, seeing Addison's admiration. "Is she always like this?" Tate whispered to Davis who nodded, laughing.

"They're starting on floor!" Addison shook her cousin who just laughed. She had never seen Addison like this, completely in her element. Addison's eyes never left the floor; she was enthralled with the magic and sport. Four years earlier, she had hoped and prayed for Tate's victory. Everything was all about Tate. But this time, Addison could just enjoy the majesty of the Olympics and gymnastics while anticipating what it would be like to compete for herself in four years' time. Addison watched every single athlete who was competing in this subgroup—not just the Americans.

"Uncle Ray, could I do that?" Addison asked as Camryn Harper flipped through the air for her second pass.

"I don't see why not. It's going to take some work, but you can already do most of that pass," Ray laughed.

"Even with the double double?" Addison asked.

"That's the part that's going to take some work. But I know you can do it," Ray grinned. But Addison's eyes had not left the competition floor. When she wasn't watching the Americans compete on floor, her eyes were jumping between the rest of the apparatuses. There was just so much to see, and when it was over, Addison had a whole list of new things she wanted to learn.

"Well, the Americans qualified in first, but we'll see if they can actually pull out the gold this time," Ray said, rolling his eyes.

"I don't understand why Brittnee is so upset," Addison said as they flashed Brittnee's crying face on the big screen. "She's in fifth place."

"Yes, but Camryn is in first, and Oakleigh is third," Tate said as though it explained everything.

"So?" Addison shrugged; the top 24 gymnasts made the all-around final.

"Only two athletes from any particular country can make a final," Tate explained patiently.

"What!? That's the dumbest thing I've ever heard," Addison exclaimed. "Brittnee was incredible! And she doesn't get to compete just because Oakleigh scored a tenth higher than she did?"

"Yep," Tate said, popping the p for emphasis. "Welcome to elite gymnastics; it's the best," she deadpanned, rolling her eyes.

«Tate—" Julie reprimanded her daughter.

"She's not wrong," Ashley laughed, the coach in her coming out. "The sport demands perfection and values youth. There are so many changes that need to be made, and we are just beginning to make them. But even Brittnee's fifth place finish will be worth it if they can pull out the team gold."

* * * * *

"Congratulations," Brittnee cheered as she hugged Catesby. Addison couldn't help but notice the difference four years had made for Brittnee. Even though she was once again knocked out of the all-around final by her teammate, she was able to genuinely celebrate each of their victories. "Nice job, ladies," she added. The team had put together a massive score that put them safely in first place.

The girls were escorted out of the arena, but before being dismissed, they had a team meeting with all the coaches and officials from the American gymnastics federation. The meeting ended in time for them to see the next set of qualifications, but the only ones who opted to watch the competition were Addison and Catesby. They found a spot with Coach Ray and settled in for the rest of the afternoon.

"You're sure about this?" Ray asked Catesby.

"If she's going to be here, I'm going to be here," Catesby answered, nodding towards Addison, who sat with a notebook clutched in her hand. She had written her scores in the notebook, and they knew she was going to document who was in each final.

"You know you qualified for all four event finals, right?" Catesby asked her best friend.

"It's not over yet, but hopefully. I'm not really worried about anything other than bars and maybe beam. Plus, this way I get to see the majority of the gymnasts I'll be competing against," Addison shrugged.

"You take things entirely too seriously. You realize that, right?"

"This is the O-lymp-ics, Cates," Addison retorted, rolling her eyes and turning back to face the arena where competition was beginning. The Chinese team was in this subgroup, and Addison cheered for Xiao Mei as they started on floor.

The friends watched as the teams competed, hoping their scores were enough to keep them in the finals. At the end of it, Xiao Mei had qualified for the all-around behind Catesby, and China was in second behind the Americans by a closer margin than they hoped.

The next couple subgroups included the Russians and the Romanians, whom Addison was looking forward to seeing. The funniest moment of the day came during the German vault rotation. One of their gymnasts ran to vault, but at the last minute realized that her steps were off. Instead of running off to the side so she could vault again, she hopped on the springboard, then the vault, and then the mat.

"What was that?" Catesby laughed.

"You know, I saw someone do that in a team final, and cost their team a medal. So please, if that ever happens to you, just run sideways," Ray pleaded as he shook his head.

"Got it," Addison answered seriously even though she hadn't stopped giggling. They talked and laughed, enjoying the competition. Through it all, Addison kept up with her list of event finalists and the top six in the all-around. She was getting to see the best gymnasts in the world compete on the biggest stage.

"What's that list?" Ray asked, pointing to the opposite page of the notebook.

"Skills I want to learn," Addison smiled.

"You're already putting together new routines, aren't you?" Ray rolled his eyes, and Addison just shrugged.

"Oh, she'll have three new routines and my freshmen collegiate routines figured out by the end of the day," Catesby laughed.

"And you'll thank me," Addison smiled, turning back to the action just in time to see one of the Belgian gymnasts roll out of her tumbling pass and tuck her head in time to protect her neck. "Oh no, that's not good."

"Let's hope she's okay," Ray said as she was escorted off the podium.

"That was terrifying," Catesby said.

"That, for the record, is exactly how you handle that situation. You let me know, and I will get the medical team. Don't move without my permission." Ray looked both of them in the eyes.

"Understood," Addison said.

"Yes, Coach," Catesby responded. He nodded, and they turned back to watch the competition.

"What's your list looking like?" Ray asked as he took the notebook from Addison and studied both sides. With only the final rotation of that subgroup and one more subgroup left, her lists were shaping up quite nicely.

| Skills to Learn | ⊘ |

(VT) Rudi
Tsukahara
layout

1. Me – 62.366
2. Cortes – 60.607
3. ~~Giana Russo (ITA) – 57.6~~
4. ~~Mia Maloney (CAN) 57.2~~
3. ~~Xiao Mei – 57.5~~
4. ~~Giana Russo (ITA) – 57.5~~
5. ~~Mia Maloney (CAN) – 57.2~~
3. Katina Markoff (RUS) – 60.1
4. Mila Falin (RUS) – 58.2
5. Xiao Mei – 57.59
6. Giana Russo (ITA) – 57.56

(UB) Front Tuck to
High Bar Mount
(I need to be doing this)

Clear hip full
Bhardwaj
Deltchev

Nabieva!

Piked Stalder
Gienger layout

(BB) Back Handspring or
maybe switch leap
Mount?

Stag leap!   Y turn
Tour Jete   Illusion
Onodi   (so pretty)

Double Double!

Team

1 USA
2 ~~Canada~~ China
3 ~~Italy~~ ~~Canada~~ Romania
4 ~~Australia~~ ~~England~~ Russia
5 ~~France~~ ~~Australia~~ Canada
6 ~~Netherlands~~ ~~France~~ England
7 ~~Netherlands~~ Italy
8 Australia

Double Arabian? (FX)
Butterfly?

Shushanova   Triple
Full   Double?
Double Y Turn   Double
                        Front
                        Piked

(VT) 1 Me - 16.05
~~2 Zoe King (AUS) 14.9~~
~~3 Lara Keller (SUI) 14.8~~
2 Katina Markoff (RUS) 15.6
~~3 Alexandra Luca (ROU) 14.99~~
~~4 Sofia Wagner (GER) 14.95~~
~~5 Zoe King (AUS) 14.94~~
~~6 Lara Keller (SUI) 14.8~~
3 Anika Kota (IND) 15.2
4 Veronica Lopez (MEX) 15.04
5 Alexandra Luca (ROU) 14.99
6 Sofia Wagner (GER) 14.95
7 Zoe King (AUS) 14.94
8 Lara Keller (SUI) 14.8

(UB) 1 Cortes - 15.86
~~2 Me - 15.83~~
2 Chen Jun (CHN) 15.83
3 Arabella Saunders - 15.7
~~4 Lilly Dupont (BEL) 15.4~~
~~5 Me - 15.33~~
~~6 Xiao Mei - 15.30~~
4 Natasha Petrov (RUS) 15.6
5 Emma Schimdt (GER) 15.4
6 Lilly Dupont (BEL) 15.43
7 Me - 15.33
8 Xiao Mei - 15.30

(BB) 1 Waverly - 15.6
2 Me - 15.8
~~3 Marie Brodeur (FRA) 14.9~~
~~4 Mia Maloney - 14.6~~
~~5 Giana Russo (ITA) - 14.5~~
~~3 Xiao Mei - 15.06~~
~~4 Marie Brodeur (FRA) 14.9~~
~~5 Mia Maloney - 14.6~~
~~6 Giana Russo (ITA) 14.5~~
~~5 Crina Andrei (ROU) 14.8~~
~~6 Mia Maloney - 14.6~~
~~7 Giana Russo (ITA) 14.5~~
3 Ana Santos (BRA) - 15.3
4 Xiao Mei - 15.06
5 Marie Brodeur (FRA) 14.9
6 Crina Andrei (ROU) 14.8
7 Mia Maloney - 14.6
8 Giana Russo (ITA) 14.5

(FX) 1 Me - 15.7
2 Britt - 15.2
~~3 Mia Maloney - 14.6~~
~~4 Sharna White (AUS) 14.3~~
~~5 Maisie Armstrong (GBR) 14.6~~
~~6 Sharna White (AUS) 14.3~~
3 Katina Markoff (RUS) 14.8
4 Sorina Muller (ROU) 14.6
5 Alexandra Luca (ROU) 14.6
6 Mia Maloney - 14.5
7 Maisie Armstrong (GBR) 14.5
8 Sharna White (AUS) 14.3

"The good news is the team final is pretty much set. The Japanese team would have to score higher than Australia in the next subgroup, which is highly unlikely. But with so many of the individual gymnasts left, these finals are still wide open. This skills list is impressive," he added, his shoulders shaking with silent laughter.

"I'm going to have to work on something once the Olympics are over," Addison stated simply.

"No break for you?" Catesby laughed.

"Have you met me?" Addison's eyes went wide. "No! Worlds are next year. Plus I'm going to have to figure out how to cope with you ditching me to go compete for Georgia."

"I have been dreaming about being a GymDawg for as long as you have been dreaming about being an Olympian. Your mom was a coach, and my mom went to UGA. And I'm not ditching you. You're my best friend. I could never ditch you, Addi."

"The good news is I will get to see you when I come watch you compete," Addison smiled.

"Okay, okay," Ray interrupted, refocusing them. "I'm glad y'all are making plans for next season, but we still have medals to win here in Rome." Addison was thankful for time with her uncle and her friend as they figured out who would be competing in each of the finals that were to come over the next week.

"There they are," Scarlett said, motioning to the guys in the USA gear. The girls were excited to get to watch the Men's team compete.

"Girls, this is Eli Dawson and Noah Archer. They are the alternates for the Men's Team," Brittnee introduced the boys they were joining as she sat down next to Eli to watch the competition. She had gotten to know most of the men's team at the last Olympics.

"Hey Wave, how's Markus doing?" Noah asked as everyone settled in. Waverly's boyfriend, Markus Harris, had hoped to be in Rome with them, but an injury kept him home.

"He's good. Annoyed that he's not here, but he's healing the way he's supposed to, which I'm thankful for," Waverly answered over Addison's head.

"Good! I've talked to him a little, but being here has put me so far off my normal rhythms," Noah laughed. "Sorry, I'm being rude. I'm Noah Archer," he smiled at Addison, who was bobbing forward and back so Noah and Waverly could have their conversation with her sitting between them.

"I'm Addison—"

"Jessup. Yeah, I know," the blonde athlete said.

"You do?" Addison was a little taken aback.

"You're a national champion—not to mention the fact that you qualified first for the all-around final yesterday. Why wouldn't I know who you are?" he challenged.

"You have a point. I guess you should," she shrugged. A smile crept across her face, and Noah gave her an affirming nod.

Addison pulled out her phone to text her cousin as the events kicked off. She was trying to get Tate to tell her what the media was saying about her while Waverly and Noah kept giving her little bits and pieces of information about the men's events. With so much running through her mind, she was exhausted and kinda confused. But when the day ended, she did know the men's team had missed out on the bronze medal by one tenth of a point.

"I noticed you and Noah Archer getting all cozy," Scarlett teased on their way to find some dinner.

"He was explaining gymnastics to me," Addison said, she wanted to hide behind something. The last thing she wanted was for her name and a boy's name to end up that close together.

"He is cute," Brittnee added, more to rile Addison up than anything.

"I—I—I don't have time for boys. I have medals to win," Addison stuttered, and they all laughed.

"You can't be all about gymnastics all the time," Waverly said, and Catesby burst into laughter. "Or you can, apparently," she shrugged.

"It's just that I've been planning and working for this—being here at the Olympics—for my entire life. I literally don't know what life without gymnastics is like. When I'm not at the gym, I'm hanging out with my family or Catesby, and they're all gymnasts, too. So my whole life is about gymnastics, but maybe not like you think?" Addison lamely tried to explain.

"We get it, don't worry. It's just the world of elite gymnastics, where our lives look so different from most people our age. You'll figure everything out, I promise," Waverly assured her, putting a hand on her shoulder. "But for the record, boys are not so bad."

"Says the girl who's about three seconds away from getting engaged," Brittnee laughed.

"How did you meet your boyfriend, Britt?" Scarlett countered.

"Gymnastics," Brittnee answered, laughing again. "His dad was a recruiter for Denver, and they came to, like, all my meets." She smiled. "But Austin is great. He's helped me see there can be life after gymnastics."

"You're really retiring after this?" Waverly asked.

"It was a miracle I made it here. My shoulder is shot, and my knees are about to give out. Plus, I have a scholarship waiting for me at Utah that I already deferred for a year," Brittnee answered.

"I forgot you're going to Utah," Scarlett said.

"Are you going to do college gymnastics?" Brittnee asked.

"I decided to go completely pro so no college sports

for me," Scarlett pursed her lips. "I mean, I thought about going to UCLA, but I knew I had to take the opportunity when it came up."

"Well, I'm headed back to Florida for one more year," Waverly said. "You're going to Georgia in the fall, right, Catesby?"

"Not till next fall. I still have to graduate from high school," Catesby laughed.

"Darn. That means I won't get to compete against you," Waverly sighed.

"Better for me; that means I actually have a chance to win," Catesby laughed, bumping her shoulder.

"Yeah right," Waverly shook her head.

"You are, however, going to have to compete against me," Brittnee said as she high-fived Waverly.

"Good! At least I know I'll have some competition," Catesby winked.

"Waverly, you'll have to show Scarlett and me around NCAA Nationals when we all go watch Cates and Brittnee," Addison said.

"If I come," Scarlett added, rolling her eyes.

After dinner, the girls all headed back to their suite. "I'm headed to bed. We have a big day tomorrow," Waverly said as soon as they walked in.

"What's tomorrow?" Brittnee laughed. "Night, everyone." They chorused their goodnights and headed to their rooms.

As Catesby and Addison brushed their teeth, Catesby brought up boys again. "Noah was pretty cute, and you seemed to hit it off," she said.

"Not you too," Addison sighed.

"I know you better than almost anyone, and I know that boys are literally the last thing on your mind. But it wouldn't be the end of your career if you liked a boy," Catesby insisted.

"He's cute, sure. But we have just started competition.

We have team final tomorrow, the all-around final, and then event finals. I can't think about boys right now." Addison threw the pillows off her bed in frustration.

"Okay, okay," Catesby surrendered. "I won't bring him up again."

"He was cute, though, wasn't he?" Addison said as she pulled the sheets back and climbed in to bed.

"Yeah," Catesby laughed.

"It really wouldn't be the end of the world if I liked a boy?" Addison reached for her stuffed fox.

"Definitely not—even if it's not Noah," Catesby added.

"Goodnight, Cates." Addison rolled over, a smile on her face. Maybe there was a boy she could be interested in.

CHAPTER THIRTEEN

"What leos are we wearing?" Scarlett's voice cut through the chaotic shuffle in their suite the next morning.

"The one that Waverly wore for the photo shoot, remember? This is team final," Brittnee called back. The leotard was shiny blue on top with sheer sparkly stripe starting from the v-neck and continuing down the sleeves. Under the stripe, it was shiny red with white side cut-outs.

"Of course. My brain is gone this morning," Scarlett laughed.

"You better find it! We have gold medals to win," Addison chimed in, which made everyone laugh.

As a finishing touch, Catesby secured an NC State scrunchie around the end of Addison's French braid. Addison touched it, thinking of how good it felt to have a piece of her mom with her.

* * * * *

Addison: Age 10

"You ready for this?" Ashley asked Addison as they ate breakfast together the morning of her elite qualifying meet.

"Beyond ready! Sometimes I hate having an August birthday," Addison sighed.

"You'll thank me when you get to go to the Olympics at sixteen–almost seventeen," Ashley countered, rolling her eyes. "So, I have something for you." She set a small gift on the table between them.

"Shouldn't the gifts come after I qualify for elite?" Addison laughed, staring at it.

"Not this one," Ashley grinned, watching as Addison opened it with glee. Her daughter dumped the black and red NC State scrunchie into her hand. She looked at her mom, eyes full of questions. "This is my good luck charm. I've had it since I was about your age and made my first cheer team. I wore it to every competition, try out, and anything else. It worked for me, so I wanted to pass it along to you."

"Mom, I don't know what to say," the ten-year-old gasped. "Thank you."

"You're so welcome." Ashley reached across the table and touched her daughter's arm. "You ready?" They both stood up from the table.

"Let's do this," Addison smiled. "But first, will you do the honors?" Addison held out the scrunchie for her mom. Ashley brought her in for a tight hug and wrapped the scrunchie around the end of her French braid.

"Perfect. A little Wolfpack magic for my blue-loving girl." Ashley kissed the top of her head.

"I love you, Mom," Addison said.

Ray was waiting on them with Addison's competition bag when they walked outside to catch the bus to the competition. "Today's the day you become an elite gymnast," he announced, a smile spreading across his face. "I always knew we'd get here, and I want you to know that I'm so very proud of you."

"Everyone's so sappy today," Addison sighed.

"It's a big day," Ashley reminded her. "It's a day we've been working towards for essentially your whole life. So we're allowed to be sappy." Addison just rolled her eyes. She knew it was going to be this kind of day from the moment her mom insisted on breakfast just being the two of them.

When they made it to the hotel ballroom where the competition was being held, Addison checked in, proudly announcing herself. She was handed her bib and coaches credentials, which she promptly handed to them. The trio walked into the ballroom and settled on some chairs near the floor. Ashley secured the number on the back of Addison's blue ombre leo. The color fade was so pronounced, it was white at the top and faded into almost a navy blue at the bottom.

Once everything was in place, Addison started her warmup so she would be ready when competition started. She had spent the last six months perfecting these compulsory routines that everyone in the competition would be doing. In order for her to qualify to compete as an elite gymnast–where she could represent USA in international competitions, she had to score a 35 out of 40. Addison was hoping for a perfect 40 and knew exactly what she needed to do to get it because she had been doing these routines for months.

She was starting on floor, which she was thrilled by; it had always been her favorite event. The competition started, and she sank into her middle split to stay warm. She used the sounds of the music and feet hitting the mat in rhythmic succession to go over her routine in her head. When it was finally her turn, she nailed the compulsory routine and wasn't the least bit surprised when it came out to a perfect score.

The rotation ended, and she headed to vault. She was doing a Yurchencko layout, which she stuck cold. She was on track to get the perfect 40 she was after. Bars was next, which was the one event she was actually worried about. She was up first in the rotation, which meant she didn't have as much time to prepare as she hoped. The routine started well; she was hitting all her markers and doing what she needed to do until giants at the end. She missed her turn on one of the handstands and landed in a super low squat on the dismount.

"Breathe. It's still a great score," Ray whispered when the 9.6 was shown for her score. He knew that she freaked out when she didn't get the score she was hoping for.

"I'm still going to be an elite, and that's all that matters," Addison winked, knowing she was still above the 35 she needed.

"That's my girl," Ashley laughed.

Addison prepped for her final rotation: beam. She found a spot to practice and marked her beam routine a couple times while she waited. When the final rotation started, Addison was set to go last on the beam because she went first on bars. She kept getting more antsy the longer she had to wait, but she was doing her best to stay calm. When it was finally her turn, she wiggled all over to release the pent-up energy. Then she climbed on the beam and started her routine. She hit all the major things she was supposed to with a couple minor bobbles along the way. She stuck her dismount and was swept into a hug from her mom. She stayed wrapped in her arms until the 9.8 was shown.

"I did it! I'm an elite gymnast!" Addison breathed a sigh of relief. All the hard work she had put in had finally paid off. Step one to becoming an Olympic gymnast was complete. She still had a long way to go, but at least now she was able to compete with the best.

"You did. I guess my good luck charm works for you, too," Ashley smiled.

"I guess it does," Addison laughed. They wrapped up everything at the competition and headed to meet the rest of the family for lunch. They opted not to come to this competition, just to enjoy some time together before Tate's turn at Nationals the next week that was in the same city.

"So?" Tate asked as everyone sat around the table.

"I did it! Not a perfect 40, but 39.4. I will take that score if it means I don't have to deal with compulsories ever again," Addison grinned.

"And I don't have to coach you through compulsories ever again," Ray and Ashley high-fived. It had been a struggle but they had survived.

"I'm so proud of you," Davis said.

"We all are," Luke assured her.

"Olympics, here I come," Addison said.

"Slow down! We still have a long way to go," Ray cautioned. But the grin didn't leave Addison's face as her mom winked at her.

* * * * *

"Can I interest you in some gold sparkly eyeshadow?" Waverly appeared in their doorway, pulling Addison from thoughts of her mom.

"Yes, please," Catesby laughed. Waverly fixed their eye shadow the way she had for Brittnee and Scarlett. They were pulling on their warmups and double-checking their bags when someone knocked on the door.

"Everyone ready?" An American Gymnastics Federation

official in a Team USA tracksuit had come to escort them to the arena. They all answered yes, slipped their backpacks on, and headed out the door.

"We're in the rotation with China, right?" Brittnee asked.

"Yep. They qualified in second. We'll be starting on vault," Addison answered.

"She might be all about gymnastics, but it means she knows everything that's going on," Catesby said.

"At least I'm good for something," Addison retorted, bumping Catesby's shoulder.

"You're good for more than that! We need you to win that gold medal. You are doing the all-around today," Scarlett reminded her.

"I hate all of you," Addison laughed. They continued to laugh and cut up the whole way to the arena. But once they made it inside, they switched into competition mode. They made it through warmups in the practice area before entering the main arena for the competition to start.

"Breathe; focus on you," Ray whispered in Addison's ear as they prepped for the touch warm-up. Addison joined Scarlett and Catesby on the podium and did her two warmup vaults.

"Let's go, Scarlett!" Brittnee called as Scarlett stood on the end of the runway waiting on the green light. Addison closed her eyes and pictured her vault in her mind, the perfect two and half twists with a stuck landing. She opened her eyes when she heard the sound of feet hitting the mat and was just in time to see Scarlett finish her vault with a salute to the judges before dashing off the podium.

The first Chinese athlete was up next, and she hit her vault easily. Addison cheered as Catesby hit her Amanar. She was grinning as she hopped off the podium. Then Addison prepped while the next Chinese gymnast vaulted.

Addison was twisting in her mind as Ray situated the

board in the right place for her. She waited, her eyes on the light, which had yet to turn green. It changed. She turned to salute the judges before racing the camera down the runway. She flipped onto the springboard, pushed off the vault table, and soared through the air. She landed with a slight hop, throwing her hands in the air before she heard the cheers of her teammates. They had finished their first rotation.

Though the Chinese team did not have the depth the Americans had on vault, they would more than make up for it on bars. After the last Chinese gymnast completed her vault, the teams rotated, and everyone competing on bars got their grips on. China was up first this rotation. The first gymnast was clearly very talented, sailing through all her pirouettes and releases with ease.

Waverly was first for the Americans, and she hit her routine easily. Xiao Mei was next, showing off her beautiful routine. After Xiao Mei, Addison stood at the chalk bowl getting her mind set as her coaches chalked the bars. She stood on the springboard between the bars, and when she saw the green light, she bounded up to the high bar. She made it through the releases and the transition to the low bar. She was pushing herself back to the high bar when she fell.

She hit the mat hard and sighed, taking stock of her body as she walked back over to the chalk bucket. She re-chalked and grabbed on to low bar. She redid the transition so she would get credit for it, and she nailed it the second time. The routine ended without any more problems. She even stuck the dismount.

Addison saluted the judges, hopped off the side of the podium, and started taking her grips off. Immediately, she pulled her headphones out of the front pocket of her bag and hit play. She had to get the fall out of her head. She listened to the songs that pumped her up and tumbled a little before the teams rotated to beam.

Brittnee and Waverly were deep in conversation, and they let Addison have the first warm up for the beam rotation. She tried to focus, but she couldn't help wondering what they were talking about.

"Focus on you," Ray told Addison as she climbed off the podium. He had seen her glancing at her teammates during the touch warmup. "Do your best. Do your job." She nodded and closed her eyes, picturing herself doing the perfect dismount. She heard the familiar sounds of the beam creaking, and she knew Brittnee had started. When she opened her eyes, Brittnee was just starting her sheep jump. Her left foot missed the beam, causing her to fumble, but she fought through it and stayed on the beam. Addison turned to look at Catesby, who gave her a thumbs up. At least it wasn't a fall. She heard both Scarlett and Waverly cheering their teammate on.

"Focus, Addi," Ray's voice cut through the noise. She didn't know where he was, but it didn't matter. She watched as Brittnee nailed her dismount.

"You good?" Gwyn asked as Addison put her headphones away.

"I will be. I just need to get on the beam," Addison said.

"Okay. What do you need from me?" Gwyn said.

"Nothing. I can do this. It's a new rotation, a new apparatus," Addison insisted, giving Gwyn a high-five as she rushed up the steps to re-chalk. Addison took long, deep breaths, trying to keep herself calm. As her routine began, she focused on connecting each element to the next. It worked until she did her Arabian half. She landed slightly off-kilter and had to push her arms down by her sides to stay steady. Thankfully, she stayed on the beam and was able to finish the routine with grace as she stuck her dismount.

"Look at you! Great job!" Gwyn hugged her, and Addison smiled. The Chinese gymnast who was on the beam after her had major bobbles and nearly ran off the podium trying to stop her dismount. Addison let out a sigh of relief. She understood now why Brittnee and Waverly had been whispering; they were talking about scores. She was thankful they respected her routine enough to not discuss it where she could hear them. Waverly's routine was normal for her, and the team all settled in to watch Xiao Mei's routine. She was the Chinese team's anchor for a reason; it was incredibly beautiful routine.

The teams moved to floor for the final rotation, and Addison knew the competition had to be close. She switched her music to simply be "Fight Song" on repeat, slid into her middle split, and blocked out her surroundings as much as possible. A few repetitions of "Fight Song" later, she felt a hand on her back and sat up. Ray nodded, letting her know that it was time to get ready. She quickly stuffed her phone and headphones back in her bag.

"Flip, fly, stick," Ray called as Addison walked up the steps.

"Flip, fly, stick," she repeated as she joined her teammates for the touch warm up. Once that was done, she went back to her headphones and middle split until it was her turn to close out the competition.

"You good?" Scarlett asked her as she shoved the headphones into her bag again, a questioning look in her eye.

"I am. I got this," Addison assured her, her face set. She sucked in a breath, jogged up the stairs, and quickly re-chalked. She paced as she waited for the green light. When it came, she saluted the judges and walked out onto the floor to hit her opening pose. Then came the first downbeat, and she backed into the corner for her opening pass. She hit it perfectly and felt herself relax ever so slightly. Perfection on her first pass was always a sign that her routine was going to go well. She lost herself in the routine and enjoyed the moment, finally landing her last pass and finishing her routine with her usual style. Then she quickly hopped off the podium to stand with her teammates. While they waited, she remembered watching the Montreal team win gold four years earlier.

★ ★ ★ ★ ★

Addison: Age 12

"USA! USA! USA!" Addison and Tate cheered along with the crowd. Addison was decked out in full USA garb and could hardly wait for the competition to start. She waited impatiently for the walk in, dreaming about which routines she was most excited to see again. Tate shook her head; they were so much alike.

"I'm sorry to bother you, but are you Tate Markum?" A blonde surfer dude asked before competition started.

"Yes, I am," Tate smiled brightly. Being recognized in public was still a little strange for her.

"See, I told you!" he hissed at a teenaged girl a couple rows up. "Could she take a picture with you?" he asked, flashing Tate a grin that almost blinded her.

"Of course!" Tate walked up to the girl and smiled for a photo.

"Thanks! I'm kinda sad you aren't competing," the girl offered.

"Me too, but I know the right people made the team. Cheer them on today," Tate told her.

"Definitely! Go USA!" The two fans waved and disappeared into the crowd.

Tate sat down just in time to see the American team enter. They were last into the arena and headed for the vault with the Russians, who had qualified in second. Camryn Harper was starting the competition off with her Amanar, which she hit beautifully. Oakleigh's vault was slightly off, but she managed to pull out a decent score. Mac, who was the best vaulter on the team, finished off the rotation strong. The Russians didn't have the depth the Americans did, but they still managed to stay within striking distance.

In the next rotation, the Russians would go first on the bars, and they had some strong bar workers on their team. Tate and Addison watched and waited with bated breath as the Russians dazzled the crowd with their routines. When it was America's turn to compete on bars,

Brittnee was up first. She only struggled a little, putting up a decent score. Rosa bounded up to the high bar to start her routine, which was going fine until she transitioned back up to the high bar and had to muscle up. Addison turned to look at Tate, who bit her lip, giving away her nerves. The rest of the routine was flawless, though, and her score was still a good one. Oakleigh was finishing them off because it was her strongest event. Tate cheered loudly for her best friend and former teammate, who started on the low bar. She nailed her routine, her Tkathevs sailing high above the bar.

"I wish my bars looked like that," Addison sighed.

"Just keep up the hard work. Your routines might not look like Oakleigh's, but I know they can be stronger," Ray told his niece. Bars would probably never be Addison's strongest event, but there was always room for improvement.

The Russians ended the rotation two tenths ahead of the Americans. Tate stared at the scoreboard, doing some math in her head. She might as well have been competing for how closely she was following everything.

"Breathe," Ray reminded the girls. "This is what makes gymnastics exciting. We haven't made it to beam yet." Addison just nodded. There were still two more rotations to go.

Brittnee was starting for Team USA on beam, and she showed why she made the team. Her beam routine was full of difficulty, but she performed it beautifully. Rosa was next, doing her routine flawlessly and putting up her highest score. Camryn finished them off with her own impressive routine.

When the Russians started, they almost immediately started to fall apart. There was a wobbly routine, a near fall on a dismount, and finally an actual fall. Addison felt herself breathing again; the Americans had widened their lead heading into floor.

The Russians rallied after the disastrous beam rotation, each of their athletes hitting their routines. But Addison knew the Americans' strongest event was floor. Mac was up first with her fun and bouncy routine, followed by Brittnee with her power tumbling, and finishing with Camryn's balletic, graceful routine. Camryn landed her final pass with tears in her eyes. Tate and Addison jumped out of their seats and cheered at the top of their lungs. The Americans had won the gold medal. During the medal ceremony, Addison dreamt she could feel the weight of the medal around her own neck as she listened to the national anthem play. She knew within the deepest parts of her being that she would have to get a gold medal for herself.

* * * * *

Addison instinctively reached up to grab the medal around her neck, but it wasn't there. They hadn't won the gold medal yet. "Was it enough?" Addison whispered in her uncle's ear as he hugged her. He shook his head as her score popped up. It was an incredible score, but it only put them in second; China stayed in first.

"Hey, look at me," Waverly demanded of her teammates. "We have so much to be proud of. You all worked hard today; China just had a better day than us." Waverly pulled the girls together for a group hug.

"She's right," Catesby smiled, but she couldn't help the tears that glittered in her eyes. They had worked hard, but a couple mistakes had left them short.

"I know this isn't what we wanted, but I'm proud of each of you," said Ray. The officials from the American Gymnastics Federation met the team in the tunnel with their medal stand warmups. The girls changed and fixed the makeup that had come off by both sweat and tears. Then they marched out to have the silver medals placed around their necks. As they listened to the Chinese national anthem, Catesby squeezed Addison's hand. The best friends looked at each other, knowing that it was even more important for one of them to get gold in the all-around final.

CHAPTER FOURTEEN

"Let me guess—your letter is from Tate this morning?" Catesby asked as Addison reached into the nightstand to pull out her bag of letters.

"Of course! It's all-around day." Addison held the letter written in Tate's swirly handwriting. As she read, she noticed Catesby underlining something in her Bible. Figuring Momma Ginny had put a verse in Catesby's letter for the day, Addison turned her attention back to the letter in her hand:

Addi Anne,

The day has finally arrived for you to compete in the all-around final. You have accomplished so many of your dreams and this one is well within your grasp. Do your best, work hard, and let the muscle memory do its thing. Remember that no matter what happens, you have achieved something that very few gymnasts get to. I hope you always know that I am so incredibly proud of you. I cannot wait to celebrate with you and recreate our pictures from eight years ago.

You are the best gymnast in the world, even if the world doesn't know it yet.
I love you,
Tate

Addison smiled, re-reading the note again. Of course Tate would know the right things to say to her on this day—the day she would finally prove to the world what she had known for a while: that she was the best. It was just what Tate had done herself eight years earlier.

* * * * *

Addison: Age 8

"She's wearing the blue and red leo," Julie said, checking the text from Tate again.

"She's changing it up. She normally goes with a solid color for the all-around final," Davis commented. Luke and Julie's heads snapped to him, he was not usually one to comment on fashion choices.

"He's right, you know," Addison shrugged. "Let's hope it helps; this could be the day that Davis is finally right."

"Right about what?" Davis asked, confused.

"Tate being the best gymnast in the world," Addison smiled.

"Three years of coming in second has not been easy on her," Julie sighed.

"This is her year. She's done so great this year, she even beat Jenny at Nationals. That just leaves Viktoria," Addison reminded them. In all three of Tate's years as a senior, she had come in second: her first year to fellow American, Haley Hayes; the next year to Viktoria Florescu, a Romanian gymnast; and the last year to Jenny Scott, who was now her Olympic teammate.

"I know. Let's hope you're right," Julie winked as they heard the announcement that competition was set to begin.

Tate stood behind Jenny as they waited for the march in. Her heart was pounding; she was so ready to start. An Olympic official led them into the arena, and Tate let out the breath she had been holding. As much as she loved her teammates, she was much happier competing for herself. Today was her turn; she could feel it. She reached up and tightened her ponytail. Nothing could stop her now.

"Breathe. Keep it normal," Ray instructed, smiling at her as the touch warm up started. Tate's warm up vault went better than she expected; it reiterated that she was ready for competition to begin. As she impatiently waited on her turn, she bounced on her toes, trying to get rid of the nervous energy.

Finally, she was allowed to bound up the steps to chalk up. She saw the green light and sprinted down the runway, flipping to the springboard and pushing hard off the vault. She flew through the air, doing the two and half twists she needed before gluing her feet to the mat. She had done the best vault of her life, and it showed. She was in the lead heading into bars.

Though Tate managed to make it through her bars routine without a major mistake, Viktoria was just better than her on bars, and Tate slipped into second by one tenth.

Beam was her event. It had nearly devastated her when she fell during qualifications, but she was determined not to fall again. She pushed through her fears and hit every part of her routine perfectly. She knew what her beam routine was supposed to feel like, like it did when she hit everything during practice. She knew as soon as she stuck her dismount that she had aced it. Ashley was there to wrap her in a hug when she got off the podium, knowing how hard she had worked on her routine.

Tate was in the lead going into floor, but she knew she would need a high enough score to hold both Jenny and Viktoria off if she wanted that gold medal. She was the first competitor on the floor, and she performed the floor routine of her life. All that was left was to wait. Both Ashley and Ray did their best to help the time pass and not let the nerves take over.

When Jenny finished, Tate stayed on the top of the scoreboard. Only one routine left. Tate did some quick math in her head and grinned; Viktoria would have to be nearly perfect to beat her. Tate's eyes were glued to the scoreboard when Viktoria finished and hopped off the podium. She was willing her name to stay in first place, and when the scores settled, it did. Tate Markum was finally, officially the best gymnast in the world. The arena erupted in cheers, applause, and a round of USA chants, yet Tate swore she could hear Davis and Addison's cheers rising above the crowd.

The athletes were escorted out of the arena, and Tate congratulated Jenny and Viktoria. She had a moment to collect her thoughts as she changed into the medal stand warm up. Though she had seen the scores with her own eyes, she was still in shock that it was real. Then, more quickly than she was even ready for, the three gymnasts walked back out into the arena, and Tate had a gold medal slipped around her neck. This was the moment she had been working for her entire life.

"I gotta get me one of those," Addison whispered from the stands, transfixed by the medal ceremony.

"Do your best and work hard." Her Aunt Julie hugged her, watching as Tate ran to slip the medal around her dad's neck. Tears formed in all of their eyes; Ray and Tate had both worked so hard for this moment.

"You really think I can do it?" Addison asked.

"You can do anything you put your mind to," Luke reminded his daughter from her other side. "That could easily be you in eight years."

"You think so?"

"I know so," Davis said, sticking his head over Luke's shoulder. "Because you're an even better gymnast than Tate."

* * * * *

Addison shook off the memory and returned her letters to the nightstand. She still had to get ready for the biggest day of her life. She brushed out her crazy curls in an attempt to tame them before deftly French braiding it herself. She secured it with a regular ponytail before wrapping the NC State scrunchie around the end. She let Waverly do her makeup again. This time, the eye shadow was a simple white with a hint of sparkle on her eyelids. She finished in the bathroom and pulled out the leo she was most excited about wearing. Blue and silver with red, white, and blue sparkles, it felt like it was made specifically for her. Finally, she pulled on her warmup and repacked her bag. On the bottom went the warmup for the medal stand. Assuming she made it that far, she needed to have it. On top of that, she put the red and blue leo that matched Catesby, just in case something happened to the one she had on. Next went the grips bag, chalk spray bottle, and her water bottle. Finally, she unplugged her headphones and checked her phone. There was a good luck text from her dad and a scripture verse from Momma Ginny. She didn't expect anything from her aunt or cousin, because she knew Aunt Julie didn't want to distract her, and Tate was too superstitious.

"Ready?" Catesby asked, her blonde hair pulled up in her signature half bun, half ponytail. They matched in their warmups, but the best friends were wearing different leotards underneath.

"Let's do this," Addison grinned, sticking one of her earphones in and turning on her competition playlist. They headed to the cafeteria to grab breakfast and meet up with Ray.

"Go tumble," Ray told Addison a few short hours later, once she and Catesby were good and warmed up.

Everything was going fine until Xiao Mei walked over to say hello. Addison could hear all the languages surrounding them and looked around to see nothing but Olympic Rings. The realization of how big and important this competition was set in. She tried to shake off the nerves and the pressure that suddenly appeared, but she blew through her vault warmup and landed on her butt. Coach Ray was there when she looked up.

"What was that?" he asked, concerned. He knew her well, and he could tell she was far from her normal competition behaviors.

"I don't know," Addison answered, still working on getting rid of the nerves.

"Breathe. This is just another competition. You've worked hard to get here, and you are more than capable of winning today. You know that, right?" Ray looked her in the eye. She nodded. "You okay?"

"Yeah, I'm good." Addison blew out a long breath. Ray patted her on the back and walked back over to talk to Catesby. He normally didn't have to do much coaching for Addison on competition days, because she pushed herself harder than he ever could.

Addison stepped back in line for the vault, trying to get back in the right headspace by visualizing her Amanar and blocking out the world around her. When it was her turn, she performed the vault just like she hoped she would for her normal warm up.

"There it is," Ray said, high-fiving her on her way to beam. On beam, she was a little shaky and wobbly. She was still fighting to keep the pressure of the Olympics out of her mind. She somehow pulled off a decent warmup, even though something about it felt off.

As the Olympic officials made the final preparations for competition to begin, Addison lined up with the rest of the girls in the top rotation. They came from all over the world, and again Addison had to work to remind herself that today's competition was just like any other. The athletes were led into the arena and up on to the vault podium by the officials.

The girls started the touch warm-up, and Addison could feel some of her nerves dropping off. She reminded herself that competition was where she shined. Her warmup vault went like she hoped it would, and she let out a sigh of relief, believing that morning had been a fluke. On the sidelines, she flipped and tumbled, getting her mind ready for the biggest competition of her life.

When the competition began, Xiao Mei was up first, and she hit her vault with no problem. Catesby was next; she soared through the air beautifully and took a couple steps on her landing.

"Flip, fly, stick," Ray told Addison on her way up the steps. She nodded and re-chalked. She took a deep breath, and when the green light popped up, she took off down the runway. She did everything she was supposed to and glued her feet to the mat, willing herself not to move. When she threw her hands in the air, she grinned, knowing this was exactly how she wanted to start the all-around competition.

"Three more, just like that," Ray encouraged her, grinning. Addison felt herself relax ever so slightly. She could do this. It was just another competition—and competing had always been her favorite part of gymnastics.

The gymnasts moved on to bars, where Catesby was set to go first. Addison loved Catesby's routine. Her teammate had always been great on the bars, but the last couple years, she had really come into her own. Watching her best friend do her thing, Addison was still amazed, even after seeing it a couple hundred times. When Catesby hit her dismount, Addison headed up the stairs.

Addison's routine had been a labor of love and something she was extremely proud of. The hardest part for her was always the transition from the low bar and back to the high bar; that was where she had fallen during the team final. She was only four feet and eight inches tall, and the biggest place it hurt her was on bars. This time, she had a little fumble getting back to the high bar, but nothing major. So even though the routine wasn't perfect, it was good enough to put her where she needed to be at the halfway point of the competition.

On beam, Addison was set to go first. When the touch warmup ended, she stared down the beam. She was in full competition mode, and she wasn't going let the beam defeat her today.

The green light popped up, and she saluted the judges and started her mount. She did the flourishes with ease. Her wolf turn was a little wobbly, but it was far from her worst one. Then she danced her way through to the first set of leaps before the dreaded full turn. With a sigh of relief, she bobbled some but managed to stay on the beam and upright before her acro series, which she could do in her sleep. Then it was time for more leaps, including the ring leap. She was not always the best at hitting it precisely, but she threw her head back and saw her foot for a split second, so she knew she was okay. She moved a little, taking a deep breath before her Arabian with a half turn.

Suddenly, she felt the unsteadiness that came from landing wrong. Steadying herself, she stayed on the beam. She finished up with her front aerial to get to the end of the beam for dismount just as the warning bell dinged. She aced the two back handsprings and did her double twisting tuck dismount perfectly, sticking the landing with her chest up. She saluted the judges and scrambled off the podium. It was over. It wasn't perfect, but it was good enough.

Addison caught pieces of her competitors' routines as she prepped for floor. She was trying to stay focused, but it would be a long wait. When she saw one of the Russian gymnasts walk off the podium, she knew Xiao Mei was next. Addison sank into a middle split and watched her friend compete.

There was no question: Xiao Mei was at home on a beam. When she finished, Addison clapped in admiration. It was impressive, the things she could do on a ten-centimeter-wide balance beam. Catesby was the last one to go on beam, and it was not her favorite event. But Addison cheered her on, cheering and clapping during the hard parts. It ended up being one of the best beam routines Addison had seen her do.

Even though Addison had a couple minor mistakes on the last two events, she figured she was pretty close to the top from what she had seen so far. She just had to hit her floor routine, which she knew she would. Her floor routine also had the built in advantage that it was three-tenths higher than anyone else's routine in the competition. She had to wait for the other competitors to finish their routines again, so she pulled out her headphones and turned up the music to tune out the arena. In her mind, she was tumbling through the air and hitting everything perfectly. This was her moment.

Ray pulled her out of her trance as Catesby was getting ready to go. Addison cheered her on. When Catesby finished, the best friends brushed hands in a good luck moment as Addison re-chalked for her own routine. She paused, listening to the sounds of the equipment being worked all around her and the cheers of the crowd. Then she saw the green light and started her routine.

The downbeat hit, and she launched into it. "Fight Song" had been just that for her since she first heard the song, and it made the perfect floor music for the Olympic year. Addison flew through the air, losing herself in the routine. As she finished her final tumbling pass, she could feel the tears threatening to leak out, but she held them back as she hit her final pose. She saluted the judges and jumped off the side of the podium to stand with Ray, Catesby, and Gwyn.

All the feelings from coming up short in the team final came rushing back. But this time when her score popped up, it sent her name flying into the top spot. The tears came then, and if Ray had not been holding her, she would have collapsed on the floor.

"You did it," Ray whispered. When her tear-filled eyes met his, his smiled and added, "Your mom and Davis would be so proud."

"Thank you," Addison mouthed, suddenly aware of all the cameras on her. Ray set her on the podium, and someone handed her an American flag. Catesby even climbed up with her since they had gone one and two—just like they had planned.

After a few minutes of celebration, the gymnasts were escorted out of the arena. Catesby redid Addison and Xiao Mei's makeup, the three girls laughed as they helped each other look presentable for the medal stand. Addison and Catesby pulled on their medal stand warmups, and all three athletes were escorted out: Xiao Mei, Addison, then Catesby.

Addison held her breath when the Olympic official slipped the gold medal around her neck and cried silent tears as the national anthem played. This was a moment she would remember for the rest of her life.

"I can't believe this is real," Addison breathed, holding on to the gold medal around her neck a few hours later.

"You are the best gymnast in the world, and now the whole world knows it," Ray winked.

"About time," Addison giggled.

"And it's not even over yet. Four event finals to go," Ray reminded her as he hugged her tightly. "Addi, I'm so incredibly proud of you. Not because you won, but because you did what you set out to do and did it with your own spectacular style."

"Thank you. It feels good to know that the world knows what I've known for a long time. All that hard work and perfectionism finally paid off."

"No, that happened when you made the Olympic team," Ray reminded her, and she just rolled her eyes.

"And thank you, Uncle Ray. I couldn't have done this without you—any of it."

"It is a joy and an honor to be your coach, Addi. Don't ever doubt that for a second," he smiled. "I keep thinking how excited your mom would be."

"I miss her so much. I swear, sometimes I can hear her cheering me on." Addison blew out a breath, sitting down to start packing her bag. "As amazing as it is to be here at the Olympics with all my dreams coming true, I would give anything for her to be here with us."

"Me too," Ray's eyes were shiny.

"It has not been easy to be away from Daddy for this long, either," Addison added, pulling her knees into her chest.

"Oh, Addi." Ray knelt down next to her. "Your dad loves you so very much. He would do anything for you; he *has* done so much for you. I know this is hard on you—harder than it is for your teammates—to be away from your family."

"At least I have you," Addison smiled.

"You've always got me," Ray assured her. "Let's call them, shall we?"

"That's the best idea you've had all day!" Addison pulled out her phone to video call her dad.

"There she is, the Olympic all-around gold medalist," Luke exclaimed. He was beaming with pride, and Addison's eyes immediately brimmed with tears. "I miss you too, sweet girl," he added softly.

"Sorry; this is supposed to be a happy call," Addison said, wiping her eyes.

"It is! My daughter is the best gymnast in the world," Luke reminded her, and Addison's smile reappeared. This was all Addison wanted—to be able to celebrate with the people who were important to her. Celebrate the biggest accomplishment of her life.

CHAPTER FIFTEEN

"Event finals, day one. You ready?" Catesby asked from the bathroom doorway, her hair halfway done.

"Vault and bars. Are you?" Addison challenged, pulling the next letter out of her bag.

"Beyond," Catesby laughed, stepping back into the bathroom to finish getting ready. While Addison had two event finals that day, Catesby only had bars. Addison noticed the swirly cursive letters on her envelope that could only mean her letter was from one person: Ginny Holland.

Addi,

I found this card, and it was just too perfect for you. The little girl who is flipping all over the front of the card reminds me of what you have been doing your whole life. I can still remember the first time you came to our house and impressed everyone with your trampoline tumbling. Davis was so proud to be your brother that day—well, really any day when you got to do your thing. I know he would be so proud of you as you compete in event finals at the Olympics! My prayer for you today is that you do your best and trust the outcome. I know that's not always the easiest thing to do but this is gymnastics, where anything is possible. Remember that perfection is unattainable, like in life. Jesus was the one who's ever been or ever will be perfect—that's something that I remind Catesby of often.

I'm praying for you today and always.
I love you,
Momma Ginny

Addison finished reading and set the letter back in her bag. She was thankful for the people in her life, especially those who had written such encouraging letters for her to read during this crazy time.

She moved to the closet to pull out the leo she had picked for the day: the red and blue one Catesby had worn for the all-around. She changed and put everything back in her bag before switching out with Catesby to get ready in the bathroom.

"Anyone up for some make-up?" Waverly stood in their doorway.

"Yes, please," Addison grinned. Waverly did Addison's make-up perfectly, complete with sparkly gold eyeshadow. She would be watching from the stands with the rest of their teammates since the beam final was the next day. Catesby French braided Addison's hair to complete her signature look just as someone knocked on the door.

"Good morning, ladies!" Ray greeted them with a big smile when Catesby opened the door. "You ready?" The girls nodded and pulled on their backpacks, heading down for breakfast with him and Gwyn before heading to the warmup area. They did their normal warmup before getting ready for the finals that day. Addison, of course, started with a couple tumbling passes.

"Looking good. Let's see some vaults, and then you can warmup on bars," Ray instructed Addison before heading over to Catesby on bars. Addison stared down the runway; this could be her chance at another gold medal. She had worked so hard to get here. Vault had been hardest for her when she first started competing, but now she was preparing for the Olympic final. She hit the vault table at full speed and launched into the air, twisting and landing with a giant bound before doing it all over again for her second vault. She did three sets before she landed them the way she wanted.

Once her vaults were feeling right, she headed to bars. She latched on the low bar and swung herself up to the high bar. She did some pirouettes, giants, and handstands before moving to releases and transitions between the high and low bar.

"Alright, that's enough for now," Ray called. "We have to get you into the arena. Catesby, I'll see you for bars warm up," Ray added as their time together ended. Catesby headed to the seating area with an American Gymnastics Federation official while Addison, Ray, and Gwyn went with the competitors.

In the practice area, Addison entered and looked around. This was one final where she didn't really know anyone. But that didn't stop the other competitors from wanting pictures with her and congratulating her on her all-around win. She did her best to stay in a good mental space. It was always hard when people called attention to her accomplishments because it would be easy to focus on those instead of focusing on what was ahead of her.

"This is me reminding you that, because it's event finals,

there will not be any other competitions going on," Ray said as they waited to walk into the arena. "You will probably be able to hear the commentary in the arena, and there's almost no way you can avoid paying attention to the scoreboard."

"I can do this," Addison affirmed. "I want this gold, and I'm finally at a place where it could be a reality. I wasn't even really sure this was going to happen until Classic."

★ ★ ★ ★ ★

Addison: Age 16 (May of Olympic Year)

"Are you doing both your vaults?" Catesby asked as the girls set their bags in the holding area.

"Nah, just the Amanar. I'm saving doing them both for Nationals," Addison answered. A couple of girls told her how much they liked her floor routine as they rotated. She warmed up her vault, landing with a bounding step.

"Flip. Fly. Stick, Addi," Ray reminded her. Addison was mentally preparing all through her wait. Her Amanar was looking good, but it was still somewhat new. It was one of the hardest vaults a gymnast could do. When it was her turn, she saluted the judges and took off down the runway. She hit the board, then the table, and yanked her arms in. She was tiny but solid muscle. Her vault had so much power behind it that she took three steps on the landing.

"Okay, where has that been?" Ray asked as Addison rushed down the stairs, suddenly aware of the camera trained on her. "Breathe," Ray whispered in her ear. "Business as usual." Addison nodded.

"I didn't know I could do that," she whispered back, trying not to be intimidated by the camera next to her. With this being one of her first major senior competitions, she was still adjusting to the cameras. She might not like them, but she knew they were a necessary evil. Cameras meant she was on the broadcast and if she was on the broadcast it meant they were talking about her.

"If this was practice and not a competition, we would be having a very different conversation," Ray said. He always known that power was in her but it was first time he had actually be able to see it up close. If it had happened in practice, he would have congratulated her and helped learn to control it; but this was a competition and while he could and would congratulate her, her vault rotation was over.

"Good to know," Addison responded. There was so much power behind that vault. The power could help her complete the rotations, but she had to learn to control it if she wanted to stick her landing.

"Calm down; breathe. Take it one event at a time," Ray reminded her. "Go get prepped for bars."

"You good?" Catesby asked when Addison sank into a split on the floor.

"This is just not going how I thought it would," Addison said, trying to focus her mind on bars. Her eyes closed as she went over the bar routine in her head.

* * * * *

"Oh, I remember that vividly," Ray laughed as the Olympic officials got the finalists ready to walk into the arena. When the touch warmup ended, the finalists were introduced.

The first finalist and her coaches set the vault. Once she was ready and received the green light, competition began. She took off down the runway and launched herself onto the table before flying through the air. The gymnast tried to push her boundaries and limits, but she over-rotated, landing on her butt. On her next vault, she landed with a couple of steps. With all the mistakes, Addison knew her medal chances were slim.

Addison closed her eyes and listened to the sounds of the German gymnast landing both of her vaults normally from her middle split on the floor. When the announcer introduced, Alexandra Luca—her biggest competition— Addison stood to watch. Alexandra hit her Amanar and only had a couple small steps on her second vault. It wasn't a surprise when she slipped into first place on the scoreboard. Addison sighed; watching had been a mistake. She pulled her headphones out of her bag and slipped them in.

She watched as the next gymnast attempted her Rudi and had to somersault on the mat to keep from landing on her head. Addison let out the breath she was holding when the gymnast stood up to do her second vault. As much as she wanted to win, she didn't want anyone to get hurt. The girl's second vault was nearly perfect.

When Addison realized who was next, she almost took out her headphones but decided against it. Anika Kota was up—an Indian gymnast who had probably been the most excited competitor to meet Addison. She hit her first vault with a couple steps on the landing, and her second vault was as close to perfect as Addison had seen during the final. Addison clapped and cheered when Anika's name slid into second. She was thankful that her vaults had higher difficulty scores, as long as she performed as well as Anika, she'd secure a medal for herself. Addison slipped off her warmup and found a spot to tumble and get ready for her turn. She wasn't paying attention when the Mexican gymnast took her turn. She heard the crowd groan and knew it had to be rough. But the gymnast had already accomplished so much by qualifying for the Olympics on her own and making the final. When she was done, Addison and Ray walked up the steps.

Addison chalked as Ray made sure the vault was set. When she saw the green light, she took off down the runway, hitting her steps perfectly and launching into her roundoff onto the board. She pushed off the table as hard as she possibly could and yanked her arms in, twisting two and half times. She landed with two steps before throwing up her arms and arching her back into a college salute.

Then she walked back around for her second vault, bouncing on her toes as she waited on the green light. When it popped up, she took a deep breath and bounded down the runway. Her second vault was beautiful, with one big step on the landing. Addison couldn't stop smiling as she rushed down the steps. She pulled back on her warmups as she waited on her final score. It popped up, but her name only slipped into second. She grinned as Ray's arms swallowed her in a hug.

"I'm so proud of you," Ray said.

"Three down, three to go," Addison laughed. She was continuing her medal streak, and so far, it was only silver and gold. The athletes and coaches marched out of the arena, and everyone started congratulating the three medalists before the medal ceremony. As the other girls began to clear out, Addison pulled her phone out of her bag to check her texts from her family.

Tate: Silver Medal number 2! You're killing it. I'm so proud of you. Keep up the good work!

Daddy: You did it. Look how far you've come on vault. Love you!

Aunt Julie: So proud. Those vaults were just incredible. One down, one to go for today.

Grammy: I know you won't get this before and I don't know what the results are yet because of the time difference but I want you to know I'm so proud of you and I love you so much.

Addison smiled; her family was the best. She pulled on her medal stand warmup and refreshed her makeup. The medalists were escorted out for the medal ceremony: Anika, Alexandra, and then Addison.

"The bronze medalist from India, Anika Kota," came through the speakers, and Anika stepped onto the podium to have the medal placed around her neck.

"The silver medalist from the United States of America, Addison Jessup." Addison bent forward to accept the medal that was placed around her neck.

"The gold medalist from Romania, Alexandra Luca." Addison listened as the Romanian national anthem played and the flags were raised to the top of the arena. When the final notes had played, the three girls posed for pictures before being ushered into the press area.

Seeing all the reporters, Addison felt much better once her uncle showed up. She hated the press part of things, but she knew it came with the territory. Ray was great at coaching her through it all and helped keep her calm.

"Breathe and answer the questions," Ray whispered in her ear as the first reporter approached.

She relaxed ever so slightly when she saw who it was: Nelly Knox from the All-Around. She hosted one of the premier gymnastics podcasts and had been a big supporter of Addison for years. "First of all, congratulations on the vault silver," Nelly said as she approached Addison.

"Thank you," Addison answered her.

"You look like you really love this event," Nelly added.

Addison laughed, "Actually, this was a big deal to me, because when I started gymnastics, I hated vault."

"Really? Why is that?" Nelly asked, surprised.

"I think it was because I was so small that I could barely get enough spring off the board," Addison responded with another giggle.

"That makes sense; you definitely have to have some power to vault well." Changing the subject a bit, Nelly continued, "You now have three medals and the opportunity for three more. Do you think you'll medal in all four event finals?"

"I'm just going to do my best and see what comes of it," Addison said confidently, giving the answer she had practiced over and over with Tate.

"Well best of luck! I can't wait to see how many medals you get. When this is all over, you'll have to come be on the podcast."

"That would be amazing! I've been listening to you for years," Addison told Nelly, who busted into a wide grin of her own.

"Okay, one more question: you competed today with several gymnasts who were history makers, including the bronze medalist, Anika Kota of India. What do you think about that?" Nelly asked.

"I have loved meeting people from all over the world and hearing the stories about how they made it to the Olympics. Getting to compete with people who had to make their own way here is so inspiring, and I hope that it will continue to help little girls want to be gymnasts when they see someone who looks like them competing—not just in the States, but all over the world."

"Me too, girl, me too," Nelly said as she walked off to talk to the next gymnast. Addison talked to the next couple of reporters before Ray pulled her out of the line. She still needed to get ready for the bars final.

"I have a surprise for you," Ray said as they found a quiet corner. He pulled his phone out and on the screen were her dad, Aunt Julie, and Tate.

"Hi," she grinned. "I could get used to seeing y'all after every event."

"Tell me about it! It's almost as good as being with you," Luke said. "We are so very proud of you. We know today is a lot, so we just wanted to see your face between competitions."

"I'm so glad you did."

"I know you're under all kinds of stress and pressure. We love you and want to be able to hug you soon," Tate said.

"It will be here before you know it," Ray said to everyone.

"I hope so," Addison agreed, leaning into her uncle's hug.

"How are we feeling about the bars final?" Julie asked.

"Better now that I have a medal under my belt. I have no idea how this one is going to go, but it is Catesby's turn to shine. Not that that will stop me from doing my best," Addison assured her family.

"Good; never stop doing your best. That's what's going to win medals," Luke said with a wink.

"Oh, I talked to Nelly Knox, and she wants me to come on the podcast," Addison added excitedly.

"Dude, that's awesome!" Tate said. "Nelly is so fun to talk to. I always enjoyed when I talked to her, and her podcast is the best."

"Who is that?" Luke asked.

"Nelly is the host of the All-Around Podcast that I listen to all the time," Addison said.

"Ah, I'm sure I would know her voice if I heard it," Luke laughed.

"Oh, you would," Addison giggled. "Tate, I'm sure that interview will be up on their Instagram later today because she asked about competing with Anika, and I think she absolutely loved my answer. You'll have to show it to Dad."

"I'll be sure and look it up," Tate assured her. "Go get medal number four."

"Thanks, Tate; that's the plan," Addison grinned. She missed them so much. It was so good to see their faces in the middle of one of her craziest days of competition. "Thank you, Uncle Ray," she sighed as they hung up. "I needed that."

"I know you did," Ray told her. He knew that she was more nervous about the bars final than she was letting on.

CHAPTER SIXTEEN

"You ready for this?" Ray turned to Addison as they walked back into the practice area in the arena.

"Yes, let's do this!" Addison grinned. This was the final she was happy just to have made. While she would love to medal, there was less pressure, so she could just have fun and do her best. Addison did some giants before working her transitions. They had come a long way this year, especially after she and her coaches had switched them up following Classic.

* * * * *

Addison: Age 16 (May of Olympic Year)

"So, this bars routine . . ." Addison bit her lip and squinted up at her coach.

"It's that transition back to high bar that's still tripping you up," Ray answered.

"It's not like I can just take it out. It's uneven bars, not just high bar—like the men," Addison sighed.

"You can't, but it's something for us to focus on for Classic," Ray was thoughtful. "We just have to find the right thing to motivate you. Or maybe a different transition." His mind was spinning; she had to get that transition if she wanted to win the all-around and make the bars final she was working for. They spent the next few days taking Addison through different transitions to find the right one for her.

"What about the Shaposh half?" Gwyn asked Ray after a few more attempts. "She can do the Shaposh, but we need her to land facing the outside of the bars."

"I'm still here you know," Addison chuckled. "So, what? It's just a Shaposh with a half twist?"

"Yes," Ray answered. "You want to try it?" His niece responded by grabbing on to the low bar. She did a couple spins before launching her herself at the high bar, twisting her body so that her hands landed on the bar facing the way she needed to. She hopped off the high bar and did the transition a few more times before she felt like she had it.

As Addison stretched at the end of practice, she realized she was going to be able to make it through her entire bars routine. "How did you do that?" she asked her coaches. "I actually did the transition every time today."

"Gwyn and I have been doing research, but it was just a little trial and error," Ray answered with a shrug. "I knew once we found the right combination, you could do it. You've been transitioning from bar to bar your entire life; let's not forget that you broke your arm on the bars when you were four." Addison grimaced then smiled at the memory. "It was just a matter of finding the right transition with the right point value to replace what you have been doing. There is no reason for you to struggle when you don't have to," Ray added. "I'm sorry it took us so long to change it."

"I'm just glad we did! I can do every part of this routine without issue now, which means I might actually make the bar final and give Catesby a run for her money," Addison laughed.

"I think you'll make the final, but I don't know about beating Catesby. But you are welcome to try; it might help both of you," Ray winked. Her uncle knew them both so well.

As Addison went to warm up on bars at Classic later that month, Catesby winked at her. "Just remember, buns for Nationals." Addison shook her head; she couldn't imagine going through this process without her best friend.

"Yeah, right. French braids forever," Addison shot back, flipping her own braid as she headed for the chalk bucket. It was a bet they had made about scores on beam and bars. Whoever won would get to choose their hairstyles for Nationals.

Addison was up first, so she did a couple of giants into her first few releases before letting the other girls warm up. Once warmups were over, she fully chalked up and stood under the low bar on a springboard, waiting for the green flag. At only 4'8", she was the shortest gymnast in the competition, which made bars a little hard, but she worked harder to overcome it. She grabbed the high bar, hitting her handstands and pirouettes. Her releases were great as she soared above the high bar. She even nailed the transition back to the high bar, the one thing that had seemed to be holding her back.

"That was great," Ray hugged her. "You made that transition look easy."

"Looks like that Olympic bars final isn't so far out of reach, huh?" Addison grinned.

* * * * *

"Let's see those releases," Ray instructed, pulling Addison from her memories. She worked into her releases, getting them ready for the final.

"Looking good," Catesby grinned as Addison fell off the bar into a heap on the mat.

"Shut up," Addison responded, rolling her eyes. "I just won a medal, thank you very much."

"Yeah, but not on bars, Miss Graceful," Catesby laughed, and Addison joined her. There were definitely parts of gymnastics that were still comedic, like the fact that she couldn't even manage to land gracefully when getting off the bars.

The girls walked with their coaches to the Athlete's Lounge to grab a snack before march in. Addison was thankful to have time in the practice area before the competition began in the arena. Once they marched into the arena, they were introduced before the touch warm up started.

Once Addison's warmup was finished, she put her

headphones in and sank into her middle split. She spent time visualizing her routine and watching parts of the routines before hers. When the Belgian gymnast finished, it was her turn. Addison returned her headphones to their pocket and rushed up the steps to the chalk bowl. Her coaches were busy getting the bar chalked just the way she liked it while Addison went over her routine in her head one final time.

She stepped onto the springboard and waited for the green light. When it popped up, she bounded up to the high bar to start her routine. She sailed through her Tkatchev and Gienger releases before transitioning down to the low bar with a Pak. There, she completed a couple pirouettes before her Shaposh half back, which she nailed. The rest of her routine led up to the dismount, a double layout that she stuck. She was all smiles as she hopped off the podium.

"Please tell me that looked as amazing as it felt," Addison implored her coach.

"You tell me," Ray laughed, but he fell silent when he saw the score. Addison had settled into second, but the score was lower than it normally was when she hit her routine. "Dang it!" Ray muttered as he walked over to the sidelines to get what he needed.

Addison knew what happened; she hadn't received credit for a skill. Her coach was going to have to submit an inquiry in hopes that her score would be corrected to reflect the right difficulty score. Addison was anxious, but she let Coach Ray handle it. There wasn't anything she could do other than to calculate what her difficulty score should have been. It was a stressful few minutes, but her score was fixed. It did not change the standing, though, given the incredible way the Chinese gymnast had showed off her strengths; she had knocked Addison into third.

Catesby's routine was chock full of difficulty, from her

mount onto the low bar before she swung up to the high bar. She did a piked and a straddled Tkatchev before going into a Jaeger. Then she transitioned back to the low bar for an in-bar stalder before doing the giants into her double twisting double back dismount, which she landed with only a small hop. Addison cheered the loudest as Catesby climbed down off the podium. They hugged as they waited on her score. As Catesby's name jumped to the top of the scoreboard, Addison was knocked into fourth place and off the medal stand.

"You okay?" Ray looked over at Addison, who was pulling back on her warmup.

"I'm good. I made the final," she answered with a shrug as she felt the tears prick at her eyes. She swallowed, trying to force the emotions away. While making the final was a big deal to her, she had held out hopes for a medal. Even still, Addison was fairly sure most of her emotions were due to the adrenaline of competing not just once but twice that day.

Xiao Mei still hadn't performed her routine, and she was next on bars. Addison was thankful she could focus on her friend instead of the fact that she no longer had a medal in the event. Next to beam, bars was Xiao Mei's best event. Her routine was a mix of pirouettes and releases. Everything was going great until she missed her hands on her Gienger release and found herself on the mats below the bars. Addison winced; that wasn't what she wanted for her friend. Yet Xiao Mei stood up and finished her routine with grace and beauty.

Catesby and Addison watched the Russian gymnast nail her routine before it was Arabella Saunders' turn. Addison had been a fan of Arabella since the last Olympics where she had won the gold on this event. Her routine had inspired a lot of Addison's, and she was excited to see Arabella up close. The British gymnast's routine was full of big releases and beautiful transitions. It was a masterclass in uneven bars, from her straight legs and pointed toes to her height above the bar. There was a reason that Addison had fallen in love with her bars routine four years earlier.

* * * * *
Addison: Age 12

"Let's go Oak!" Tate cheered on her best friend. Oakleigh hadn't had the all-around experience she hoped for, but this was her chance at another individual medal. It was going to be a tough competition for her. Addison watched with rapt attention. While bars wasn't her favorite event to compete in, she loved getting to watch any type of gymnastics. The Chinese and Russian gymnasts did their thing, each impressive for how beautiful and strong they were.

They were still waiting on Oakleigh's turn when the British gymnast, Arabella Saunders, bounded up to the high bar. Addison was amazed at how her legs were glued together and how she easily moved from one release to the next. Addison found herself on the edge of her seat, trying to see better.

"Wow! That was incredible," Addison breathed when Arabella landed her full twisting double back dismount and stuck the landing.

"It certainly was," Ashley answered, watching her, curious as to what she was thinking.

"I think I could do something like that on bars," Addison said as she turned to her coach. "Don't you?"

"Absolutely. It's going take some work though," Ray smiled.

"I can do it. There's just no tumbling on bars," Addison added, rolling her eyes so that everyone in her family laughed. This was typical Addison; she loved tumbling so much it meant she didn't like bars as much as the other apparatuses.

"Shh, it's Oakleigh's turn," Tate announced, waving her hand excitedly.

"Hey, look! Arabella's in first," Addison noted as she pointed to the score board in the center of the arena.

* * * * *

"Are you even breathing?" Catesby asked, returning Addison to the present. Addison rolled her eyes and watched Arabella's beautiful skill and style. She even stuck her double full dismount.

Addison stared up at the scoreboard, waiting to see what was going to happen. Arabella's score sent her into second, but she was tied with the Chinese gymnast.

"There are no ties at the Olympics, right?" Addison looked over at Ray and Gwyn.

"Right, the higher E score gets it," Ray said. When gymnastics had replaced the 10.0 system with open-ended scoring, they introduced a difficulty score, as well, which was calculated based on the elements of the routine. The execution was still out of ten points and was based on how well you performed the elements. Things were tense in the arena for a few moments before the Chinese gymnast's name slipped into third.

"Congratulations," Addison said a few minutes later as she braved speaking to Arabella.

"Thank you," she chirped in her lovely British accent.

"You are such an inspiration to me! Could we get a picture together?" Addison asked, and Arabella grinned.

"Of course! And you're an inspiration to all of us," Arabella said as they got set for the picture. Addison thanked her again and headed out of the arena with Gwyn while Catesby got ready for the medal ceremony with Ray.

"Addi?" Gwyn's question was in her eyes as she looked at Addison.

"I'm okay, I promise. Tate and I talked about this being a possibility," Addison assured her coach as she wiped at the tears escaping from her eyes.

"You've had an eventful day. You're allowed to have feelings, even if you don't know what they are quite yet. This is the Olympics after all," Gwyn reminded her.

"You're right," Addison smiled.

"Alright, we'd better hurry if you want to watch the medal ceremony." Gwyn led Addison to spot where they could see. The three medalists were escorted onto the floor where the medal stand was set up.

"The gold medalist from the United States of America, Catesby Holland." Catesby stood on the top of the medal stand and had a gold medal placed around her neck. The flags were raised to the top of the arena, and the best friends both had tears running down their cheeks, even though they couldn't see each other. For years, they had been dreaming of winning at the Olympics. When the national anthem ended, the medalists posed for pictures before walking back out of the arena.

"Gold medal! You did it," Addison cheered as she embraced her best friend.

"Olympic gold medalist. That feels *so* good to say," Catesby responded. She couldn't wipe the grin off her face.

"It suits you. Both of you," Ray said. "Addison, I know the bars didn't go the way you hoped, but I'm so incredibly proud of both of you. A gold and a silver medal. Plus, Addi survived two finals today."

"Thanks, Coach Ray. We couldn't do it without you." Catesby hugged him.

"Thank you for everything," Addison smiled, tears pooling in her eyes. "I wouldn't have made it to the bars final without that transition change. Thank you, Coach Gwyn."

"You did it, not me. But I'm so proud to be one of your coaches." Gwyn hugged her.

"I'm glad you are my coach," Addison said, and Ray exchanged a glance with Gwyn. They knew better than to call attention to Addison's admission on such an emotional day, but it meant a lot to Gwyn that Addison had come around to her. She wasn't her mom and never would be, but she loved coaching Addison.

"Let's get you ladies some food, what do you say?" Ray asked, and both girls grinned. They got on the bus and headed for the cafeteria. Catesby and Addison needed a good replenishing meal after competing hard.

It was late when they got back to the suite, but there

were notes from their teammates on their beds, which made them smile. Catesby let Addison shower and get ready for bed first. Once she was ready, she collapsed on the bed and video called her dad before she even realized she had dialed his number.

"There's my girl. How are you?" Luke smiled.

"Exhausted. Missing you and Mom and Davis," Addison answered honestly. She had known this was going to be the hardest day because of the two event finals. It was a lot to have to all the adrenaline that came from a competition followed by the drain only to have to it all over again.

"I'm sure. I miss them too, but you've had a long day. Get some sleep. I love you," Luke said.

"I love you too," Addison echoed as Tate appeared behind her dad.

"You did awesome today! Congrats," Tate said.

"You were right about the bars medal." Addison rolled her eyes.

"I didn't want to be, but at least you made the final," Tate smiled.

"Mom would never believe it; me in a bars final?" Tears escaped Addison's eyes before she could stop them.

"Mom always believed that you could do anything you set your mind to," Luke gently corrected her.

"I wish she were here. She was supposed to be here," Addison said, the tears threatening to give way to sobs.

"I know she was," Luke agreed. "Get some sleep, Addi. You'll feel better in the morning."

Addison nodded and hung up. She grabbed her stuffed fox off the floor, tears spilling over as a wave of jealousy hit her. Tate had gotten to experience the Olympics with her mom, something she would never get to do. She cried even harder until she fell asleep.

CHAPTER SEVENTEEN

"Event final number three. You ready?" Gwyn asked Addison as they rode the bus to the arena for the beam final. Waverly and her coaches were sitting behind them.

"It's beam. Can you ever really be ready?" Addison laughed. Her dad had been right, she felt better this morning.

"Okay, well . . . are you prepared then? Because you might not be able to be ready, but you can certainly be prepared," Gwyn pushed back. Addison nodded, knowing her coach was right.

"Were you nervous before your beam final?" Addison heard herself asking.

"Yes, even though I had been doing well on beam. I was the favorite going into it." Gwyn could remember the day as if it were yesterday.

* * * * *

Addison: Age 5

"Deep breaths. You got this," Ashley gave Gwyn some last-minute advice before the beam final.

"And if I don't?" Gwyn glanced anxiously around the arena.

"You have been hitting your beam routine every day," Ray smiled. "Just keep things normal."

"You're right, you're right," Gwyn admitted as she shook her head, trying to shake the nerves out.

"What do you need?" Ashley asked.

"Fifteen minutes of silence and a giant cake," Gwyn laughed.

"You're going to be just fine," Ray laughed as they moved into the tunnel for the competition to start. The gymnasts and their coaches all filed into the arena for the beam final, and the competitors walked up the steps to be introduced before the touch warmup started. Gwyn chalked up and waited for her turn to hop onto the beam. When it was finally her turn, she ran through her normal warmups before hopping back off the beam and marking her starting point for her dismount.

The bell sounded to end the warm-up period, and everyone but the Chinese gymnast, who was up first, cleared off the podium. Gwyn settled into a split off to the side. She was the favorite in this final, and she knew it. She had been the beam favorite for a while, but it was a different animal for her to actually compete in the finals without the whole thing going to her head. Not that there was much she could do stop it from going to her head. It was the reason she had been so nervous all day.

Gwyn shut her eyes, listening to the sounds of the beam creaking as the Chinese gymnast finished her routine. She was doing her best to get into the right headspace for competition. Cheers erupted, and when Gwyn heard the sound of feet hitting the mat, she opened her eyes. McKenzie Carver, the other American who made the final, was up next.

Gwyn watched the routine she had seen dozens of times over the course of this year. It showed off McKenzie's light and airy touch with plenty of flips and leaps and choreography that covered the entire length of the beam. Gwyn was always amazed at how McKenzie was able to make it look effortless. She knew her teammate was capable of medaling in this final. When McKenzie finished, Gwyn cheered for her and watched as Ashley made her way over. Gwyn smiled; this was starting to feel normal.

"Take me through your routine," Ashley ordered as she returned and sat down across from Gwyn.

"Don't you have better things to do?" Gwyn laughed before walking

Ashley through each step of her beam routine. When the next gymnast finished, Gwyn stood up to get ready for her turn. She stretched, jumped, and did a couple back walkovers to warm back up. The German gymnast finished, and Gwyn walked over to get up on the podium. Ray was waiting on her at the base of the stairs.

"Breathe. Settle. Do what we've practiced five thousand times," Ray told her. She nodded and took off up the stairs to re-chalk and get in position. She waited, bouncing on her toes, for the green light. It popped up, and she started her handstand mount. She stretched through her toes and moved into her first element, a forward roll. She stood up and started her leap series before her double y turn straight into a back tuck. Then she danced her way to the end of the beam for her acro series. She did a sissonne into side sumi before starting her dismount. When she hit the mat with her feet stuck together and threw her hands in the air, a grin spread across her face. That was best she had done all year.

Gwyn rushed off the podium and hugged both of her coaches before she pulled on her warmup and waited to see her score. As soon as it popped up, her name went flying into the first place position. The three-person team celebrated together, knowing it was going to be hard to catch her. They waited through the rest of the gymnasts, but Gwyn's score held in first place.

When the Russian gymnast finished up the final, scampering off the podium after a disastrous routine, Gwyn finally let out the breath she'd been holding. She had won the gold medal after all. She managed to meet all the expectations that had been placed on her.

"Would you look at that?" Ray grinned. "You did it."

"Gold medal incoming," Ashley cheered. "Gwyn?" The young gymnast had a dazed look on her face.

"I won?"

"You sure did," Ashley answered, turning her towards the nearest camera. "Smile big and wave," she whispered, and that's exactly what Gwyn did.

Everyone exited the arena, and the three medalists stood inside the tunnel waiting. Gwyn changed into her medal stand warmup and put on a little makeup before she marched out between the other two medalists. She stepped onto the top of the medal stand and had the gold medal placed around her neck, and she stood tall as the national anthem played. This was her moment alone. She had been working towards this moment for so long, and it had finally happened. Her strength on beam was the entire reason she had made the US Olympic Team. She walked out of the arena and back to her coaches, where she placed the medal around Ray's neck.

"It's just as much yours as it is mine," Gwyn told him. "There is no way that I'd be here without you—either of you," she added, looking at Ashley.

"You did the hard work," Ashley said, hugging her tightly.

"We're so very proud of you and all you've accomplished," Ray added as he placed the medal back around her neck.

* * * * *

"You pulled it off though," Addison said, pulling Gwyn from her golden moment.

"I did, and you can too, if you don't put too much pressure on yourself," Gwyn explained, locking eyes with Addison.

"And how would you suggest I do that?" Addison asked.

"Relax, have fun, and don't worry about the outcome," Ray spoke up from the seat in front of them. "It's the same thing Ashley told Gwyn before her beam final." Gwyn nodded, and Addison did her best to take their advice. She put in her headphones and let her competition playlist help pump her up. As she listened, she closed her eyes and visualized a perfect routine.

When they made it to the arena, Addison warmed up in the practice area before doing her beam prep. She listened to advice from Gwyn about being tighter, pushing harder, and finishing her lines. After what felt like hours, they were marched into the arena to be introduced before the touch warmup. Addison finished off her warmup time by adding her signature A to her dismount spot. She put her headphones back in and settled it into a middle split.

Addison didn't pay attention to the first two gymnasts, but it was easy to tell when the Italian gymnast was finished because of roar of the crowd. Addison didn't leave her middle split, but she did finally look up to watch Waverly's routine. Her teammate hit her front tuck mount, and Addison breathed a sigh of relief. When Waverly made it through the acro series where had stumbled in the team final, Addison clapped and cheered. Finally, Waverly hit her leaps leading into the dismount, but she had too much power and landed her dismount on her butt. Addison winced. After such a great routine, that ending was not what she wanted for her teammate.

But Addison didn't dwell on Waverly's fall as Xiao Mei started her routine with a split mount. She stayed low before standing to do her leaps and acro series. Addison paid close attention to all the little details, hoping to learn a thing or two. This was Xiao Mei's best event, and she was showing the world what she was capable of. One slight wobble after a little wonky landing on her ring leap was the only mistake that Addison noticed. Her double twisting dismount was beautiful. Addison cheered loudly and high-fived her friend when she slipped off the podium. No one was surprised when Xiao Mei's name moved to the top of the leaderboard.

Only one routine left before she entered the competition. Addison spent the routine before hers doing final mental prep.

"Deep breath. Relax," Gwyn instructed, watching as Addison did what she asked. "Now break the beam," Gwyn winked.

Addison hopped up the steps to the podium and re-chalked, visualizing her routine one final time. The green light popped up, and she saluted the judges. She placed her hands shoulder width apart and jumped into her squat through mount. Then she went straight into the double wolf turn. While it was not always pretty, upped her difficulty score substantially. Thankfully, it didn't give her too many problems this time, and she stood to go into a switch leap and straddle leap as she traveled down the beam for her full turn, which she only slightly wobbled on. She took a deep breath before starting her back handspring, layout step out, layout step out back down the beam. She landed with a little bit of flourish and choreography before going into her switch side half and ring leap, making sure she could see her foot before landing. Next was her Arabian half. She stumbled a little on the landing but was able to correct herself with some arm flourishes. It was always her problem spot.

Finally, she danced her ways to the spot where she started her sissonne into a front aerial. This was it; all that was left was the dismount. She heard the warning bell sound before she launched into the two back handsprings that led into her full twisting double back dismount. She landed with two small steps and saluted the judges with a wide grin on her face. She hopped off the podium and hugged Ray. Then she quickly turned to Gwyn for confirmation of what she felt.

"That was awesome! That's the best you've done!" Gwyn affirmed, hugging her.

"Good enough to medal?" Addison bit her lip. She started pulling her warmup out of her bag to put back on as she waited on her score. When it popped up and sent her name into the second spot, she high-fived Xiao Mei and Waverly. There were only two finalists left; her medal chances were good.

Now that her routine was done, she could enjoy the rest of the final. Up next was Mia Maloney, the Canadian gymnast who competed with Waverly in college. Her candle mount was beautiful, and her routine was strong from the start. Her leaps and acro series were nearly perfect. Even with the large step on her dismount, she slid into second place, bumping Addison to third. Addison sighed. There was still one more gymnast to go. She sat and waited, tumbling a little during the final routine. When it ended, she went to stand with her friends as they waited on the score. When it appeared, it didn't affect the medal stand, and Addison cheered, hugging and high-fiving Waverly, Xiao Mei, and Mia.

"Complete medal set, plus an extra silver, not too shabby." Gwyn was grinning.

"I couldn't have done today without you," Addison insisted as she hugged her.

"See, I knew she'd turn out to be the right person," Ray boasted with a smile as he nudged his niece. "Congrats, Addi. You were spectacular today."

«How many medals is that now?" Mia asked as they waited for the medal ceremony.

"Four," Addison laughed lightly.

"Four medals?" Xiao Mei's eyes went wide, and Addison nodded.

"Congratulations on your gold medal, by the way," Addison told Xiao Mei. "You were amazing!" She gave her friend a thumbs up as they were led out by the official.

"The bronze medalist from the United States of America, Addison Jessup." She stepped onto the lowest part of the podium where an Olympic official placed the bronze medal around her neck. She waved, and the crowd erupted in cheers.

"The silver medalist from Canada, Mia Maloney." Mia stepped on the second highest part of the podium and bent forward to accept the medal before standing to wave to the cheering crowd.

"The gold medalist from the People's Republic of China, Xiao Mei." Xiao Mei stepped up to the top of the podium and received the gold medal. The flags were raised to the top of the arena while the Chinese national anthem played. The three girls posed for pictures before being ushered into the media zone.

"Addison!" Addi was attacked by a wall of sound, most of which was people calling her name. She looked around for her uncle but couldn't find him. "Addison, Addison!" As she searched for a familiar face in the crowd, she became so distracted that when Ray found her and touched her shoulder, she jumped. Thankfully, he guided her to one of what seemed like hundreds of journalists.

"Addison, I'm with Sports Now. You are continuing the EGA tradition of medaling on beam. What's it like to be coached by an Olympic gold medalist?"

"I've looked up to Gwyn my whole life, and it's been great to have a coach who has experienced the Olympics before," Addison said.

"I'm sure. What can we expect from the floor final?" the interviewer asked.

"Floor is my favorite event, and this routine is a special one for me," Addison said.

"Why is that?"

"'Fight Song' means a lot to me, and having my routine set to it has been so amazing. I helped design so much of this routine too, from the tumbling passes to the choreography."

"Why is 'Fight Song' so special to you?"

"'Fight Song' has helped me deal with so many of my thoughts and feelings about the deaths of my mom and brother. It's always reminded me to keep fighting for my dreams."

"I'm so sorry, but what a way to honor them. Your floor routine is incredible. We can't wait to see how you do in the floor final tomorrow," the journalist said as Addison fought back the tears that stung her eyes.

"Thank you. I'm looking forward to it," Addison responded as the journalist moved on.

"There she is! Four-time Olympic medalist!" Thankfully, Nelly Knox was the next journalist to talk to her.

"Thanks! One more and I get to join the ranks of so many highly-decorated gymnasts I admire, like Tate, Jenny Scott, and Camryn Harper," Addison said.

"It's an elite list for sure. Sounds like you're ready for the floor final," Nelly laughed.

"Definitely, especially if it means that I get to tie Tate's record," Addison grinned.

"I love that, even with all you have accomplished, you still just want to be better than Tate," Nelly said.

"That's what little sisters are supposed to do, right?"

"I was always that way with my sister," Nelly shrugged. "By the way, I love that you and Tate consider yourselves sisters rather than just cousins."

"She's always been as close to me as a sister," Addison said.

"Let's talk about your beam routine today."

"It was a great one, and I'm really proud of it," Addison said. "Xiao Mei is one of the best beamers, and she was flawless today, so I knew I had little chance of beating her. I'm just happy to have a medal."

"It was well deserved. What's it like to watch so many people fall and then have to compete?" Nelly asked.

"A lot of people fell? I work really hard to just focus on me. Yes, it can be scary or nerve-inducing, but I spend a lot of time visualizing my routines and blocking out the things going on around me."

"Well, keep doing that, because it obviously works for you."

"Not planning on changing it anytime soon," Addison answered.

"What can we expect for the floor final tomorrow?" Nelly changed the subject.

"Floor is my favorite and best event. I plan on bringing

my A-game and hoping my best is enough for the gold medal."

"Well I look forward to seeing it." Addison just smiled. Her floor routine alone could have given her a spot on the Olympic team. Yet here she was, one medal away from tying Tate's Olympic record—as long as everything went according to plan.

CHAPTER EIGHTEEN

"One last competition. You ready?" Catesby asked Addison as she walked out of the bathroom the next morning in the blue leo with the red belt.

"Yeah. Gonna get that one last gold medal," Addison smiled, checking her phone but ignoring anything that wasn't from her family. She was happy to find a text from her grandmother.

Grammy: Four Medals! Congratulations, my beautiful Addi. I can't wait to watch you win the floor final. I love you so much.

Addison texted her back before pulling out the last note in her bag. She knew from the handwriting that it was from her dad. She could almost feel the hug that she would be getting in person so very soon as she opened the envelope.

My Dearest Addi,
*   I am so close to getting to see you and hug your neck. You are competing in the final event of artistic gymnastics today: the floor*

final. Here's the thing. . . I don't have any glamorous words of wisdom because it's the floor final. You, my daughter, are the tumbling queen. You have been since you were little. Tumbling has helped you learn how to process so many things in your life. I know how much this floor routine means to you and just how hard you have worked on it. Keep fighting and keep living. Mom and Davis are cheering for you louder than anyone in the stadium possibly could.

    I love you to the moon and back,
      Daddy

Addison grinned with tears in her eyes. Her dad always knew the right things to say and how to encourage her without adding extra pressure. She placed the letter with the rest before repacking her bag for the final day of competition. She pulled on her warmup pants, grabbed the jacket, and headed into the common room of their apartment.

"You're going to do great. Relax," Waverly said to Brittnee as she finished up her makeup. "Ah, there's my next victim," Waverly added as she spotted Addison coming out of her room.

"Nice leo choice," Brittnee laughed, showing off the same sleeve under her warmup.

"Blue is my signature color," Addison shrugged, switching spots with her teammate.

"And floor is your signature event," Brittnee said, and Addison high-fived her. "I can't believe this is it."

"Me neither," Addison sighed. Waverly worked her magic, and Addison was again amazed by her abilities. "What am I going to do without your makeup skills in my life?"

"I'll teach you; it's not that hard. Eyes closed, please," Waverly winked as she applied the gold sparkly eye shadow. "All done! Go rock that final. We'll be cheering you on."

Brittnee and Addison were met by their coaches, and they all grabbed breakfast before heading to the practice area in the arena to get warmed up. Addison slipped in her headphones as soon as they entered. She knew she had to stay in the right headspace, and she didn't want to deal with people wanting to chat and take pictures. Her competition playlist helped keep her focused as she visualized her routine.

The athletes were escorted into the arena and introduced before the touch warmup began. After her warmup, Addison put her headphones back in before settling into her middle split to wait for her turn. She spent most of the first two routines visualizing her own and not paying attention.

Mia Maloney was up third, and Addison stood, stretching with her music blaring in her ears while Mia competed. It was easy to see how her college experience had influenced her routine and why she was the NCAA floor champion. Addison clapped when she finished and then found a spot to tumble while she continued to wait her turn. She was halfway watching when Alexandra Luca, who had won the vault final, crash landed out of her Arabian pass. Addison winced; that was not good. When Alexandra stood up to finish her routine, she almost immediately fell back down again; she was hurt. Alexandra did not finish the routine and instead was escorted off the podium. Addison blew out a breath and visualized her own routine, working to push the fall and injury from her mind. As much as she didn't want anyone to be hurt, thinking about it too much would just throw off her own concentration and make it more likely that she'd fall, as well.

Ray walked over to make sure Addison was ready as the second of the Romanians finished up her routine. Addison put her headphones away and stepped out of her warmup pants. The Romanian gymnast hopped off the side of the podium, and Addison trotted up the stairs. She re-chalked and waited on the green light from the judges that meant she could start. When it popped up, she saluted, and walked out to start her routine.

She hit her opening pose, and the music started. She danced her way into the corner and launched into her opening pass. She stumbled going into the punch front that led into the double double, which she landed on her knees. Shaken, Addison stood up and did her leap series into the opposite corner. She took a deep breath and went into her second pass, which she hit. She danced and spun her way into the corner for her third pass. She could feel herself running out of steam. Addison did her third pass, but she landed short and almost fell again, bending at the waist. She didn't know what was going on. She did the choreography to get set for her final pass. Worried about her earlier fall, she did the easy version of it and flipped her way into her final pose. She hit it, but landed breathing heavily. Quickly, she saluted the judges and hopped off the side of the podium.

"Are you okay?" Ray was at her side.

"Physically? I'm exhausted, but nothing is sprained or broken. But I have no idea what just happened." Addison sighed. "How horrible was it?"

"It's not going to be pretty with a fall, a major bend, and an easier final pass. I don't know if you'll even make the medal stand." It was Ray's turn to sigh, and Addison hung her head. This was not how her Olympic experience was supposed to end. This was the floor final, and she had blown it. Ray was right; her score only put her in fourth, and Brittnee still had to go. Addison knew she should be upset, but she was more frustrated with herself than anything.

She turned her attention to Brittnee, who was hoping

for an individual medal. She cheered on her teammate and was smiling when she finished. It was spectacular routine. Brittnee's name slid into second place; she had done it. Addison hugged her as the finalists all walked out of the arena.

"Do you want to do press?" Ray asked after the medal ceremony ended.

"Is not doing it an option?" Addison was shocked he was even asking.

"I don't know, but if you don't want to answer questions, I will ask," Ray assured her.

"It's going to suck because I didn't even medal. But since this is the last competition of the Olympics, I feel like I need to," Addison said.

"Okay. Do you want to tell me what you're thinking about that performance before you have to tell the reporters?" Ray offered.

"Honestly? I'm just exhausted. This whole Olympic experience has been mentally and physically draining. And I'm beyond frustrated that my final Olympic appearance was not my best. But I have four Olympic medals, including the all-around gold. I am proud of all I've accomplished, even though I wish today went better," Addison added, surprising herself with how well she was able to express her feelings.

"Sounds like all the money your dad paid Dr. Rooks to help you sort through your feelings was worth it," Ray laughed.

"That really happened though, right? I crashed landed a tumbling pass and didn't get a floor medal at all?" Addison asked him pleadingly, hoping the answer would be different this time.

"Unfortunately," Ray sighed. Addison took another minute to gather herself while the medal ceremony wrapped up.

"Well, that didn't go as planned." Addison was not the least bit surprised to see Nelly Knox waiting on her.

"Not exactly. Shall we talk about that floor routine?" Nelly asked cautiously.

"We can, but I don't know that I have any more answers than you do," Addison shook her head. "I've been working on that routine for almost two years, and those kinds of stumbles have never happened to me."

"We all have rough days. Plus, that opening tumbling pass is hard!"

"Oh, yeah, and I've got the scars to prove it. That was the pass I tore my Achilles learning," Addison laughed.

"I can see why! Okay, because I have to ask . . . You have four medals. What's next?"

"I'm so ready to see my dad and walk in closing ceremonies with my friends on my birthday. But as far as gymnastics goes, I'm just getting started."

"Good for you," Nelly grinned. "And happy birthday! For real, though, I want you on the podcast."

"I'm sure we can work that out," Ray answered as he took the card she held out. "The All-Around has always been so supportive of Addison and the rest of the EGA gymnasts." Nelly thanked them, and Addison moved onto the next reporter.

"Congratulations on your accomplishments here in Rome. You are one of the stars of these Games, as evidenced by the crowds' cheers today even though you didn't medal. What do you think about that? Especially considering not many people knew who you were earlier this year?"

"It's exciting because the world finally knows that I'm the best. As far as people knowing my name, they certainly do now. Because other that being injured for most of last year, my name was always in the mix for these Games," Addison explained to the reporter who clearly didn't cover gymnastics regularly.

As he moved away, she glanced around, hoping to get out of the media zone quickly. But then she noticed that Nelly was talking to Brittnee. Addison moved closer, curious about the conversation they were having.

"You finally have that individual medal you were hoping for. Are you surprised it came in the floor final?» Nelly asked.

"Yes and no. This is the final I competed in four years ago when I got fourth, so it feels a little like, 'See? I knew I could do it.' But also, I'm not the same person or gymnast I was four years ago. Winning this one was a little bit of a surprise, but I'm definitely not complaining," Brittnee smiled.

"You said you aren't the same person or gymnast you were in Montreal. What has changed for you?"

"Everything," Brittnee scoffed. "Probably the biggest thing is that I'm the leader now. I've had to step into the big sister role, be there for my teammates, and teach them how to advocate for themselves when necessary."

"You've gone through some pretty public coaching changes in the last couple years and been vocal about the abuse you experienced. Is it safe to say that this experience has been better for you?"

"Oh my gosh, yes. I'm so thankful for Kristen and Louis! They have really helped me become a better gymnast. They've helped me heal and restored my joy for the sport." Brittnee released a breath, fighting tears.

"I'm pretty sure I know the answer to this but just in case: are you going to try for Seoul?"

"I've learned to never say never. But I'm headed to Utah when I get back to the States, and I could not be more excited," Brittnee grinned.

"We will be cheering you on as you transition into college." Nelly thanked her and shut the camera off. "How's Scarlett?" she asked, her voice low.

"She's okay. It's been a rough Games for her," Brittnee said, matching the journalist's tone. "I'll be interested to see how the press tour goes, but I've already talked to her. And I know Coach Ray has picked up on something being off with her coaches. I don't know that he's talked to her yet."

"I hope he will. Please tell her that we're in her corner and want to help however we can," Nelly said. "Keep me updated?" She pressed a piece of paper into Brittnee's hand before walking off to see if there was an update on Alexandra Luca.

She didn't have to wait long because someone from the Romanian Federation addressed everyone to let them know that Alexandra had torn her ACL. Addison sighed. Alexandra was older, and a tear like that would likely mean the end of her gymnastics career.

Addison used the commotion to leave and grab a bite to eat. She had salmon, broccoli, and rice with cherry juice and ice cream—one of her favorite post-meet recovery meals. After dinner, she headed to her room, thankful to find it empty. She loved Catesby, but it was nice to have some alone time. She pulled her journal out and lay on the bed. She was exhausted after two long weeks of competition, but she also didn't want to forget anything. She started her journal like her therapist had taught her, as a letter to her mom.

Dear Mom,

Well, that certainly didn't go according to plan. Who would have thought that I would choke in the floor final of all things? Maybe it was because it was the last one or maybe it was the pressure. I don't know that I'll ever know. But I do know that it sucked, and I don't care for that to ever happen again. I'm more frustrated and mad than upset, but I wish I knew what happened. As you and Uncle Ray like to remind me, this is gymnastics, where anything is possible.

Overall, I'm happy with how things turned out. I'm officially the best gymnast in the world. I did it. I won the all-around! I made all four event finals. I only medaled in two, but I made all of them, including bars! Can you believe it? I got vault silver and beam bronze, too, so I have a full set of medals. Plus, we got silver in the team final. I know, I know, it should have been gold. But China was just better, and we had some mistakes, like my bars fall, to contend with.

I wish you were here. I know you would be if you could, but it doesn't make it any less true. Uncle Ray is doing his best. Gwyn has actually been helpful and shared some of her experiences with me. It's just not the same without you around to comfort, support, and encourage me. I haven't even wanted to talk to Tate the last couple days. I think it's more because she got to go through this experience with you and I don't than that I haven't had time.

I love you,

Addi

Writing a letter to her mom always helped her reflect on what was going on in the moment. Yes, she hadn't earned the six medals she hoped for, but she had still managed to qualify for all four event finals. She was closer than she ever thought possible to a bars medal. No, they hadn't won the gold medal in the team final, but they had fought so very hard and earned the silver.

Through it all, she had done what she wanted to do the most: prove she was the best. She had done that by the all-around gold medal. It was something she had known for a while, but winning the gold meant she was able to be more herself. She was sure of her place in the gymnastics community, but now she could say it without coming across as cocky. She had the medals to back up her confidence.

She put her journal away and pulled the covers up. Sleep came quickly, which she was thankful for because she was so very ready to see her dad.

CHAPTER NINETEEN

"Daddy!" Addison ran into his open arms. "I missed you."

"I missed you, too." Luke held her tightly. "I don't like being separated from you for that long."

"Me neither." Addison broke the embrace. "Aunt Julie!"

"There she is, in the flesh." Julie hugged her niece. "You good?"

"Yes, I'm great. No injuries, new friends, a whole slew of new tricks to learn, and four medals," Addison laughed.

"Four medals," Tate said, appearing by her mom. "Look at you go!"

"Thanks. I'm still so frustrated that I didn't tie your record yesterday," Addison admitted, but she didn't dwell on it. "Do you want to see the medals?"

"Of course!" Julie said as Ray pulled them out of Addison's bag.

"Team Silver," Ray let them all see and hold it. "Now, I know we were hoping for gold but—»

"Things happen. And you certainly rallied," Tate finished.

"That you did," Luke agreed.

"This is beam bronze," Ray offered as he examined the next medal in the stack.

"Not sad I lost to Xiao Mei. She's so talented," Addison said about her beam medal.

"She's definitely a beamer," Tate agreed.

"I don't think I realized that Xiao Mei is the same friend you're always talking about," Luke laughed.

"I had to tell him during the all-around final," Tate said.

"Xiao Mei is awesome. Now that I know a little Mandarin, we can actually have some conversations. They are pretty basic, and we've still resorted to our translation app a couple times, but still," Addison shrugged.

"I guess it's some good motivation for doing well in that class," Luke said.

"She was the whole reason I decided to take Mandarin. One advantage of online school," Addison added with a high-five to her dad.

"You must really value that friendship," Julie commented.

"I do." Addison switched out the medals.

"This is vault silver," Ray said.

"You sure pulled that one off," Tate praised Addi as she flipped the medal over in her hand to look at the designs on both sides.

"Oh, here we go. All-around gold," Ray said as he pulled out the next medal.

"Matching medals!" Tate high-fived her. "Photo shoot when we get home?"

"I've already booked one for you," Julie grinned.

"Thanks, Mom," Tate said with a grin. "On a different note, Camryn's here, which means the most recent three US all-arounders will get to do an interview together."

"That's great! Speaking of interviews, Nelly wants me to come on The All-Around," Addison said as she remembered her conversation the day before.

"I'll work on getting it scheduled," Tate said. "Since I'm

basically Addi's manager. I should tell you that my agent, Melinda, has people reaching out to her about Addi." Tate had been running Addison's social media for the last year or so, that way Addison didn't have to worry about it and was able to focus on the gymnastics part of things.

"I guess this is as good a time as any to have this conversation," Luke said. He had put off the conversation about Addison going professional for as long as possible.

"I'm ready. I want to go pro," Addison immediately answered. She turned to Tate. "Does Melinda have room for me?"

"Yes, but even if she didn't, I'm pretty sure she would make room for you based on our conversation and your performance," Tate said.

"Will you be my manager for real?" Addison asked. It was a conversation that they had been having since the beginning of the year when Tate had volunteered to run things for Addison in addition to the all the traveling that Tate was already doing, going to gymnastics clinics all over the country.

"I don't know," Tate answered, studying the carpet in front of her. She had loved what she was doing for Addison, running her socials and handling the media requests. As thankful as she was for gold medal, Tate had always preferred to be in the background.

"Please! You basically run my calendar as it is, and this would mean I could pay you," Addison pleaded.

"It would be nice to get paid for what I'm already doing," Tate laughed, if Addi could pay her, it would mean less traveling and she might could even pick back up some classes at the gym. "Uncle Luke, you're awfully quiet."

"You're sure about this?" he asked his daughter earnestly. "Going pro isn't just something you can undo, and it would mean giving up your college eligibility," he added.

"I don't want to go to college," Addison said, which

earned her a disapproving frown from her dad. "It's going to be a miracle if I actually graduate from high school," she insisted. "Plus, do you really think *I* could handle college and gymnastics at the same time?"

"You have a point," Luke admitted with a helpless laugh. She was right. She had been saying the same thing to the college recruiters who had been trying to talk to her since she was twelve.

"So it's official? I'm going pro?" Addison's face lit up.

"You're sure Melinda can take her?" Luke turned back to Tate. Melinda Shannon had been Tate's agent since she went pro ten years earlier. She had been easy to work with and knew how to represent a gymnast.

"I talked to her yesterday, and she's already drawn the paperwork up," Tate said with a knowing grin.

"Get her to send it over," Luke sighed. "And if you're really going to be Addison's manager, you should draw up your own contract."

"I will work on it," Tate nodded, this was what she had been waiting for.

"This is crazy and exciting. We've only been talking about this forever," Addison laughed.

"It's a big deal," Ray said. "Yes, there are many good things about going pro, but it brings its own set of challenges."

"I hear you. This is going to change things," Addison agreed.

"It is, but for what it's worth, I know this is the right decision. The advantage of Tate going first is that you know you're getting an incredible agent," Ray smiled.

"Alright, we're doing this," Luke laughed lightly, fully accepting his daughter's choice.

"We are," Addison affirmed as she hugged her dad.

She was still giddy as Catesby's family walked over. As they approached, her eyes were drawn to Columbus,

Catesby's older brother, who she swore was cuter in the three weeks since she had seen him. But her crush had been growing since the day Gwyn became her coach.

* * * * *

Addison: Age 15

"Addi? Are you okay?" Columbus found her sitting on the bench outside EGA with her knees pulled into her chest.

"It's been a long, terrible day," she answered as she looked up, her eyes red and puffy.

"Do you want to talk about it?" Columbus sat down next to her.

"No." Addison hid her face again.

"Well, I'm just going to sit here with you for a few minutes," Columbus said.

"You don't have to do that," Addison replied without lifting her head. But Columbus didn't move; he just sat with her. After a couple minutes, Addison turned her face so she could see him. "What are you doing?"

"Davis would want me to check on you. Just trying to do what he would," Columbus admitted.

"Yeah, well, Davis isn't here, is he?" Addison's eyes went as cold as her response.

"I miss him, too," Columbus said, and Addison sighed. "You're not the only one hurting."

"I'm not so sure about that," Addison said. "It just seems like everyone is fine even though everything keeps getting worse."

"What happened?" Columbus gently pried.

"We have a new coach, so my mom has officially been replaced." Addison grimaced.

"Addi–»

"If you even think of saying that my mom can't be replaced, I will take your keys and drive off in your car."

Columbus barked out a laugh, "You are so much like Davis."

"You're not helping," Addison said with a trace of a smile in her voice.

"Oh, your life would be so boring without me," Columbus bumped her shoulder, which earned him an eye roll.

"I know what you're doing," Addison challenged, the smile slowly moving from her voice to her face.

"Well, it's working," Columbus commented with a shrug. "If you're not going to go back in, do you want to go to the ball field with me?"

"Wait, why are you here?" Addison suddenly dropped her knees, sat straight up, and looked around. She hadn't thought that it was weird he was here but now—had Catesby texted him?

"Relax, the little girls have a class after school so I just dropped them off, and when I came out you were sitting on the bench," Columbus defended himself and Addison visibly relaxed; she knew that Columbus dropped Catesby's youngest siblings off for gymnasts class every Tuesday.

"I just needed a few minutes; the Gwyn news was a little too much."

"Gwyn—like Sullivan? The Olympian?" Columbus's eyes went wide.

"Not you too," Addison deflated.

"I don't understand," Columbus said. "Your whole life plan is to go to the Olympics. You love Gwyn, and she can help you get there, right?"

"Did you miss the part where she replaced my mom?" Addison stared at him in disbelief.

"You need an assistant coach, especially if you and Catesby are going to make the Olympic team," Columbus challenged her, shaking his head. "Why can't it be Gwyn?"

"Because it was supposed to be my mom!" Addison's anger flared.

"Sorry, that was stupid. You clearly weren't ready for that," Columbus backtracked.

"I did warn you earlier," Addison crossed her arms and turned her head away.

"You're right, you did. At least you didn't try to drive my car. So, ball field?"

"I'm still in my leo," Addison motioned to her bare legs.

"Do you want to go or not?"

"Give me two minutes." Addison ran back inside the gym and returned in a t-shirt and shorts with her phone. "Let's go!"

"You sure?" Columbus asked.

"I think a change of scenery would do me some good." Addison fell into step with him on the way to his car. They drove to the ball field in contented silence, but Columbus didn't miss how she tensed up as they drove through the intersection that changed her life forever. Even though the light was working and it was a beautiful spring day, she still felt anxious every time she drove past it.

"It will get better," Columbus said softly. Addison offered him a small smile but turned toward the window.

A couple turns later, they pulled up at the baseball fields where Davis and Columbus had spent so much of their time. Addison perched herself on a picnic table while Columbus headed onto the field with his friends. A light spring breeze blew, Addison closed her eyes, taking in the beautiful weather. It wasn't long before normal baseball sounds filled the air: metal bats hitting balls which swished through the air, leather gloves catching them, gum smacking, and cleats pounding against the packed dirt.

Addison smiled; she had missed this. It has been almost a year since she'd been to a ball field. But then that was because Davis wasn't here to watch anymore. Instead, she watched as his friends played the sport he loved as much as she loved gymnastics. He should have been out there playing, but his friends still were. Life was moving on; she could see it. So why was she so against it at the gym? Gwyn was an incredible gymnast, and she had clicked with Catesby. Uncle Ray had picked her for a reason, and Columbus was right, they had to have an assistant coach.

"You ready? I can swing you by the gym," Columbus asked when they were wrapping things up.

"Yeah, thanks." Addison hopped off the picnic table. "I needed this."

"I figured. I can't imagine everything you're dealing with right now, but I hope you know that you can always count on me," Columbus said as they headed back.

"Thanks, that means a lot. And you were right about Gwyn—we have to have an excellent assistant coach . . ." she trailed off.

"But you miss your mom," Columbus smiled brightly.

"Something like that." Addison's stomach flipped, and it had nothing to do with the fact that they were driving through the fated intersection. She pushed down her feelings and ignored it. There was too much at stake, for both of them. She thanked him again and hopped out at the gym. There would be time for boys later.

* * * * *

"We had to come talk to the four-time Olympic medalist," Ginny Holland greeted Addison, pulling her away from the memory.

"Momma Ginny!" Addison hugged her tightly.

"Congratulations, Addi. You are such an incredible gymnast," Catesby's dad said.

"Thank you," Addison grinned, her eyes drifting back to Columbus.

"I can't believe you have four medals. I mean, I can because you're, ya know, you. But yeah," Columbus faltered.

She had never heard him stumble over his words before. She cocked her head as the feeling of antsy butterflies she usually only had before competition set in, and before she could stop herself or even realize what she was doing, she looked over her shoulder and threw a perfect back tuck.

"Sorry," Addison muttered when she landed and caught Catesby's "what-was-that-for" look. "Thanks, I'm pretty proud of myself."

"As you should be! I know Davis would be bragging about it to anyone who would listen," Columbus said.

"Oh my gosh, he would be insufferable," Addison smiled thinking of her brother.

"Definitely! But with good reason. You are very talented," Columbus stepped forward closing some of the space between them.

"Columbus." It came out as more of a whisper as she looked up into his blue eyes. She would pay good money for his long eyelashes.

"Unfortunately, it's time to say goodbye," an American Gymnastics Federation official suddenly announced. "The athletes have to get to an interview in just a few minutes."

Addison quickly tried to step away, but Columbus touched her arm, stilling her. "Until next time." He wrapped her in a hug, and Addison knew something had shifted between them. Her whole body felt electrified by his hug, and her stomach flipped like it had that day in the car with him. This time the feelings wouldn't be so easy to push down, especially when she felt his eyes on her as she walked over to her family. Addison said goodbye to her family and Catesby's. Tate promised her she would get her the agent contracts soon.

"I love you. I will see you soon," Luke promised as he hugged his daughter. "Have fun and stay safe."

"Always." She didn't want to leave but knew she had to.

As the girls were getting ready for bed that night, Addison finally had a chance to tell Catesby about her family's decision. "Oh, big news! I'm officially going pro."

"What? Addi, that's so exciting!"

"I can't believe it's finally happening."

"Are you signing with Melinda?"

"Yep, and Tate's going to be my manager, hopefully," Addison laughed.

"Wow! Big things," Catesby sing-songed.

"How was time with your family?"

"Not long enough, but good. They were just as excited to see you though—especially Columbus," she added with a knowing glance.

"Huh," Addison grunted noncommittally. She didn't know how to have a conversation with her best friend about her best friend's brother.

"So, can I ask about the back tuck? During the conversation with Columbus?"

"Do you really want to?" Addison pulled her knees into her chest.

"I know he's my brother, but you have never shown any interest in boys—like, ever. Plus, I kinda thought you liked Noah Archer. I'm just trying to work my way into what's going on in your head," Catesby elaborated as she sat down on the end of Addison's bed.

"Okay, okay," Addison sighed. If there was no way out of a conversation about boys, maybe she could at least redirect it. "Noah is great. He's cute, kind, and explained men's gymnastics to me, but I'm pretty sure he just sees me as a little sister. I *am* only sixteen," Addison sighed again.

"That would make sense. Waverly said that Noah and Markus are best friends, so he's around Kaylin a lot. She's literally a little sister, and she is our age," Catesby reasoned.

"Wait—what?" Addison was confused.

"Oh, the guy that's Waverly's dating? It's Markus Harris. His little sister is Kaylin. And Noah is Markus's best friend."

"I knew that Kaylin's older brother was a gymnast. I just didn't know he was the guy dating Waverly. Or that he was friends with Noah." Addison sat working it all out for a minute. "Sorry," she said, shaking her head when Catesby nudged her. "That was a little mind-blowing. Where were we?"

"You were explaining how you and Noah—»

"Oh, yeah. We're nothing because I'm sixteen and he's a lot older than me," Addison finished, rolling her eyes.

"But Columbus?"

So the distraction hadn't worked. "Columbus is . . . I can't do this. He's your brother," Addison squeaked as she fell back against the wall.

"But there is something going on there?" Catesby asked.

"I think so? But it was one conversation for like two minutes. And of course, my awkward self had to go off and tumble because I was nervous talking to a guy I've known forever. Just because I suddenly realized he is super cute. And that hug," Addison groaned.

"That's why you flipped? You were nervous?" Catesby was fighting laughter.

"Stupid gymnastics! That's what I get for tumbling to deal with all my nerves. I end up embarrassing myself in front of a cute boy," Addison laughed, and Catesby joined in.

"You are the best gymnast in the world. Tumbling in front of a cute boy—that feels so weird to say about my brother, but whatever—should not be embarrassing."

"It is when you do in it the middle of a conversation without even thinking about it," Addison sighed.

"Oh, Addi." Catesby shook with silent laughter. "We all have weird things we do."

"Have you ever nervously done a backflip in front of a boy you like?"

"No, but I have done plenty of embarrassing things in front of cute boys. Do you not remember the fiasco from Columbus' graduation party?"

"Are you talking about what happened with Dallas?" Addison raised an eyebrow.

"Yes! I dumped an entire pitcher of tea on him because he caught me off guard by saying, 'Hey Catesby.' So much for a graceful gymnast," she cringed, covering her face with her hands.

"So we all do embarrassing things," Addison laughed.

"At least my brother didn't have to change clothes because of something you did," Catesby bemoaned.

"Okay, I will be less hard on myself," Addison said, and Catesby barked out a laugh.

"Good luck with that."

"Thanks for your vote of confidence," Addison said, kicking at her.

"You are harder on yourself than anyone could possibly be on you. For the most part, it works for you. It helped you become the best gymnast in the world, but when it comes to other parts of your life, you could cut yourself some slack. And especially when it comes to how you interact with cute boys. You've rarely ever thought of boys, much less practiced talking to them. So take it easy on yourself. Even if one of them happens to be my other best friend and brother," she finished with a wink.

"You're okay with this? Me and Columbus?" Addison wanted to be relieved, but she was still hesitant.

"It's a little weird, but he's had a crush on you for a while, so I've had time to think about it," Catesby laughed.

«He—what?" Addison blinked.

"I'm saying you weren't the only one embarrassed by that interaction today. He sent me like eight texts about it," Catesby laughed.

"Thanks, Cates," Addison smiled with relief, thinking of the text from Columbus she hadn't had the courage to respond to that was still sitting unread on her phone. "I know it's weird."

"It is, but I think I can handle it." Catesby hugged her. "I just kept thinking what Davis would have said if he were there to experience that interaction."

"Oh, I would never have heard the end of it!" Addison laughed. "But I think he would be okay with the whole me and Columbus thing."

"Are you kidding? He would be pushing y'all together. So just be yourself, nervous tumbling habits and all."

CHAPTER TWENTY

"I have contracts for you," Tate announced at breakfast a few days later. They were still in Rome, waiting for the closing ceremony and getting through all of the mandatory media coverage in the meantime. "Your dad's already signed and approved them."

"I sign this and it's official? I'm a professional athlete?"

"Yes. I'm working on getting a call set up with Melinda so we can all talk through the many offers she's already fielding for you," Tate explained.

"Thank you for everything." Addison signed the paperwork, grinning the whole time.

This was a huge milestone for her, something she had been working towards since Tate turned pro ten years earlier. Being the best gymnast in the world was always her goal, it had been for her whole life, and now she was going to be able to earn money doing it. She knew it was going to take hard work and scheduling, but she was ready for the next step in her career.

"These are just for Melinda, right? What about you? Did you decide about being my manager?" Addison asked, handing the papers back to Tate.

"I'm going to do it. Mom, Dad, and I had a long conversation about it last night. I don't have anything for you to sign yet; I'm still working on that part. But I've got you scheduled for an interview on the All-Around with Nelly, an interview with Gymnastics Today, and a photo shoot of the Olympic stars with Sports Now."

"Seriously?" Addison's jaw dropped. "How?"

"Perks of me running your social media," Tate laughed. Addison was so focused on gymnastics that sometimes she forgot about everything else.

"I'm so thankful you do, it's just so overwhelming for me," Addison sighed. "And thank you, I'm so excited about you being my manager."

"I'm excited about it too," Tate put the contracts for Melinda back in her bag.

"Now that that's done, we need to talk about my boy problems," Addison said.

"Boy problems? You? Okay, start talking. Now," Tate demanded, leaning in.

"I met Noah Archer during one of the men's competitions, and he was really kind and taught me all about men's gymnastics because I knew nothing. He's cute but so much older than me. And then when I saw Columbus the other day, he was being weird and flirty. Something is happening there. Catesby even told me that he has a crush on me." Addison pushed around the leftover food on her plate.

"Addison likes a boy. I knew this day would come," Tate laughed. She could read her cousin so easily that she knew the conversation about Noah was just a decoy. "You and Columbus, huh?"

"I don't know," Addison squirmed. "We had one weird and charged interaction."

"But do you like him?"

"I think so? He's cute and fun. And he knows me, knows that my life revolves around gymnastics."

"That's always nice. I don't think there is anything wrong with seeing where this goes. But do remember that this is your best friend's brother, and the last thing you want to do is ruin two relationships that are important to you."

"So, be careful?"

"On all fronts," Tate said.

Addison nodded, pulling her phone out of her jacket pocket. She found the text from Columbus that she yet to respond to and did.

"You ready for this interview?" Tate asked when she looked back up.

"Let's do it!" Addison stood up, and they headed to the television studio. She was so excited that all three of the most recent all-around winners were going to get to interview together at this Games. Addison remembered watching Camryn win the all-around four years earlier.

★ ★ ★ ★ ★

Addison: Age 12

"We can't be late! Hurry! They are already warming up!" Addison ran ahead of her family to find their usual seats in the arena for the all-around final. For Addison, this was the most important competition of the Olympics. Tate sat down next to her and couldn't help but notice the camera man flip his camera to her. She smiled and waved. Tate was the reigning all-around Olympic gold medalist.

"Is that weird?" Davis nodded towards the camera.

"A little, but this is the all-around final, and since I'm here, they are going to show me," Tate shrugged. "I just want Oakleigh to medal; she's worked so hard."

"Yeah, but Camryn Harper's going to win," Addison shot back, her lips pursed.

"Hopefully, but remember this is gymnastics so . . . "

"Anything is possible," Ray finished for Tate as Addison turned to watch the action. The gong sounded, and the athletes did their final prep for competition. The whole family waited and watched as Oakleigh and Camryn both hit their vaults with grace and strength. Camryn had a slight lead going into bars, and Oakleigh was in second.

The Russian gymnast, who was in third, soared into second when Oakleigh fell trying to do her piked Thatchev after transitioning back up to the high bar. Camryn's bar routine was beautiful, and she managed to stay in first. Tate was doing math in her head, trying to figure out if Oakleigh could still get a medal as the gymnasts rotated.

Beam was always a test of nerves more than skill. Something about that four-inch wide, suede-covered wooden beam tested even the most seasoned of gymnasts. Camryn was up first, but she didn't let it get to her. She leaped, spun, and tumbled on the beam, performing one of the best beam routines that Addison had ever seen her do.

"Dang, that was impressive," Addison commented.

"Definitely. This is Camryn's competition to lose at this point. Her floor routine is just incredible," Tate said. They turned their attention back to the beam to see one of the Russians fall. It was the same gymnast who had outperformed Oakleigh on the bars. The cousins looked at each other; Oakleigh might still have a chance at the bronze after all. Through the other routines, there were falls, bobbles, and wobbles, but there were also beautiful turns, leaps, and acro series.

"Come on, Oakleigh!" Tate called, standing up to try and get a better view of her best friend. Addison glanced at her cousin with fascination; she had never seen Tate like this. But then she had never actually watched a meet with Tate. Usually at least one of them was competing.

Turning her attention back to the beam, Addison watched Oakleigh start her mount. She was looking steady as she leaped down the beam before coming back with her acro series, which was one of the most beautiful combinations Addison had seen all night. Addison seemed to stop breathing as Oakleigh went into her full turn. It looked like she was going to come off the beam for a second, but she saved it by turning it into a double turn. Addison felt herself relax as Oakleigh finished the routine without another major mistake. She glanced up at the scoreboard and smiled as Oakleigh's score set her back in third with only one more rotation to go.

Addison watched the routines with rapt attention, always fascinated by the different ways the athletes flew across the floor. There were gymnasts who flipped more than they twisted, gymnasts who preferred forward tumbling over backwards tumbling, and vice versa. Oakleigh was the first of the Americans up, and Tate could hardly sit still. She took to pacing up and down the stairwell closest to them.

"Tate, you have to stop! They're going to show you pacing on the broadcast," Ashley hissed at her. Tate nodded and stood still, constantly shifting her weight as her best friend hit her floor routine. Oakleigh's routine was set to a fun upbeat song that gave her plenty of opportunity to show off her sassy style and personality. Her passes were jam packed, and she landed the last one with tears in her eyes, knowing she had performed as well as she possibly could. Tate cheered the loudest, and when she sat down, she immediately pulled out her phone to congratulate Oakleigh before the score was even up. When the score did come up, it sent her into first place, and Tate jumped back up. With only two athletes left, Oakleigh was guaranteed to get a medal; she just had to wait to find out the color. The Russian gymnast had managed to settle into first after her routine—even after her beam fall, knocking Oakleigh to second with just Camryn left to go.

Addison tried to figure what kind of score Camryn would need to win, but she couldn't do it in her head, so she gave up. She leaned forward, as If those few inches would somehow make her more a part of the action. Camryn's floor routine was beautiful, full of high-flying tumbling, long leaps, and balletic choreography. Addison quickly decided she wanted to try to copy Camryn's opening tumbling pass, which included a double double that seemed just out of Addison's reach. Camryn hit each of her passes with the precision everyone had come to expect from her, and she landed the last one with the biggest grin on her face before moving into her final pose. She finished, saluted the judges, and jumped off the podium to stand with her coach.

Addison found herself standing as she waited on Camryn's score, and the next thing she knew, Camryn's name was sitting in first place. Tate jumped up and hugged Addison and then Davis. Camryn Harper was the all-around gold medalist, continuing the legacy that Tate herself was a part of. And to top it all off, Oakleigh received the bronze, even with her fall on bars.

"So, what do you think? Is that going to be you in four years?" Ashley leaned over to ask her daughter, nodding towards Camryn, who was draped in an American flag on the podium.

"Definitely," Addison breathed. "I can't wait for it to be my turn."

* * * * *

"Camryn! I'm so glad to see you; thanks for doing this!" Addison hugged her, shaking off the last of the memory.

"Of course! Any chance I get to hang out with you and Tate, I'm going to take it. Even if there are cameras involved," Camryn winked.

"Thank you. I know; it's never really fun to be in front of cameras," Tate agreed as she hugged her.

"Five minutes," a production assistant announced, walking into the green room to get the girls. All three followed her out to the main studio where they didn't have long to wait for their interview. The host greeted them as they got settled before the interview started.

After a quick countdown, they were live. "Welcome back," the host crooned. "I'm joined by the three most recent all-around gold medalists from artistic gymnastics—all of whom are from the United States. Tate Markum won the all-around eight years ago in Melbourne, Australia. Camryn Harper won the all-around four years ago in Montreal, Canada. And Addison Jessup won the all-around here in Rome just a few days ago," he introduced them as the cameras focused on each girl. "Addison, let's start with you. What's it like to be sitting here with these two gymnastics legends?"

"They might be legends, but to me they are just Camryn and Tate. Tate is my cousin—but more like a sister thanks to how we were raised—and I've been watching her forever. And Camryn, well, she inspired the opening pass of my floor routine," Addison explained.

"Camryn inspired your opening tumbling pass?" the reporter asked, surprised.

"She did! Her opening pass four years ago, the one with the double double, is what got me to start training mine," Addison said.

"Camryn, what's it like to know that you're inspiring gymnasts who are younger than you?"

"It's one of the things I don't think ever really seems real. I am so incredibly grateful for the opportunities gymnastics continues to give me," Camryn answered humbly, shaking her head in awe.

"So Addison, Camryn inspired that double double, but who has been your biggest inspiration? I'm pretty sure I know the answer," he added, laughing, "But I have to ask!"

"Tate, hands down. I've been watching her my whole life." Addison grinned, wrapping her arm around Tate and leaning into her.

"Tate, what has it been like to watch Addison go after her dreams?"

"It's amazing! She has worked so very hard to get here, and for her to get to show the world what I've always known is something I will always cherish," Tate answered.

"The thing is, Addi's always been an incredible gymnast," Camryn cut in. "She made the national team as an eleven-year-old and has won the floor title in almost every competition she's been in. Yet everyone acts like her making the Olympic team and winning four medals was something unexpected. It really wasn't. Addison's been inspiring gymnasts for a long time. While I might have inspired a tumbling pass, Addison's floor routine from her first year as an elite inspired me—that's how good it was."

Addison broke into a wide grin. She was glad someone else was explaining that her wins were normal; they weren't a fluke. She was a consistent gymnast who was the best and could do anything she set her mind to.

"And to think you saw that floor routine for the first time at the worst competition of my life," Addison laughed and then remembered how bad her Olympic floor final had gone and winced. The fact that her routine had inspired Camryn was new information for her.

"Hey, that floor routine was amazing. You just overshot your landings," Camryn shrugged. "But yes, how sharp and precise you were made me want to be as clean as you. And the height! You had more amplitude than I had ever had. My coach even pointed it out, and he wasn't the only one."

"Your tumbling is very clean and high. Is that something that you have to work on a lot?" the reporter asked, trying to regain control of the interview.

"Have to? Probably not, but I love it. Tumbling is my favorite thing in the world, so I will work on a pass or even just a skill until it is absolutely perfect. That perfectionism is a blessing and curse," Addison answered honestly.

"Perfection is what's expected in gymnastics though, right?" the reporter asked, and all three girls nodded.

"It is, but it's also not easy to obtain," Tate explained. "They don't give out perfect tens in elite gymnastics anymore. While all gymnasts strive for perfection, they never obtain it. What Addison means when she says that perfectionism is a blessing and a curse is this: Addison has the *work ethic* to perfect a routine, which is a blessing. But it's a curse because she feels like she *has* to perfect it, which is impossible."

"You obviously did something right, though, considering the outcome," the reporter said, turning back to Addison again.

"Uncle Ray reminds me often that gymnastics is like life: you should always strive for perfection, even if perfection is unattainable," Addison said.

"All the time," Tate agreed, rolling her eyes. "Love you, Dad!"

"Camryn, do you agree?"

"Absolutely. I don't know that I've heard it put that way

before, but the perfectionism gymnastics brought out in me comes through in places like school, too, where I work hard to have top grades," she said.

"Well, ladies, keep inspiring and striving for perfection. Unfortunately, that's all the time we have. Thank you for joining us today!" the reporter said as they broke for a commercial. "Thank you so much, Ladies," he added as the girls were led back to a green room to take off their mics before leaving the studio.

"That was pretty good," Camryn laughed.

"Thank you for saying all that," Tate said as she hugged her.

"I didn't say anything that's not true," Camryn replied. "Addi, keep being you and showing the world that you deserve all the attention you're getting."

"Thank you," Addison echoed, hugging her tightly.

Before they headed out of the studio to go their separate ways, the three all-around champions found someone to take a picture of them together. Then Addison and Tate headed to meet up with Luke for a quick call with Addison's new agent. She left the conversation even more excited and looking forward to what the future would hold.

"Tomorrow, you have interviews with Mary Margaret from Gymnastics Today and Nelly Knox," Tate said, fueling both Addison's excitement and nerves.

"And the rest of today?" she asked hopefully.

"You get to spend with me," Luke answered with a grin.

"Best news ever!" Addison hugged him tightly.

«I thought we could explore a little of Rome, if you're up for it," her dad suggested.

"I'm always up for exploring with you," Addison grinned. Leaving Tate to meet up with her own parents, the father and daughter pair headed out of the main Olympic area and caught a cab to the Spanish steps.

"We have a full tour of Rome planned for later in the

week with everyone, but this is not on it," Luke said when they arrived. As they stared up the massive staircase, he added, "I know you've gotten your workout for today in, so I won't make you climb the 135 steps, unless you want to?"

"You don't think you can handle it?" Addison looked sideways at her dad.

"No, not at all," he answered. "I'm not in shape like you are, but you know Davis would be racing you up those stairs before you even had time to think about it." Luke laughed, picturing his son running up the stairs before them.

"Oh, I know! And Mom would be so mad. Yelling at us about getting hurt," Addison could almost hear her complaints. She looked at the stairs again. "I think I'll pass on the climb. But I could do some shopping."

"Come on," Luke laughed, and they walked through some stores together. The two talked and laughed as they filled one another in on all the things that had happened over the last few weeks. She had missed spending time with him. Over the last two years, they had become so close with everything that had happened. The few weeks they had already spent in Rome were the longest they been apart since the deaths, and it felt so comforting to be back together. Once they finished checking out all the shopping, they found a pizza place nearby.

"Pizza in Italy is just better," Luke said as they were served.

"My thoughts exactly," Addison giggled. "What's been your favorite part of all this?"

"Seeing your dreams come true," Luke answered without hesitation. "I know that sounds cliché, but this is what you've spent all your time and energy on. To know that all your hard work has paid off and you have accomplished what you set out to do just helps me know it was the right choice. Your mom and I talked all about this experience. I know she would give anything to be here with you."

"I know. I keep thinking of all these things she would say to me if she was here," Addison said.

"I think that's one little piece of her that lives in you. I hope you always listen to it," Luke smiled, tears brimming in his eyes.

"I have been, don't worry," Addison assured him. When they finished their dinner, he took Addison back to the Olympic village. "Thank you for today," she said, delaying their goodbye. "It's been wonderful."

"It has. I hope your interviews go well tomorrow. Don't worry," he added, seeing her nerves start to return already, "I will see you for our track and field outing in a couple days." Luke hugged her, and Addison turned to be escorted up to her room. It was harder than she liked to admit being away from her dad for the last three weeks. But she only had to make it through her interviews before she saw him again.

CHAPTER TWENTY ONE

"Hi Addison! I'm Mary Margaret Webb with Gymnastics Today," the journalist greeted Addison as she and Tate sat down across from her. "Thanks for agreeing to talk to me today. Congratulations on all you've accomplished here in Rome."

"Thank you," Addison said. "It's all been such a dream come true."

"I'm sure. Do you mind if I record this for my own personal use?" Addison nodded, and Mary Margaret hit record on her phone. "How long have you been doing gymnastics?" she asked, starting right into the interview.

"My whole life," Addison laughed. "I guess technically since I could walk, but I was at the gym when I was like a month old."

"Perks of being a coach's kid, huh?"

"Something like that," Addison smiled, thinking of her mom.

"When did you know that gymnastics was your sport?" Mary Margaret asked.

"I think it was at my first competition. I had been watching Tate compete my whole life. When it was finally my turn, it was every bit as magical as I hoped it would be," Addison answered, breaking into a wide grin.

"Why is that, do you think?"

"There is a rush and excitement that comes with competing. I still can't get enough of that adrenaline," Addison explained.

"Clearly," Mary Margaret laughed. "Did you ever have a time you wanted to quit?"

"Oh yeah, at my very first international competition as an eleven-year-old. I was not mentally prepared, so I completely bombed, and I did not handle it well. I wanted to quit, mainly because I was embarrassed," Addison said as the memory of that competition filled her mind.

* * * * *

Addison: Age 11

"It has to be perfect," Addison whispered, more to herself than anyone else.

"Just breathe." Ashley put a hand on her back, steadying Addison as she waited for her turn to warm up on beam. She was trying to get in the zone for competition but couldn't seem to find a safe and quiet space in her mind.

"Tighter, pull in quicker," Ray called when she landed her warmup dismount a little wonky. Addison walked over to the edge of the podium to talk to Ray before her turn started. "You can do this," he reminded her. "Take a deep breath. It's just a competition. Just like you've been doing." Addison nodded. She looked over at her cousin, who was in the same blue leotard with red and white sections across her stomach and the American flag stitched onto the sleeve. Her uncle was wrong; this wasn't just another competition, and that's why she had to be perfect. She was the first athlete up for Team USA.

"Let's go, Addi!" Tate yelled as Addison started her mount. She was shaky from the start. She wobbled and bobbled, and Ray wasn't the least bit surprised when she fell trying to land the back handspring that started her acro series.

"You got this," Ray coached, looking straight at her as she jumped back up to finish her routine. It was still shaky, but it looked better than the front half. She had two steps on the dismount, but with a sigh of relief, she completed the routine.

Ray and Ashley exchanged a glance knowing her mental state needed to be addressed. As Addison sank into a middle split with her face to the ground, Ashley walked over and tapped her daughter on her back. They were going to fix this before Addi's next event.

"You okay?" Ashley asked.

"Did you see that routine? It was awful!" Addison lamented.

"It was, but floor is next; focus on that," Ashley smiled, knowing her daughter's love of tumbling. "It was one bad routine. Everyone has them. You have to move on. Try walking through your floor routine in your mind." Addison nodded and went back to her middle split as Ashley went to help prep Tate for beam. But Addison couldn't stop the beam routine from playing through her mind, even as she watched Tate.

Tate was the first senior up. It had been a journey for her to get back into Olympic shape. She started off strong but fell landing her aerial and bent at the waist following her full turn. If Tate couldn't stay on the beam, Addison had no hope.

The rotation ended, and the Americans moved to floor. Addison trudged over to get in line for the floor warm up, and amazingly, her passes were even more powerful than normal. Ray chose his words carefully, encouraging her, pointing out the only good things he saw. In this event, Addison was supposed to anchor the juniors. She paced and even threw a few tricks while she waited on her turn.

When her name was announced, she rushed up the steps to the podium and waited on her music to start. She was even more powerful and bouncy than she had been in her warmup, so she landed all four passes out of bounds and crash landed the last one. She hopped off the podium and waited on her score. When it popped up, she was even more disappointed than she expected to be.

"You can do this," Tate admonished, sitting down next to her cousin. "You just have to focus on what's next and not worry about what you already did." Addison, who already had two bad rotations, shrugged her off, unable to get out of the mental hole she had dug for herself.

Addison's last rotation was vault, which she had been working so hard on. Even though she was pure muscle, she was tiny, coming in at 4'4". It had been hard to find a vault with enough difficulty to use when competing on the international stage. But now, with how bleak her mental outlook was, it was going to be nearly impossible to stick. Tate, Ray, and her mom were all trying to help, but their words only seemed to frustrate her more. Her warmup was okay, but she ended up sitting down her actual vault. Addison had never been more glad for a competition to be over. Back in her hotel room, she showered and crawled into bed, crying herself to sleep.

"I'm quitting gymnastics," she announced to her family as they sat at breakfast the next morning. Luke looked at Ashley. He knew Addison had a rough day, and he also knew that quitting was not the answer, but he didn't want to push her.

"We'll talk about it when we get home," Ashley simply said, hoping that her attitude would be fixed by then. They headed to the arena to watch the competition. While it would normally cheer Addison up, it only served to make her attitude worse. Yet anytime she brought up quitting, the answer was always the same: "We'll talk about when we get home."

By the time they made it back to North Carolina, Addison's mood was improving, but she was still threatening to quit. Luke and Ashley agreed that Luke would work from home that Monday. It was not going to be a fun day, and they did not want anyone else to have to deal with her.

The Jessup's had enrolled Addison in online school so she would have more flexibility to be at the gym as much as necessary now that she was a member of the junior national team and competing internationally. When Monday morning rolled around, Addison behaved exactly like Luke thought she would. After breakfast, she plunked down at the table with Davis who was out on spring break and pulled out her schoolwork.

"Don't you have practice?" Davis looked at his sister incredulously.

"I'm quitting," she said matter-of-factly, not looking up.

"You can't quit!" Davis exclaimed. He stared at her, waiting for a response.

"I can," she finally answered, her brother's shock starting to crack her resolve. "This weekend was awful. How am I supposed to show my face in the gym after that?" she added in a whisper.

"Addi, do you know how many bad games I've had? How many times I've struck out?" Davis laughed. "It was one competition. Now you practice so the next one is better. It's that simple."

"He's right, you know," Luke chimed in.

* * * * *

"Why didn't you quit after that competition?" the journalist asked, pulling her from the memory.

"Because quitting then would have been for the wrong reasons. The practice after that competition, we really worked on my mental game. I had to stop looking at the scoreboard during competitions. I started tumbling to calm my nerves, and I learned how to visualize my routines."

"Clearly, all of that has been helpful. I'm pretty sure I know this answer, but who is the best coach you've had?"

"I'm definitely biased, but my mom and Uncle Ray. I would not be here without them," Addison answered, but her wheels kept turning. "And Coach Gwyn. I don't know that I would have said that a year ago, but she has been so great during this experience."

"Why do you say that? What's changed?"

"When she got hired, it felt like everyone was trying to replace my mom. While I know that's not the case, I haven't always acted like it. But having a coach who has experienced the Olympics was invaluable. Gwyn really helped me through some of the rough moments."

"Rough moments? Like the floor final?" Mary Margaret asked.

"There were some things early on that she helped me with, and I could not have done the beam final without her. And yes, she helped me process the bars and floor outcomes," Addison answered.

"She sounds like a great coach. Next question: what is your least favorite thing to do at practice?"

"I feel like the answer I'm supposed to say is conditioning, but surprisingly, it's something I enjoy because I know it's important for the rest of my gymnastics. Before I tore my Achilles, I probably would have said bars, but that's not the case now," Addison really had to think to come up with an answer. "I think it's re-doing basic things that I know I know how to do."

"Interesting. What's your favorite thing?"

"Do you even have to ask?" Addison laughed as Mary Margret shrugged. "Tumbling, hands down. We've learned that practice goes so much better if at least one tumbling pass is under my belt before I start anything else."

"What is your single greatest moment in a competition?"

"Winning the all-around gold medal. That was the culmination of everything I've spent my life working on."

"Such a huge accomplishment. What about your lowest moment?"

"Being named the alternate at Worlds last year was rough. I had worked so hard after tearing my Achilles, and I thought I'd done it when I made the selection camp," Addison said, remembering the disappointment that came with that decision.

* * * * *

Addison: Age 16 (October before the Olympic Year)

"Traveling alternate will be Addison Jessup. Congratulations, ladies! Let's bring home the gold," the official from the American gymnastics federation addressed the group of gymnasts standing in front of her. Addison felt her stomach drop, but she quickly reminded herself that it was a miracle she had made it to the Worlds trial at all. She should be grateful to be the traveling alternate for the Worlds team. She looked over at Catesby, who was grinning and gave her a thumbs up. Addison smiled back while tears formed. She blinked them away, refusing to ruin this moment. The girls were dismissed, and the best friends found their coach.

"Way to go! I'm so proud of both of you. Addison, I know this isn't what you wanted, but at least you're going with us," Ray said as he pulled his niece into a hug.

"I still can't believe we're going to Worlds. Worlds this year, Olympics next year," Catesby said with excitement.

"Yeah, but you're not the alternate," Addison pouted, her emotions starting to show.

"Addi, this was the first real test for your Achilles and you only did bars and beam. You're the alternate, which means you were sixth on the list with only two events! That's incredible! Especially after the year you've had. Take the win," Gwyn reminded her.

"She's right; you were incredible today," Catesby agreed before adding, "And you're not even back to full strength yet, you have time before the Olympics."

"I get to go to Worlds and be on the floor with the team," Addison echoed, to remind herself more than anything.

"Exactly," Ray grinned. "It's going to be great."

* * * * *

"I know that couldn't have been easy, but you clearly made the best of your disappointment," Mary Margaret said, abruptly ending the memory playing in Addison's mind.

"I did. I'm so thankful for my coaches and friends," Addison added.

"Speaking of friends, who are some of the friends you've made because of gymnastics?"

"My teammates, of course. But the most important one is Catesby. We met on our first night of competition team practice almost ten years ago. As the story goes, Dad asked if I had made any friends, and I told him that the girl behind me wouldn't stop talking," Addison explained with a grin.

"That's precious! I know Catesby is important to you. How do you stay motivated?"

"I have goals that I'm always working towards, whether it's a competition or a new skill. This year, I made a vision board with Catesby and Tate that hung in our kitchen along with Tate's all-around gold medal," Addison said. "Having the vision board where I could see it every day reminded me what I was working towards." She could still clearly picture it.

"That's awesome. I know having Tate's gold medal to look at would be motivation in and of itself. How do you deal with self-doubt?" Mary Margaret moved to the next question.

"I tumble . . . a lot," Addison laughed. "It helps clear my mind. And all the people I have in my corner who remind me to keep going and keep pushing to be the best I can be."

"You clearly have so many people who love you. How do you relax?"

"Spending time with my family. Dad and I live next door to Uncle Ray, Aunt Julie, and Tate. My grandparents live across the street. We love to watch movies together, and one of my favorite things to do is to cook breakfast food with my grandparents," Addison giggled.

"I love that you are so close to your family. Now that competition is over, what's next for you?"

"I'm just getting started!" Addison exclaimed. "I can't wait to see where gymnastics takes me."

"Do you have plans to enjoy any other events here in Rome?"

"Yes! I am so excited about getting to see some track and field events in person, and I'm hoping to watch some beach volleyball."

"That sounds fun; I hope you get to! One last question: I've heard that your seventeenth birthday is the same day as the closing ceremonies. Does that mean we can expect to see you walking in it? We didn't see you at the opening ceremonies."

"Absolutely. We didn't get to walk in opening ceremonies

because of when our competition started. I can't think of a better way to celebrate my birthday," Addison said.

"Me neither. Well, this was a wonderful interview. Thank you, Addison." Mary Margaret switched off the recording app on her phone. "I'm such a huge fan, and you are so talented. I can't wait to see what the future holds for you."

"Thank you. This was my first real interview now that I'm going professional, and you made it easy," Addison gushed as she breathed a sigh of relief.

"I'm thrilled to hear that," Mary Margaret smiled. "Enjoy the rest of your time in Rome, and happy early birthday."

"Thank you," Addison said as Tate stood from the table behind them.

"Not too terrible, huh?" Tate asked as they walked out of the little cafe.

"No, it was actually pretty good. I'm glad we did that one first, because I have a feeling things with Nelly are not going to be that easy," Addison laughed.

"I have a feeling you're right," Tate said. "Just remember, everyone will be able to hear what you say at the next one." She had never been a fan of interviews but they were part of the territory that came with being at the top.

"Oh joy." Addison ran her hands down her face.

CHAPTER TWENTY TWO

"Hey Addison! Welcome, welcome." Nelly motioned her and Tate into the hotel room where she had set up her makeshift recording studio. "I know it's intimidating, but I want you to be comfortable," Nelly explained as she helped her get situated with the mic and headphones before doing a quick sound check.

"First of all, welcome to the All-Around, Addison Jessup," Nelly said as she started the official interview.

"Thank you! I'm so excited to be here. I'm a huge fan of this podcast." Addison never even thought to wish for the chance to be on Nelly's podcast, but now that she was, she was thrilled.

"Well, that's good, because I'm a huge fan of you!" Nelly laughed. "I eventually want to talk about Rome and your experience here, but first let's talk a little bit about your journey to get here. It has not been an easy one."

"No, it hasn't. But being here, in Rome, was always part of my plan," Addison said confidently.

"Oh, I have no doubts after seeing how hard you worked to get here," Nelly said. "You have been competing as an elite gymnast since you were eleven, and your name has always been in the conversation for these Games. Your cousin has an all-around medal, and you train at a gym that produces Olympians. Was going to the Olympics just something you always knew would happen?"

"Definitely not!" Addison responded. "Don't get me wrong—I always wanted to get here, but it never felt like it was guaranteed or that I wouldn't have to work for it. Yes, I watched Tate go to the Olympics, but that meant I knew exactly what it took to get here and just how hard it is."

"I'm sure there were days when you thought you'd never actually get here," Nelly prompted her to continue.

"Absolutely. The last few years have been the worst of my life, and there were so many times it felt like this dream was slipping through my fingers," Addison admitted.

"Let's start with what was probably the worst year. A couple years ago, your mom and brother died in car crash," Nelly directed the conversation with a look at Addison, who nodded, letting her know it was okay.

"Yeah, it was sudden and awful and all the horrible adjectives you can think of," Addison sighed, tears starting to form.

"And to make matters worse, your mom was also your coach. So not only did you lose your mom, but you also lost your coach."

"It was a lot," Addison agreed. "For about a week, I couldn't do any gymnastics, because it just reminded me too much of Mom. Then when Uncle Ray hired Gwyn, I walked out of practice in anger. But now I'm thankful Gwyn was here. I can't imagine this whole experience without her," Addison added, noticing Nelly scribbling something on the pad in front of her.

"Having a former Olympian for a coach would definitely have its perks. But let's talk about your mom and brother again. You've said multiple times that your floor music is a way to honor them. Why is that?" Nelly asked.

"'Fight Song' has been my theme song since I first heard it. For me, it's a reminder to keep going and keep fighting, even when I want to give up." Addison didn't know how many times she had listened to the song in the last two years.

"What are some ways that you keep fighting?" Nelly pushed.

"Well, breakfast food is a big deal in our family. It was my mom's all-time favorite, so it is very common for me to help my grandparents fix breakfast food no matter the time of day whenever someone in my family is missing Mom and Davis. The other big thing that my dad and I do to honor my brother is go to baseball games. Davis played baseball. He loved it, so Dad and I try to go to at least one live baseball game a year." Addison let out a steadying breath. "But the biggest thing for me is tumbling. I will go into the gym by myself, turn up my favorite music, and tumble until I can't anymore." Addison remembered the day after Nationals.

* * * * *

Addison: Age 16 (June of the Olympic Year)

"Good morning, sleepyhead," Julie said when Addison walked into the kitchen.

"What day is it? I feel like I've been asleep for a week."

"It's only Monday, but it is almost two," Julie said with a laugh. "You were clearly exhausted. Let me fix you something to eat. Would you like breakfast or lunch?"

"Can I have pancakes?" Addison asked. Part of being an elite athlete was taking care of her body, and that meant putting the right fuel into it. Pancakes were staple for her because they were carbs, and carbs were fuel.

"Of course." Julie smiled and set about fixing pancakes for her niece. "You are so much like your mom."

"Pancakes were always her favorite," Addison agreed, smiling back.

"You know, one time I watched Ashley eat about ten pancakes in one sitting. In fact, they served them at your parents' wedding." Julie set a plate with two pancakes, a couple boiled eggs, and some fruit in front of Addison.

"You tell me that all the time!" Addison whined, rolling her eyes. They had the same conversation whenever she asked for breakfast at non-breakfast times.

"Yeah, well, never forget: your parents' reception was all breakfast food," Julie told her for what felt like the millionth time.

"Well, breakfast food is definitely one of Dad's favorite things, too. I always know he's missing Mom when he insists on having breakfast for dinner." Addison cut into her pancakes. Julie turned, unable to stop the tears that spilled down her cheeks. Ashley should be here, experiencing this with them. Davis too.

"Aunt Julie?" Addison said and Julie turned back around. "I miss them too." Julie wrapped her arms around Addison, and they cried together. "Sorry," Addison said after a few minutes. "That was not how I meant for today to go."

"Never apologize for grieving, Addi," Julie reminded Addison as she finished eating.

"Can you give me a ride to the gym?"

"Itching to tumble, huh?" Julie laughed as Addison nodded. "Go change. It's about time for me to head that way." Addison managed to find a clean leo, along with a t-shirt and shorts to wear over it. She laced up her tennis shoes and pulled her curly hair up into a ponytail.

"Addi, you ready?" Julie called.

"Have you seen my bag?" She didn't find it in Tate's room or the guest room.

"It's in the garage," Julie said as Addison walked into the kitchen. Julie handed her a water bottle before they walked out the door.

"You didn't have to come in today," Ray told Addison when they arrived at the gym.

"I needed to tumble and get a workout in," Addison said with a shrug as she headed back to the elite gym.

"Just don't hurt yourself. Trials are in less than two weeks," Ray called, but she just waved him off. Addison was thankful to find the gym empty. She hooked her phone up to the speaker and let Lindsey Sterling play as she tumbled. It was the only time the whole world fell away and the pressure to be perfect was gone. She only had to worry about landing each trick and moving on to the next one. When Addison was out of tricks to throw, she collapsed on the floor and let the sobs come.

Most of the time, Addison could keep the grief at bay, but days like today when she should have been celebrating her National Championships win and prepping for Olympic Trials with her mom, it was nearly impossible. She switched the playlist to her memories one and cried until there were no more tears.

* * * * *

"What special ways to honor your brother and mom. And we all need ways to keep our heads clear," Nelly's kind words brought Addison back into the interview. Nelly had tears sparkling in her eyes and didn't wear the pitying look Addison normally saw when this was the topic of conversation.

"Definitely," Addison agreed, allowing a smile to come to her face again. "Tumbling has been that for me for a long time."

"So, two years ago your mom and brother died. Then last year you tore your Achilles in February and were out for the majority of the season," Nelly said, moving the conversation forward.

"Yeah. Like I said, the worst two years of my life." Addison shook her head. "I had been working on my opening tumbling pass, and I had finally conquered the double double. I was in the middle of putting it all together when I crash landed out of the back handspring and completely ruptured my Achilles. We decided the best course of action was surgery, and I was unable to train for months; it was awful. Not only was I was dealing with losing my mom and Davis, but my outlet was gone. I was in physical therapy and actual therapy multiple times a week, and it felt like my Olympic dreams were getting farther and farther away."

"But you made to Worlds Selection Camp," Nelly reminded her.

"I did," Addison nodded. "Uncle Ray and I decided that, because I wouldn't be fully ready for Nationals, it was best not to compete. But I was ready for a later camp, which let me be a part of the Worlds Selection. I was so excited. It felt like my chance to come back and show everyone I could still compete—even if it was just on bars and beam. And I made the team, but as the traveling alternate. I learned a lot about myself and about how to be a team player."

"Like what?"

"Oh, I had to be a cheerleader and watch everyone else, which is not how I normally handle myself at competitions. But it was fun." Addison smiled at the memory.

* * * * *

Addison: Age 16 (October before the Olympic Year)

"You got this!" Addison cheered from the sidelines as her teammates started the beam rotation for qualifications. Addison was able to take part in podium training with the team a couple days before. It felt great, but now her role was to be the team's number one cheerleader. In typical Addison fashion, she knew everyone's routines backwards and forwards. She knew when they needed encouragement and when they were showing off what they could do. As much as she hated being that close to competition and not competing, she was doing the only thing she knew to do for the situation she was in. She spent the day watching and cheering until the final scores had been posted.

"I made the all-around final," Catesby cheered. "I can't believe I actually did it!"

"I can! You've worked so hard, and you deserve this," Addison grinned.

"I couldn't have said it better myself," Ray said, nudging Addi. "You know, if this whole gymnastics thing doesn't work out, you would make a great coach."

Addison rolled her eyes and laughed, "Since Mom isn't here to say it?"

"Because it's true. Look how well it worked out for Gwyn," Ray said.

"Your mom always could spot a great coach. I guess it takes one to know one," Gwyn said. "And Cates, what a day. You were incredible! Congratulations."

"Thank you. All of you," Catesby said. "Team final is next, though. Gotta get that gold."

"Hey Addi. You okay?" Luke asked when he answered his daughter's call the morning of the team final. "It's early, especially for you."

"I know. I just don't know if I'm ready to go cheer for everyone without competing again," Addison said. "I wish Mom was here; she'd know what to say."

"She would," Luke agreed. "I know you would rather be competing, but no matter what, you're a Worlds team member. You're still working towards the Olympics, and right now, that means being the best cheerleader possible. Put on your leo, French braid your hair, and be the coach I know you can be."

"Dad," Addison giggled.

"If you want to make the Olympic team, you're going to have to prove you can be a team player. Acting as a cheerleader when you can't compete is the perfect way to show that."

"You sounded just like Mom," Addison admitted.

"Well, I was married to her for a long time," Luke reminded her. "You can do this."

"Thanks, Daddy. I love you!"

"I love you, too!" Addison hung up and did just what her dad said. She pulled herself together and headed to be the supporter her teammates needed.

"Are you okay?" Ray asked his niece on their way into the stadium.

"I'm great." She smiled and trotted to catch up with the rest of the gymnasts. This was their day, and she was going help them win that gold medal. She cheered, clapped, and gave words of encouragement as the other girls competed. Without the need to keep her mind on her own routines, she was free to spend time staring at the scoreboard and offering encouraging words to everyone. She didn't have to tumble or listen to music once.

"Is she always like this?" Brittnee asked Catesby.

"I've only ever seen her like this at practice," Catesby admitted. "But I've also never been to a competition where she is not competing." Addison smiled. Her dad had been right; she just needed to be a team player.

By the time Brittnee was ready to go on floor, everyone had noticed Addison's attitude change. They all knew she was part of the reason they were one routine away from another gold medal, and she hadn't even touched the equipment. When Brittnee hit her final pose, the whole team erupted in cheers, and all six athletes stood clutching hands, waiting for the score to appear. It appeared, and they all jumped for joy. It was a gold medal for Team USA yet again.

* * * * *

"So how *do* you typically handle yourself when you compete?" Nelly asked as the memory faded.

"Well, I walked right into that one, didn't I?" Addison laughed. "It's not that I don't want to support my teammates," she clarified. "I am just very serious. In order to keep my mind focused on my own routines, I don't pay attention to the scoreboard. I'm typically in a middle split with my headphones in or tumbling to try and keep the nerves at bay."

"That makes sense. You were the alternate at Worlds, but then you dominated competitions this year and even won the guaranteed spot on the Olympic Team. What was that like after the last couple years?"

"It felt so good be back. It was like all the things everyone had been saying about me for years were finally coming true. And I was able to prove what I already knew: that I am the best gymnast in the world," Addison said. When she looked over at Tate to be sure it was okay to say that, her cousin gave her a small thumbs up. This was Addison's moment to shine.

"Best gymnast in the world, huh?" Nelly smiled. "Well,

you've proved that to be true here in Rome. You qualified for all four event finals and have four medals: team silver, all-around gold, vault silver, and beam bronze. What can you tell me about your goals for this Olympics?" Addison looked over at Tate again, curious what she should do. Nelly backed up a little from the mic, attempting to cover it with her hand. "What is it?"

"I just don't know how honest to be," Addison followed Nelly's lead and covered her own microphone.

"Be as honest as you want; the Olympic competition is over for you," Tate said.

Addison let out a breath and readjusted to the mic. "I had some big goal for Rome. While not all of them were accomplished, the biggest one was. I've wanted to win the all-around since I watched Tate win it eight years ago."

"Let's talk about the night Tate won the all-around for a moment. Can you take me back there?"

"I am the biggest gymnastics fan," Addison began. "As an eight-year-old, I was also a belligerent Tate Markum fan. Because I watched her train, I knew every detail of her routines, sometimes even better than she did," she added with a wink at her cousin. "I had seen her come in second in the all-around for three years, and I wanted her to get that medal as much as she wanted to win it. When the final competitor finished and her name stayed in first, I . . . I lost my ever-loving mind. Tate had finally done the thing she had been working towards my whole life. As I watched that gold medal get placed around her neck, I knew I had to have one for myself. I don't really know how to tell you why, but that's what happened," Addison explained.

"Sometimes, moments like those can bring the most clarity," Nelly said. Then she brought the conversation back to Addison's career. "Let's get back to you. You made it through qualifications, and you ladies were set. Team USA was in the lead, you qualified in first for the all-around, and you managed to make all four event finals. The team final is up first, and you fall on bars. Where is your head?"

"I've fallen on bars so many times. I was mad at myself, but in the end, China had a better day. Don't get me wrong: I wish our team medal was gold, but we worked so hard and were glad to medal."

"Definitely," Nelly nodded. "So you recover from the fall at team final and head into the all-around. Did you know you had it in the bag?"

"Pretty much," Addison admitted. "I did my routines the way I had been doing them all year, and I knew I had the capability to come out on top. The top three highest all-around scores of the year were mine before the Olympics."

"You know your stuff," Nelly agreed. "Take me through event finals."

"Vault was a big one for me. I hated vault when I started competing, because I was so small. Earning the silver medal showed me just how far I've come. Bars was always a long shot. The fact that I made the final is still kinda mind-blowing. Beam is beam, so literally anything is possible, but I'm thrilled to have the bronze there. That was always Xiao Mei's gold. And floor . . . I don't know what happened," Addison trailed off.

"That performance was not normal for you. You've only lost on floor one other time," Nelly said. "But we don't talk about that competition, right?" She winked, and Addison laughed.

"No. No, we do not."

"Do you have any insight as to what happened this time?"

"I think I was tired. The Olympics is the longest competition I have been a part of, and over the course of a few days, I competed more than I ever have. It wasn't nerves or pressure, just pure exhaustion," Addison explained, it was the only explanation that anyone had been able to come up with that made any sense.

"You've been competing at a high level for almost a month. I'm sure you were exhausted," Nelly said, smiling sympathetically. "You're here in Rome, on this Olympic team, with your best friend and training partner, Catesby Holland. What it's been like to experience all this with her?"

"It has been absolutely incredible. Being at the Olympics with my best friend has been the greatest experience I could have asked for. We have been talking about it for years, and we worked so hard to go one/two in the all-around final," Addison said.

"That was the plan?"

"Absolutely."

"Tell me about your friendship with Catesby," Nelly urged.

"Catesby and I have been friends for ten years. We are very different but complement each other very well. She has pulled me out of my shell some, and I think I have calmed her down ever so slightly. That's not even talking about gymnastics, where our strengths are opposite. We work together to make each other better gymnasts and better people," Addison explained.

"What is it like to train day in and day out with someone who's on the same level as you?"

"I'm so thankful that I have her so I don't have to do it by myself. Without Cates, I'm pretty sure I would be even more uptight and anxious about everything. But to have someone who is experiencing the same thing I am has been wonderful. Unlike so many people, she gets it and is working towards the same goals," Addison said.

"That's one of those things most people don't think about: having someone who is experiencing the same things. A lot of elite gymnasts are the only ones training in their gyms," Nelly explained for the sake of her audience. "Which is why it's good to go to camps and hang out with other national team members."

"Camp can be hard and stressful, but I love that I get to know other gymnasts," Addison said.

"There has been a lot said about the culture of abuse in gymnastics and how things need to change. What do you think?" Nelly asked cautiously.

"While that has not been my experience, I know that there many gymnasts who have suffered all types of abuse, and that is not okay," Addison said firmly. "I'm so grateful for a coach who puts my well-being above everything else. And there are plenty of changes that could be made to help gymnastics be safer for everyone." She had expected this question. The topic of abuse in gymnastics had received a lot of attention over the last few years, and Brittnee had even switched coaches because of it. When she had heard Brittnee and Scarlett talking about the things that were going on with Scarlett's coaches, she knew it was still an issue for many athletes.

"I'm glad to hear that you have coaches who want what is best for you," Nelly smiled. "Let's talk about how big a gymnastics fan you are, since you've already mentioned it multiple times."

"Oh, I'm the biggest gym nerd you will ever meet. During qualifications, I sat and watched all of the sessions after ours. I have to know who I'm competing against, but I left with a fun set of new skills I wanted to learn."

"Amazing! Thinking of new skills to learn while you are competing in the Olympics." Nelly shook her head jovially. "Can you tell me some of the gymnasts you love?"

"Oh gosh, well . . . I'm friends with Xiao Mei, the Olympian from China. She is just incredible on beam. Arabella Saunders inspired so much of my bars routine. Of course, I'm a huge fan of Brighton Kerry, Coach Gwyn, and Tate. I always enjoyed watching Jenny Scott, Oakleigh Turner, and Camryn Harper. And it has been awesome to get to know Brittnee, Waverly, and Scarlett better because

I have looked up to them for so long. There are plenty of Russian and Romanian gymnasts that I've studied and tried to emulate—too many for me to name."

"You really are a gymnastics fan, aren't you? How did you become friends with Xiao Mei?"

"We met a few years ago at a competition and have developed a friendship since then. She inspired me to take Mandarin for my foreign language so we could attempt to communicate better," Addison grinned.

"I love that!" Nelly laughed. "Do you have a good balance between gymnastics and normal life?"

"Gymnastics is my life. When I'm not training or competing, I'm watching videos and visualizing routines. Tate and Catesby are always reminding me to turn off that part of my brain and have fun. But I've been a competitive gymnast since I was six. I love this sport so much. While I'm not your typical teenager, I can't wait to spend a Sunday watching movies with my grandparents, go to an NC State baseball game with my dad, and hopefully go to a Georgia gymnastics meet with Catesby once the season starts," Addison said.

"That sounds like a lot of fun! I hope you get to do all those things and more. What would you say to young girls hoping to get where you are?"

"Keep going and keep pushing. Set small, attainable goals alongside your big dreams. Celebrate the little wins as well as the big ones," Addison said, listing things she did to keep herself motivated.

"Are those things you do?"

"Yes. I always have goals I'm trying to accomplish, whether it's 'make the Olympic team' or 'do ten beam routines without falling on my Arabian,'" Addison laughed.

"That Arabian hasn't always been your friend," Nelly said, giggling.

"No, but it's a lot of fun," Addison agreed.

"Fun? Flipping on a 4 inch wide beam is fun? That's really

the world you want to use?" Nelly was laughing even harder.

"Yes! It's fun. Not as fun as tumbling on floor, but I like beam . . . for the most part." Addison joined in the laughter, and it took a few minutes for both of them get their laughter under control.

"Sorry; I don't know why that was so funny to me," Nelly said when she finally calmed down.

"I get it; it's beam. It's the event that can make or break a gymnast because of nerves, but I really don't mind it," Addison emphasized.

"You're not wrong, I just can't believe you actually said that about beam," Nelly said again, shaking her head.

"It's true! At least for me," Addison shrugged. "We've talked about so much, including the fact that I have four medals, and you're hung up on the fact I called a skill on beam fun?"

"Okay, okay, I get it. You like gymnastics and are very good at it," Nelly surrendered.

"Very good," Addison said, pursing her lips.

"Oh, this isn't the Addison we usually see," Nelly said, sitting back in her chair to take in Addison's changed demeanor.

"I had a plan for this Olympics, and for the most part, it went according to plan. I couldn't say it before the Olympics because then I would seem cocky and full of myself, but now . . . I've done it. I'm officially the best gymnast in the world. I can finally be sure of myself without worrying about it seeming like I'm trying too hard, because I have medals to back it up."

"Oo, I like confident Addison, and I hope she's here to stay," Nelly said, nodding.

"Me too," Addison agreed. "I'm excited to get to be myself more." This was who she wanted to share with the world: the girl who was confident, sure of herself, and not afraid to go after the things she wanted. Addison was a fierce competitor. She usually knew everyone else's weaknesses and knew exactly what she needed to do to beat them.

"As you should be," Nelly said. "Our time is winding down, so I have to ask: what's next for you?"

"Worlds next year and Seoul. My senior career is just getting started," Addison answered without hesitation.

"I can't wait to see what the future holds for you. You are always welcome on the All-Around," Nelly said.

"Thank you. I'm sure I'll be back," Addison said.

"I'll hold you to it." Nelly ended the recording. Addison thanked her before she and Tate walked out of the room. When they were in the hallway, she breathed a sigh of relief. She was thankful to have the interviews behind her and ready to experience what was next, even if it involved the boy she might have a crush on.

CHAPTER TWENTY THREE

"You good?" Catesby asked Addison as she redid her messy bun for the third time in about ten minutes.

"I think so," Addison sighed. She adjusted her Team USA tank top and jean shorts nervously.

"Oh my word," Catesby said, shaking her head as it dawned on her. "This fidgeting is about Columbus, isn't it?"

"Maybe." Addison reached for her phone. "Let's just go." The girls walked out to meet Ray to head to the track and field stadium for the day. They both were excited about getting to see some other Olympic events, plus both of their families would be joining them.

"Hey Daddy!" Addison exclaimed when she saw Luke. She hugged him tightly before they scanned their tickets and walked in to find their seats. Tate, Julie, and Catesby's family were waiting on them.

"Hey Addi," Columbus said as she took a seat next to him.

"Hey Columbus," she grinned. "Do you know much about what we're going to see today?"

"I think it's sprints. I've heard there are some really

good Americans," Columbus answered. They fell into easy conversation with each other as they watched the races going on. Addison was happy to just get to be around her family and enjoy an Olympic event that she wasn't competing in. Now that her competition was over, the pressure was off, and she could relax.

The two families cheered on Team USA. Zeke Bauer won the gold medal in the 400 meter, and Addison was astonished at how fast he could run.

"This is so much better than any track meet I ever competed in," Columbus laughed as they waited for another race to start.

"When did you run track? Wait, with Davis? When y'all were like freshmen?" Addison asked, clearly confused.

"Yeah, we were suckered into it by our baseball coach. Horrible decision, hence, why we never did it again," Columbus said.

"Well, the baseball thing certainly worked out. Dad and I are planning to come see a few games this season," Addison told him.

"I would love that," Columbus said. He smiled and Addison's heart fluttered. Columbus sitting this close to her with his adorable grin was a little too much. The truth was, if she wasn't sitting, she probably would have thrown some tumbling trick.

The men finished, and it was the women's turn. Addison was excited to see Ruby Meza, who had made headlines for returning to the sport after becoming a mother. Ruby was running the 400 meter and easily won her heat. Addison watched the other heats, chatting with her family while they waited. There were two other Americans who advanced on to the final with Ruby. When Ruby won the 400-meter gold, it was a full American medal stand.

"I wish that could be the case in gymnastics," Addison sighed, still staring at the medal stand.

"Yeah, it would be nice for the best to actually get to compete together," Catesby said, forever hating the two-per-country rule that was a part of gymnastics but not other sports.

"I'm pretty sure it was an attempt to stop the Soviets from sweeping all the events in their heyday," Addison explained, ever the gymnastics expert.

"That would make sense," Catesby nodded as the final notes of the national anthem played. Once the medal ceremony was over, the group headed out of the stadium.

"Today was perfect; thank you," Addison gushed as she hugged her dad again.

"It really was," he agreed before they went their separate ways. "Have so much fun at your photo shoot tomorrow!"

"Is this really happening?" Addison asked, turning to her cousin as they walked to the first official event for Tate as Addison's manager. "I'm going to be in an Olympic stars photo shoot that's going to be on the cover of Sports Now?"

"Yep! You packed all your leos, right?" Tate asked for the fifth time.

"It's the same as the last time you asked. Yes, I have them all. You have my medals, right?" Addison shot back, her lips pursed.

"Okay, I will stop asking," Tate laughed. "I'm nervous too! This is my first major responsibility as your manager."

"Do you know who all is going to be in this shoot?"

"No, but I could probably make some educated guesses," Tate said.

"Do you think I'm going to get to meet Christopher Mann?" Addison thought of the swimmer who had won a bunch of medals.

"Definitely! Breathe, Addi." Tate gently pushed her, since she had stopped moving just outside the door. They walked in, and a girl with short black hair with an all-access pass hanging over her Sports Now polo greeted them.

"You must be Addison. Let's get you to hair and makeup so you can start your day."

"Thank you. This is my manager, Tate Markum," Addison introduced her cousin, who just grinned as the woman handed them both all-access passes. It was the first time Addison had introduced Tate as her manager. And it felt right. The woman escorted the girls past people setting up lights and backdrops on their way to a makeup chair.

"Let's get your makeup done." The woman got Addison settled in front of a mirror with a makeup artist.

"Well, aren't you beautiful? I'm going to just go for a natural look, but it will still probably be more makeup than you're used to," the makeup artist explained as she started color matching Addison. They talked and laughed, the artist making Addison feel comfortable as she worked. "Alright, I'm all done," she declared, moving so Addison could see herself in the mirror properly.

"Wow, that's me?" Addison barely recognized her own reflection. "Thank you," she managed to squeak.

"Of course! Have fun," the makeup artist said as she walked off to work her magic on the next person.

"Hey Addison! I'm going to do your hair," another girl announced as she walked up pushing cart full of hair stuff. "Let's talk about this hair." She tugged at Addison's hair tie.

"It's wild and unruly because of all the curls. My signature style is a French braid," Addison said as the red curls came tumbling out of the bun on top of her head.

"You sure have some hair, don't you?" the hair stylist laughed. "Let's see what we can do with it." After a few vain attempts to tame the curls, they opted for a styled braid that the stylist made look better than Addison ever had. Tate wiggled her eyebrows at Addison in the mirror jokingly.

"Oh my word! I wish I knew how to make a braid look this good." Addison lightly touched the braid. The hair stylist gave her a couple pointers as the woman who initially greeted them walked back in.

"Aren't you stunning? Let's see those leotards," she requested, leading them to a dressing room. Addison pulled out the collection of leos she was given for the Olympics. Her favorite was the blue ombre with sheer silver sleeves complete with red, white, and blue sparkles. It was the one she had chosen for the all-around final, so it was now iconic. A couple of the people in Sports Now polos looked over all her leos and had her try on a couple, but they ultimately landed on the blue ombre, too.

"You look incredible," Tate affirmed as she snapped a picture to send to the family. "You ready for this?"

"I'm a little nervous but mostly excited," Addison said as they followed someone to the green room. Addison looked around the room at the other athletes sitting or milling around, all in uniform or Team USA gear. She recognized a few people like, Christopher Mann and Marlowe Tripp, who were swimmers.

"You're the gymnast, right? The one who won all those medals?" a tall black guy asked as he walked up to meet her.

"Yes, I'm Addison Jessup. And you're Zeke Bauer!" Addison gasped. "I saw you win the 400 meter earlier this week!"

"Well, I'm honored." He flashed his wide smile.

"Hey Zeke, who's this?" a beautiful dark-skinned girl asked, coming up behind Addison.

"I'm Addison. I'm a gymnast," she introduced herself.

"It's nice to meet you, Addison. I'm Ruby. I'm a runner," she winked. "Wait, you have lots of medals, right? You're freaking talented."

"Thank you! I saw you compete the other day, and so are you," Addison grinned. "It was so inspiring to see how much you still have to give to your sport even after you've become a mom." Ruby thanked her, and the pair took

Addison under their wing, introducing her to a couple of the other athletes before someone in a Sports Now polo called the room to attention.

The athletes were escorted into a big room with backdrops and lights. The Sports Now people put each person into position and helped them arrange their medals so they were all visible. Addison stood on a platform that she guessed would be photoshopped into beam or maybe a vault for the final photo. The photographers captured group shots, individual shots, some with the people from the same sports, and a few with the athletes who had won the most medals.

"You okay?" Tate asked when Addison was on a break.

"I didn't know how tiring this would be," she admitted.

"Are you at least having fun?"

"Yes, but it's been a long day." Addison laughed. She enjoyed getting to meet other Olympians, but she had about reached her wall. Thankfully, there were only a few more shots before she was done.

"Thank you for today," Addison said to Tate honestly. "It was an incredible experience, even if I am exhausted." The two girls hugged.

Tate dropped her off at the suite, calling over her shoulder as she left, "See you tomorrow for our sight-seeing adventure!"

"Ciao! I'm Vanessa, I'll be your tour guide for today." An Italian woman greeted the group outside the Colosseum at the start of their sight-seeing adventure early the next day. They all introduced themselves as they stood in line to head inside the giant arena.

"This is so cool," Columbus said as he moved to stand next to Addison. "I heard you had a photo shoot yesterday."

"I did! I'm going to be on the cover of Sports Now. How is this my life?" Addison giggled.

"That's awesome! Was it as cool as it sounds?" Columbus asked.

"Yes. I met Christopher Mann, Zeke Bauer, Ruby Meza, and several other Olympians. It was a long day, but still, it was really cool. I'm excited to see the final pictures," Addison raved, but she was distracted by the ancient building they were standing in. She couldn't believe it had been around for thousands of years.

"Whoa," Catesby's younger brother breathed.

"Right? This place is incredible," Columbus agreed as Vanessa began to explain some of the history. They walked around, snapping pictures and listening to Vanessa, enthralled with the majesty of the Colosseum.

Luke couldn't help but notice how Addison stayed by Columbus's side. He nudged Ray and Julie and nodded towards the two teenagers in front of them. Ray just shook his head, but Julie broke into a wide grin.

"Looks like someone has her first crush," Julie whispered a bit too loudly. Tate spun around to glare at the adults, who burst into laughter.

After the Colosseum, the group headed to the ruins of the Roman forum. Vanessa told them all about how it was the center of ancient Roman life and pointed out a few of the storefronts that would have made up some of the marketplace. Catesby's siblings were asking her all kinds of questions as they walked around the ancient parts of Rome.

Finally, Vanessa led them through the Pantheon before they walked about ten minutes to finish up the morning part of their tour at the Trevi Fountain. "They say if you throw a coin in, you're likely to come back to Rome again someday," Vanessa explained. Every person in the group threw a coin over his or her shoulder, and they all took pictures at the popular tourist site.

"Cates, will you take one of me and Addi?" Columbus handed his sister his phone and wrapped an arm around her shoulders. Addison willed herself to stay calm and to smile as Catesby snapped the picture of the two of them.

"Lunchtime?" Catesby's youngest sister asked, turning to Ginny.

"Lunchtime," Ginny agreed with a laugh. The families headed to a nearby restaurant for pizza and pasta. Catesby's younger siblings were excited about eating something they recognized.

"This is so good," one of the twins gushed as they all ate their lunch.

"I love pizza. It's always my favorite thing to get when we're in Italy," Catesby said. There was an annual gymnastics competition in Jesolo, Italy, that both she and Addison had been to multiple times.

"I love pizza anytime, but it's even better in Italy," Addison laughed, and Catesby reached across the table to high five her.

"Before we go over to the Vatican, I thought you might also like to tour a gelato shop," Vanessa said with a wink, and everyone cheered in delight. She took them around the corner, and they had the chance to learn how gelato was made. They all had samples before deciding to get a few favors for themselves.

"My word, this is amazing," Columbus said, licking his cone of chocolate hazelnut gelato.

"This is the best I've had in a while," Addison shook her head.

"Oh, you have authentic Italian gelato often, do you?" Columbus asked with a nudge.

"Every day, don't you?" Addison looked at him incredulously before rolling her eyes. Columbus reminded her so much of Davis and the fact that they were best friends.

A few hours later, the group was walking through the Vatican. "This place is amazing," Columbus whispered to Addison as they walked towards the Sistine Chapel.

"I just want to look up the whole time. Who knew ceilings could be this cool?" Addison agreed.

"Just wait until we get into the actual Sistine Chapel." Columbus took her hand to pull her along, but when they made it to the chapel, he didn't let go. Addison looked down at their joined hands as her heart flip-flopped in her chest. "Addi?" Columbus caught her attention again, and she realized she missed something.

"What?"

"I asked what you thought about this ceiling," Columbus repeated with a laugh.

"It's incredible," she answered, redirecting her gaze away from their hands and back to the beautiful ceiling Michelangelo painted. "I can't believe someone actually painted it." As they walked around to see the rest of the art housed in the Vatican, Columbus kept her hand in his. His attention was all new to Addison, but she wasn't mad about it. It proved to her that there really was something between them.

"I guess that's going to be a thing now?" Tate asked Catesby, nodding towards Addison and Columbus. They were walking together, holding hands, and whispering.

"Apparently he's been nursing a crush on her for a while now," Catesby explained with a dramatic eye roll. "I think it all came to a head after she won all those medals."

"You're okay with it?"

"It's weird because he's my brother. And I'm terrified that if things go wrong, it's going to ruin our friendship, but she looks so happy," Catesby sighed.

"She does, doesn't she? I think the only reason Uncle Luke is even remotely okay with it is because it's Columbus," Tate said.

"Oh, I'm sure you're right." Catesby shook her head. "This is so weird though, right?"

"Beyond," Tate agreed. "But I'm sure it will get less

weird. At least it did for me when Oakleigh started dating Tyler. But then, Tyler's not my brother."

"Thanks, Tate," Catesby smiled. "Who knows if they are even going to be anything? This is still so new."

"There is that. They have plenty of time to figure it out," Tate assured her.

"They sure do," Catesby agreed, watching her brother and best friend smiling and giggling together.

As they settled back in their room for the night, Catesby tossed a pillow at Addison. "You seemed to have fun with Columbus today," she said.

"I did," Addison grinned. Then she sobered. "Sorry. Is this weird for you?"

"A little, but it's okay," Catesby said. "I can't believe this whole trip is almost over," she added to change the subject.

"I know," Addison agreed, taking the bait. "But we still have closing ceremonies and my birthday to look forward to."

CHAPTER TWENTY FOUR

"Happy happy birthday!" Catesby sang through their room the morning of closing ceremonies.

"Happy birthday, Addi!" the rest of their teammates chorused.

"Do we have closing ceremonies outfits?" Addison asked, ducking her head to hide her smile by digging through her Olympic stuff.

As if on cue, someone knocked on the door. "Good morning! Can you tell me the name of everyone in this suite, please? I have outfits to give you," the Olympic official with a giant pile of bags said. Waverly listed all their names and received a bag for each of them.

"For tonight," Waverly announced as she passed them out. They pulled out the red, white, and blue outfits and laughed at the ridiculousness of them before deciding on the color of shirt they wanted to wear.

"I can't believe this is it," Scarlett sighed. "The Olympics are over. I just got used to the idea of being an Olympian, and now . . . it's just done."

"Weird, right?" Brittnee laughed. "We are all getting

ready to walk in closing ceremonies and then fly home."

"And what? Go back to life as normal?" Scarlett chuckled.

"Apparently," Waverly shrugged. "While I'll miss this, I am excited to get to spend more time with Markus."

"We all better be invited to the wedding," Brittnee insisted, laughing again.

"We're not even engaged yet!" Waverly rolled her eyes. "But yes, of course. You all will be invited to my wedding."

"That's all I ask," Brittnee acquiesced.

"Are you excited about college?" Waverly changed the subject.

"Yeah, I am," Brittnee answered with a smile. "I think it will be good for me. I'm excited about being a part of a real gymnastics team. But first, I think I'm going to have shoulder surgery."

"It's that bad?" Scarlett asked, concerned.

"Oh yeah. I'm still amazed I made it this far without surgery," Brittnee conceded.

"That sucks; I'm sorry," Catesby said.

"As long as it makes the shoulder better, it will be worth it," Brittnee shrugged, rolling her shoulder a few extra times for good measure.

"Last year was awful in so many ways, but surgery was one of the best decisions I made when I tore my Achilles," Addison said. She paused and looked at Catesby, who nodded. There was something they had decided they wanted to do with their teammates. She took a breath and began, "It's our last night, and since we have some time, I wanted to share a tradition we have in my family. We do it for every big trip. It's five questions, and everyone has to answer them. You are allowed use the same answer as someone else, but you have to answer. There is no such thing as a wrong or a stupid answer, so don't worry about it. Do you want to do it?" Addison asked, and they all agreed. "Okay then, first question: what has been your favorite part of the Olympic experience?"

"I love when we do this!" Catesby grinned, kicking off the answers. "Getting to compete in the all-around and winning the bars final."

"I know we didn't win the gold, but I loved the team final," Brittnee said, jumping in with her answer. "It was so close; we *had* to work together. And of course, getting my floor medal."

"This whole experience has been incredible," Waverly said. "I know this might seem weird, but I enjoyed podium training, because there wasn't all the pressure that came with competing."

"Winning the all-around—and getting to be on the All-Around podcast, simply because I've listened to Nelly for so long and the interview wasn't terrible," Addison laughed.

"I'm still jealous you got to do that. I love Nelly," Brittnee said.

"I don't know if I've had the same experience as all of you," Scarlet sighed. "I had all these hopes and dreams, but none of them came true. I have watched all of you compete and medal in the finals. It's been exciting, yes, but it's been hard. So, my favorite part? I guess, by default, team final, because I was actually able to contribute."

"Oh Scar," Brittnee breathed, making up her mind to talk to her again before closing ceremonies. She didn't want to call her out in front of everyone about something that was so personal.

"What is one routine that you will remember forever?" Addison said, continuing the questions. "It can be yours or someone else's. For me, it's my floor routine from the team final and how good it felt."

"Oh, what a fun question!" Waverly exclaimed. "Xiao Mei's beam routine was freaking impressive, especially in the beam final."

"This is hard!" Brittnee said.

"Gold medal winning bars routine," Catesby said without much hesitation.

"Brandon Fischer's Pommel Horse from the final. It was positively beautiful," Scarlett said. "Is that weird?"

"There are no rules, just a routine that you will remember," Addison smiled. "That's the beauty of these questions."

"That routine was beautiful, Scar. Crap, I have to answer, don't I? Um, my floor routine from the floor final, because of the silver medal," Brittnee fumbled.

"What is your favorite thing you did, saw, or ate while you were here?" Addison asked next.

"You do this after every competition?" Brittnee looked between Addison and Catesby.

"After every major trip. In our family, they normally revolve around some kind of gymnastics competition. Or it used to include baseball tournaments, too," Addison explained. Then she quickly answered the question before she could tear up. "I loved getting to be a part of the Olympic stars photo shoot."

"Have you seen any final photos from that shoot?" Waverly asked.

"Not yet. Tate said she will text when she has them," Addison said. "Hopefully soon."

"Getting to explore Rome with my whole family was my favorite thing to do," Catesby grinned. "This is the first time they have all been at a major international competition."

"I love that," Waverly said. "I think my favorite was eating real Italian gelato."

"It's so good, right?" Catesby laughed.

"So good," Waverly smiled.

"Getting to watch opening ceremonies with all of you," Scarlett grinned.

"It was definitely a fun night," Waverly agreed. "Just you, again, Britt."

"Sorry, I'm just terrible at making decisions. I think my favorite was getting to go to the gold medal beach volleyball match," Brittnee said.

"I forgot you did that! How cool!" Addison said excitedly. "The gold medal team was at the photo shoot with me."

"You met all the cool people!" Scarlett threw her hands up.

"I'll introduce you tonight," Addison winked. "What's something you think you will tell your kids about this trip someday?"

"I think we're all going to have the same answer for this," Brittnee said, finally able to answer first. "That I was an Olympian." They all laughed and nodded; Brittnee was definitely right.

"Okay, final question: what about this trip has changed or challenged you?" Addison asked.

"These are some really great questions. It's so cool that you do this all the time," Brittnee said. "I think the biggest challenge for me has been being the leader of this team."

"You have been the best leader," Waverly said with conviction. "I'm so thankful you are the captain of this team. This whole experience has been life-changing for me, because I was actually able to compete and win some medals," she added.

"I think being around all of you and your coaches has changed me," Scarlett said.

"For me, this is one of the first times I've really had to compete with a team, and I couldn't have asked for a better set of teammates. Being here and competing with you has made me a better athlete," Addison said.

"We made a great team, even if we didn't win the gold medal." Brittnee reached over to put a hand on Addison's knee.

"I have been challenged by y'all to be the best version of myself and to compete with strength and grace, no matter what the outcome is," Catesby said, tears in her eyes. "I can't believe it's almost over."

"It may be almost over, but this bond? It's forever." Waverly grabbed Catesby's hand and held it lightly. "Only the five of us have ever experienced this Olympic Games, and we are the only ones who ever will experience them, which is why I'm sure you will all be invited to my wedding, no matter when it is. And next year at Nationals, we'll all be sitting in the audience together, cheering Addison on, and they will show us nine trillion times because that's what they do."

"She's right," Brittnee laughed. "We better get ready for tonight. Wave, you up for one last round of makeup?"

"Always," she laughed.

"Great. Addi and Catesby first." Brittnee watched as the three girls walked out of the room. For just a moment, Addison stood inside the doorway, watching her two remaining teammates, wanting to confirm for herself what was going on with Scarlett.

"Do you want to talk about it?" Brittnee asked as she turned her attention to Scarlett.

"Not really, but also yes?" Scarlett fell back against the couch.

"I'm an open book, Scar, you know that," Brittnee said, wanting Scarlett to lead the conversation.

"I started to realize something was off at Worlds last year, but I won. I was a world champion, so who was I to question the methods that helped me win? But your coaches and Coach Ray . . . they are so different from my coaches. They build their gymnasts up and don't call them names. They value input from the gymnast and actually listen when you talk. The way Addison talks about gymnastics, and that whole exercise we just did . . . my coaches would never—" She ran out of words.

"Look, I've been where you are, and it's not easy to make a change, but it's worth it. Abuse in any form is never okay."

Brittnee hugged her teammate. "I'm here if you need to talk. Anytime."

"Thank you, Britt, for everything," Scarlett said before heading to her room to get ready. Addison turned from the door to let Waverly start her makeup, sitting on the floor front of her.

"Are we wearing Team Silver?" Addison called as she buttoned on her navy-blue outer shirt.

"Yes!" chorused the other girls. She found the silver in the stack of medals and slipped around her neck. They all grabbed a quick dinner before following the stream of athletes into the stadium. They didn't have to wait very long before the flag bearers were let in, followed by all the athletes.

Unlike the opening ceremonies, everyone walked together, which was so much fun. They all took pictures together and danced around the floor of the stadium. People from all over the world were coming up to take pictures with Addison. She couldn't think of a better way to celebrate her seventeenth birthday. Not many teenagers would have even thought about celebrating their birthdays at the Olympics, but for Addison, it was what she had spent her entire life working towards. The experience of being at the Olympics was even better than she hoped it would be. As she walked around the arena, dancing and laughing with her friends, she couldn't stop smiling. This would definitely be a birthday she would remember for the rest of her life.

"This is so cool!" Catesby screamed, looking at Addison, who just nodded. There was so much to take in and so many people, many of whom had Olympic medals hanging around their necks. Everyone all scrambled to get in front of the camera anytime one was nearby.

It was one big celebration; the likes of which Addison had never been a part of before. She was in sheer awe and amazement at all the athletes and all the languages that were being spoken. She lost count of the number of pictures she was asked to be in, proving to herself that she really was one of the stars of the Games.

Eventually, everyone was seated for part of the ceremony. Addison and her teammates managed to get some great seats, which Addison was thankful for. Opening ceremonies had been cool to watch on TV, but this was another level; she was actually in the stadium. They all oohed and aahed, clapped, and cheered when it was appropriate.

"This is so fun!" Addison leaned over to whisper in Catesby's ear. The next thing she knew, she was pulled to her feet to dance along with the music again. She danced and joined in with her friends, thoroughly enjoying herself.

As was tradition, the final medal ceremony for the men's marathon was a part of the program. The whole delegation of athletes cheered them on. It was louder than Addison expected it to be, especially when the gold medal was awarded. The crowd listened to the national anthem of the gold medal winning country in a moment everyone would remember. It was definitely a unique experience, because the marathon runners had all the athletes from the Games cheering them on—athletes who knew exactly how hard they had worked to get to that point.

There was a little more celebration before Italy passed things over to South Korea, marking the beginning of preparations for Seoul in four years. Addison watched with rapt attention, already looking forward to another Olympic competition, knowing how hard she would have to work to get there.

The hosts gave some speeches, thanked the athletes, made the call for Seoul, and extinguished the Olympic flame before one final dance party. Addison and her friends were some of the last ones to leave. The Olympics truly were over, set to begin again in four years with new athletes and new challenges.

As Addison and her friends walked back to their suite for one last night, she took it all in. "Good birthday?" Catesby linked her arm through Addison's.

"The best! It's hard to believe that this is over—that what I've spent my life working towards is finally complete," Addison said.

"On to the next?"

"I guess, but I also want to make sure this moment is celebrated before I move on. We have accomplished so much! Yes, I'm already looking forward to Seoul, but I don't want to just brush over everything too quickly," Addison admitted.

"Wow, look at you! Stopping to acknowledge a victory instead of just plunging ahead to work on something new. I'm so proud of you," Catesby laughed. "I'm sure Coach Ray has a plan. Plus, we still have the victory celebration hosted by the gym once we get home. I can still remember going to Tate's and how special it was."

"Uncle Ray always makes it special," Addison grinned. "Plus, I have a feeling it's one of those things he and Mom talked about."

"Definitely. I'm sure it will have plenty of Coach Ashley flair. I'm excited to see how they will tailor it to us and all the things we accomplished here."

"Me too. I realized that I'm actually excited to have a little bit of time off of training. This schedule has been grueling. I think I've talked him out of full training until January, which is a little crazy, but I think it will be good for me," Addison admitted.

"Me too. I'm not doing full training until I get to Georgia, but I will work out with you until I leave," Catesby assured her.

"Good, because I'm still not sure how I feel about you leaving me. But I know how excited you are." Addison leaned her head on Catesby's shoulder.

"It's going to be so weird without you. And I can't even try to talk you into joining me now that you're pro," Catesby laughed.

"I sure am!" Addison grinned. "I'm excited to sort through offers with Dad and Tate when I get home. Melinda has plenty of them for me."

"I love that you're so happy about it," Catesby laughed. "You deserve everything. I promise, I will support you however I can."

"Thanks, Cates. And for the record, the best part about this Olympic experience is getting to do it all with you."

"One hundred percent. There is no one else I would rather experience any of this with than you." Catesby hugged her. "Not a bad way to spend your seventeenth birthday, huh?"

"I think I can think of some worse ways to spend my birthday," Addison giggled.

"That's true. Will you celebrate with your grandparents when you get home?" Catesby asked.

"Yes, it will be a full week of birthday and Olympic celebrations," Addison smiled, thinking about how excited her grandparents were going to be to celebrate all the highs and work through all the lows with her.

CHAPTER TWENTY FIVE

"Welcome back to the good 'ole US of A," Luke said as he nudged Addison to wake her up.

"We're home?" she asked sleepily.

"Almost. We just landed at JFK. We have to go through customs and then fly to Raleigh," Luke explained.

"Uh huh," Addison groaned, sitting up. "I just want to be home."

"I know, and we're so close," Luke said. They pulled up to the gate, and Addison gathered her stuff. She followed her dad off the plane and made sure she had everything ready for customs.

"Holy crap, you're Addison Jessup! Congratulations," the customs agent exclaimed as he checked her passport. "Welcome home." He stamped it and handed it back. Addison smiled and thanked him, and they made their way to the domestic terminal where they had to go through security again and recheck their bags.

"Food. I need food," Addison said, still exhausted. It had been a month of going non-stop, and now she was really starting to crash.

"I see that," Ray laughed as they walked into the main part of the terminal. "Let's see what we can find to eat." There was a food court not far away, and Addison gave her order before finding a table. She was trying to stay awake when a little girl who couldn't have been more than eight came running up to her.

"Are you Addison Jessup? I watched you in the Olympics!" she said excitedly.

"I sure am," Addison replied, a grin spreading across her face as she shook herself awake.

"Wren . . . " A very attractive man followed the girl over to the table.

"But Daddy, I was right! It is Addison Jessup!" She motioned excitedly towards Addison.

"I'm sorry," the man said looking at Addison.

"It's okay, really," Addison assured him. "Do you want to take a picture with me?" she offered.

"Lysie!" the little girl called, and another girl came running over. "My name is Wren Johnson, and this is my sister, Elyse. Can we both take a picture with you, please?"

"Sure," Addison laughed, moving to stand between the two girls. Their dad snapped the picture and thanked her. "Are you gymnasts?"

"No, but we loved watching you," Wren said.

"Well, I'm glad to hear that. Thanks for coming over to talk to me. It's so nice to meet you, Wren and Elyse," Addison smiled brightly.

"Thank you. You're very kind. I'm their dad, Rett," the man said, extending his hand.

"They're very sweet," Addison answered, shaking his hand. She watched as they ran back over to a couple of boys and a woman with blonde hair.

"What was that about?" Tate sat down next to her.

"The little girl recognized me and wanted a picture with her sister," Addison laughed. "This is so weird."

"Welcome to being a famous athlete," Tate laughed, dropping a French fry into her mouth.

"Food! Thank you, Daddy," Addison exclaimed as she devoured the plate he set before her. They enjoyed time together before getting on the plane home. She had never been more excited to sleep in her own bed.

"Good morning, sleepyhead," Anne greeted her granddaughter the next morning as Addison walked into the kitchen, following the smell of pancakes and bacon.

"Grammy!" Addison hugged her tightly.

"Welcome home, precious girl. You did it!" Anne motioned to the vision board still hanging on the wall.

"I did, didn't I?" Addison grinned. "Where's Granddaddy?"

"He ran to the grocery store because we're out of eggs," Anne laughed. "I didn't think about the fact that your dad has been gone for two weeks, so there isn't any food in this house."

"Grammy," Addison laughed, shaking her head.

"Do you want some orange juice?" Anne asked Addison, who readily agreed and took her normal spot at the table.

"You haven't started talking about the Olympics without me, have you?" Franklin asked as he walked into the kitchen, grocery bag in tow.

"No, I wanted to wait until you were here. Perfect timing," Addison added as she hugged him.

"Good. We want to know everything." Franklin sat down at the table next to her.

"Where should I start?" Addison laughed.

"The beginning," Anne instructed as she set a plate in front of Addison, full of all her favorite breakfast foods. Addison laughed and started with their arrival in Rome. If they wanted to know everything, she was going to tell them everything.

"Tell me about your teammates," her grandfather prompted. "You know we love Catesby, but what are the other girls like?"

"Brittnee and Waverly were the team leaders. Brittnee is so encouraging and was basically everyone's big sister. Plus, she already had Olympic experience, so she knew a lot of the random little helpful things. Waverly pushed everyone to actually be a team. She competed in college, so she understands the team side of things. Then there's Scarlett. . . she's great, but I really didn't get to know her as well. She didn't have the experience she hoped for and was kinda withdrawn most of the time," Addison concluded with a shrug.

"You know, those commentators were saying the same things about Scarlett," Anne sighed. "I felt so bad for her."

"Me too," Addison agreed as she cut into the top pancake on her stack. "What did they say about me?"

"Oh, you know better than to actually care about what commentators say. They are just looking for a good story," Anne said as she casually batted her hand in the air.

"But they sure showed you a lot! I think we saw all of your routines," Franklin grinned.

"Good. They should have! I'm the best for a reason."

"Addi—»

"What? I am! I proved it! I have four medals, including the all-around gold."

"She's not wrong." Franklin looked at his wife, who simply let out a breath, knowing it wasn't worth the fight. Addison continued to take them through her Olympic experience.

"Okay, can we talk about that floor routine? It was beautiful!" Anne said when the conversation made it to the team final.

"I still can't believe that happened! I just knew that everything had to be perfect after the falls and stumbles I had earlier in the day," Addison admitted. "I don't know if I'll ever perform that perfectly again, but it was amazing."

"It certainly was," Franklin laughed. "But they showed your fall on bars over and over. It was the one thing the commentators kept coming back to."

"Really?" Addison shook her head. Why was it that news outlets insisted on showing the worst moments instead of the best? She was the best gymnast in the world, but she fell on bars, so they had to show it to let everyone know that she was mortal. And it was bars, anyway! Not even close to her strongest event.

"Really," Franklin confirmed. Addison shook her head and kept talking, taking her grandparents through the all-around. They told her that the broadcast showed Tate in the stands a lot and talked about her Achilles tear, neither of which were a surprise to her. They talked about each of the finals and how different they were because there was nothing else going on, just that one apparatus.

"We are so very proud of you," Franklin said.

"Thanks; I'm pretty proud of myself," Addison laughed. "Do you want to see the medals?"

"Of course! And I want to see all those gorgeous leos," Anne added. "I loved the blue one you wore in the all-around final."

They worked to get the kitchen put back together. Once it was clean, Addison went to get the medals and the leo collection from her room. They sat down on the couch together and looked through everything.

"Gold, silver, and bronze." Franklin stared at the medals sitting on the coffee table.

"Crazy, right?" Addison couldn't wipe the smile off her face.

"I will never get over these leotards. There is more bling on them than the ones from Tate's Olympic year," Anne laughed. "They are even more beautiful in person."

"Some of the most beautiful leos I will ever wear, I'm pretty sure," Addison agreed. She was so content, sitting curled in between two of the most important people in her life, looking at her Olympic medals and leo collection.

"What are you going to wear to the victory celebration this afternoon?" Anne asked.

"Oh, I decided that a while ago," Addison laughed. It was true; she and Catesby had decided together almost as soon as they had seen the full collection.

CHAPTER TWENTY SIX

"Who said you two could come in?" Gwyn stopped Addison and Catesby at the door of the gym, a wide smile on her face.

"But this is our victory celebration," Catesby said in confusion as people walked past them and Gwyn waved them on.

"It is. Do you have on your leos?" Gwyn asked, and the girls both nodded. "Good. Wait here!" She turned to walk back inside.

"No way! It is August; I am not standing out here in the heat," Addison said, and Gwyn spun back around.

"Okay, fine," Gwyn conceded. "But I'm going escort you to the locker room. Do not look around, and do not come out until I or Coach Ray come get you." The Olympians settled into the locker room and finished getting ready for the celebration.

"Do you have any idea what's happening?" Catesby asked, looking over at Addison.

"I'm as in the dark as you are," Addison laughed. "I

have been thinking through all the celebrations we've been to over the years, but none of them have been the same. Brighton's was all about the excitement of the Olympics. Gwyn's was like talk show, with interviews and clips from the Olympics. Tate's was this triumph of her career and winning the all-around."

"You remember Brighton's?" Catesby asked with doubt in her voice.

"I've watched the video of it. It was one of those videos that was on repeat when I was little. I've always been obsessed with the Olympics, remember," Addison reminded Catesby.

"Of course it was." Catesby rolled her eyes. They continued to talk about what they thought might be going on until the door opened.

"Are you ready?" Ray asked.

"Are you going to tell us what's going on?" Catesby responded.

"We're ready," Addison said, knowing they weren't going to get answers until they walked into the gym.

"Let's go." Ray paused at the door. "We have decorated the whole gym and did our best to honor both of you as individuals, but also to highlight your friendship. You'll have about twenty minutes, and then we'll get the next part started." The girls looked at each other before following him out.

With so many people milling around, the girls were able to blend in for a few minutes as they took in everything their coaches had done for them. The walls were covered in photos telling the story of Addison and Catesby's journeys to the Olympics. Addison marveled at the level they had gone to transform the gym. She saw pictures she knew by heart and some that were new to her. One of her favorites was her at about two in at blue leo with a clipboard and a whistle.

"'A normal sight in the elite gym. Addison's favorite thing to do was help coach the big girls,'" Catesby read. "Some things never change."

"Yeah, well, that's when Mom decided the best thing for me to be when I grew up was a coach," Addison said.

"You are going to be an incredible coach someday." Catesby hip bumped her, and Addison smiled. She knew it, too. Once she was done being a gymnast, she was going to coach, but she didn't want to admit it to everyone quite yet.

They saw pictures from early competitions all the way up to the Olympics. There were family photos, and an entire section paid tribute to the signs Davis used to make to support her at every competition, which Addison was thankful for.

"Two sets of best friends and Olympic teammates. This picture was taken at Nationals last year. Tate Markum and Oakleigh Turner with Catesby and Addison,'" Addison read.

"I forgot we took this," Catesby grinned.

"Well, Nationals was a whirlwind for you last year. But Oakleigh's the best," Addison smiled. "I wouldn't put it past Uncle Ray and Tate to have managed to get her here today."

"Maybe," Catesby said. "But just this is impressive enough. I can't wait to see what Coach Ray has planned." They kept looking around and reading about the photos that had been chosen until Ray and Gwyn called everyone into the main gym. In the middle of the floor, a few chairs were arranged, and Ray waved them over.

"Welcome to the victory celebration for Addison Jessup and Catesby Holland!" he announced, getting everyone's attention. "I hope you got enough time to explore, see, and read all about the two of them. It has been the biggest privilege to be their coach and to get to experience this with them. What Addison doesn't know is that her mother and I have been planning this victory celebration since we planned Brighton's. I know that we all wish Ashley was here with us today, but know that her fingerprints are all over this celebration," Ray said with tears glistening in his eyes. "We're going to start with a video." On the one blank wall, a blue rectangle popped up, and the video started playing.

"That's it, Addi! You can do it!" Ashley's voice filled the gym as a five-year-old Addison flipped across the screen. "First floor pass complete." Ashley's face came into view. The video showed footage of Addison and Catesby at practice and competitions over the years. It showed so clearly how much they had both grown and how deep their friendship was. For three minutes, everyone was able to reflect on the journey the two of them had made.

When the video ended, Ray continued, "I wanted it to feel like Ashley was here with us, and that felt like the most appropriate way. Addison and Catesby are a continuation of what is a becoming an Olympic legacy at this gym. So join me welcoming the rest of our Elite Gymnastics Academy Olympians: Brighton Kerry, Gwyn Sullivan, and Tate Markum." The other three girls joined Catesby and Addison in the middle of the floor. "I have asked each of them to share a little of their Olympic experience with you in addition to one of their favorite memories with Addison and Catesby. And yes, Addison and Catesby, you will be expected to do the same," Ray said before passing the microphone to Tate.

"My Olympic experience was a culmination of everything I had worked so hard for. I finally got the all-around gold, which had felt so unattainable since becoming a senior elite. But little did I know that was just the beginning for me. After my failed attempt to make the team four years later, I started to help Addison become the best version of herself. When Aunt Ashley and Davis died and she tore her Achilles, I did my best to help her through it. I spent many a night reminding her of what she was working towards. And now, I get to support her in the best way possible: I get to be her manager and help her through all the big decisions that are to come." When the applause died down, Tate continued, "Don't worry, Catesby, I haven't forgotten about you. One of my favorite memories of you is when you were working on qualifying for elite. You were struggling on beam and asked me to help you. It took us a little bit, but I helped you get the skill you were struggling with. That was the moment I knew you were going to do great things," she concluded before she passed the microphone on.

"My turn!" Brighton chirped. "My Olympic experience was simply about getting there. I got to compete with the best of the best, and I even made the floor final, which I wasn't sure was possible. I'm glad I got to go, but honestly, my coaching career has taught me the most about myself. I knew I wanted to be a coach when Coach Ray allowed me to come work here when I finished college. Addison was in one of my very first classes, and she was always pushing me to teach her more. That was the summer Tate taught her a back handspring, and she was so excited. I haven't gotten to coach Catesby yet, but I can remember the first time I met her. I was home for a little while, and Addison talked me into coming to the gym to see her newest floor routine, and Catesby was there. I got to see her do one of her first elite bars routines, and I was so impressed. Then I got to talk to her and realized that she was this fun, bubbly person. I got see Catesby encourage and push Addison to be a better gymnast and teammate. That's when I knew that, together, they could do just about anything," she finished.

"I get to go last, because I have had the pleasure of coaching these girls for the last year and half," Gwyn began when she received the microphone. "Since I have to talk about my Olympic experience, first, I'll say that the biggest thing it did was prepare me for this one. I worked so hard to get to the top, and winning the beam gold felt like a pipe dream, but I did it, and I lived to tell the tale. I went to college on a gymnastics scholarship and learned even more about myself and the sport. I got a job at a gym in the town where I went to college, and I loved it. I was able to pour everything I had learned into new gymnasts.

"Then one day, my mom called to tell me that Coach Ashley had died with her son and that there was going to be a celebration of Ashley's life at the gym. I dropped everything to come back to honor the woman who shaped me into the coach I was becoming. I got to have a conversation with Coach Ray at the celebration of Ashley's life and fill him on my life. Little did I know that, just a few months later, he would offer me a position at the gym, and I would find myself accepting.

"To say that it went over like a lead balloon would be an understatement. My first day on the job, Addison walked out of the gym, and Catesby cried through that first practice. Two weeks later, when Addison tore her Achilles in training, I began to lose hope that Addison and I would ever truly connect. But on the bright side, Catesby and I were getting along swimmingly. We clicked almost instantly, and she reminded me so much of myself. We are motivated in so many of the same ways," Gwyn said with a smile in Catesby's direction. "But getting to go to the Olympics with them was truly life-changing, for all of us. We connected and bonded over our Olympic experiences and the pressure that comes from being the one everyone expects to win." Gwyn nodded at Addison knowingly as she wrapped up her speech and handed her the microphone.

"I don't know how in the world I'm supposed to follow that," Addison said with a gulp, "But I'm so incredibly thankful for Gwyn and Uncle Ray guiding us through the last month. Getting to be an Olympian and win medals for my country has been everything I hoped it would be and more. I am finally the best gymnast in the world, just like Davis always said I would be. I've spent a lot of time thinking about my friendship with Catesby over the last few weeks. I know without a doubt that Catesby's friendship is important to me. I could not have asked for a better person to experience all of this with than her," Addison explained. She hugged her best friend as she passed off the microphone.

"This is all a little overwhelming," Catesby said, laughing, though tears were shining in her eyes. "And while I have never been a person who is short on words, I want to careful with the ones I choose. Becoming an Olympian is a dream I never fully believed would come true. I hoped, prayed, and worked so hard. When Coach Ashley and Davis died months before Addison and I were set to become seniors and get ready for the Olympics, I really didn't think it would happen. But God, in goodness and grace, brought Gwyn into my life to help me get across the finish line. I couldn't have done any of it without Coach Ray, Coach Ashley, and Addison, either, who have helped me become the best gymnast I could be," Catesby said, the tears streaming down her face by the time she finished speaking.

Ray took the microphone back from Catesby to move the program along. "Thank you all for sharing your stories with us. We are so grateful that you were chosen to represent not only America but EGA in the Olympics. I have another video that showcases all our Olympic athletes, especially the latest ones," he said as the lights dimmed and a video of all the Olympic routines played. Once it was over, a spotlight hit the giant poster of Brighton with "Olympic Team Member" printed on the bottom. Gwyn's poster lit up next, with "Balance Beam Gold, Team Silver, Floor Exercise Bronze" printed on it. Then Tate's poster lit up. It read, "All-Around Gold, Balance Beam Gold, Team Silver, Floor Exercise Silver, Vault Bronze" beneath a photo of her on the balance beam.

Then, with a drumroll, the final two posters were lit up. Catesby's poster dropped first. It was a photo of her at the bars final, flying between the bars. Printed on the bottom, it said, "Uneven Bars Gold, All-Around Silver, Team Silver." Addison's poster unfurled to reveal a photo of her flipping on floor from the all-around final with "All-around Gold, Team Silver, Vault Silver, Balance Beam Bronze" printed on the bottom.

"As I explained at the beginning, this celebration is something Ashley and I had been planning for a long time," Ray continued when the applause died down. "We talked about a variety of different things, but we always came back to one theme that would have to be a part of any celebration of Addison and Catesby: family. Family was at the core of this journey." Ray paused, clearly fighting off tears. "Now, I get the honor of passing the mic to some very important people: Luke Jessup and Ginny Holland."

Luke spoke first. "I think the first time Addison said she wanted to go to the Olympics, she was about three, and nothing's really changed in the last fourteen years. I have seen her give everything and make sacrifices that normal teenagers would never make, all in pursuit of her goal. When Ashley and Davis died, there was about a month when I was worried the dream died with them, but gymnastics became Addison's safe haven— at least until the months she couldn't do it anymore, thanks to her injury. But she overcame that challenge too, and came out the other side a stronger person and gymnast. I'm so proud to be your dad, Addi," Luke concluded. He hugged his daughter and passed the microphone off.

"In our family, we believe that God has gifted each of us uniquely with gifts to honor and glorify Him," Ginny Holland began. "It has been a true pleasure to see Catesby flourish in hers. Catesby was bouncing and flipping off all our living room furniture from the time she could walk, so we decided that gymnastics was the best place for her, and it has been the biggest blessing. She has grown into herself and become more of who God created her to be with every passing year. Our family is big and loud. You can always tell when we're around, but we push each other to be the best versions of ourselves. We do things together and love hard—Catesby most of all. We are so grateful for all the people here who have shaped our girl into the incredible young woman she is today," Ginny finished, and she handed the microphone back to Ray.

"Thank you both for sharing your daughters with us. Enjoy this video of our EGA family," Ray said, and another video played. This one was full of family moments and photos of both Addison and Catesby's families. After about a minute and half, it transitioned to show pictures from other EGA teams and their families. "We are so thankful for the legacy that has continued with Addison and Catesby. We can't wait to see what the future holds. Thank you for joining us for this victory celebration today." Ray dismissed everyone to enjoy the refreshments the gym had provided. Addison and Catesby spent the next little bit signing autographs and taking pictures while the gym cleared out. Once everyone was gone, both families headed to the Holland's house for a more intimate celebration.

"You did it," Brighton cheered, hugging Addison as they walked into the house. "You were spectacular. I'm a little sad I won't be able to talk you into joining Catesby at Georgia, but I can't wait to see what the future holds for you."

"Thanks, Brighton, for everything," Addison said.

"There you are," Columbus said when he walked around the corner and spotted Addison. "Sorry, I didn't mean to interrupt."

"It's okay. Columbus, this is Brighton. Brighton, this is Columbus, he's—well, he's Catesby's brother," Addison fumbled for the right words to describe her relationship with the boy standing next to her.

"Okay then. It's nice to meet you, Columbus." Brighton shot a questioning glance at Addison.

"You, too. My sister is a big fan," Columbus said.

"I'm a big fan of hers. In fact, I'm going to go find her," Brighton announced as she walked off, leaving the two of them alone.

"Catesby's brother? Really, Addi?" Columbus questioned.

"What else am I supposed to say?" Addison shot back defensively.

"What about your friend? I am your friend, aren't I?" Columbus raised an eyebrow.

"Of course you're my friend, Columbus." Addison touched his arm. "But with the way you acted in Rome, I just . . . I don't know where we stand," Addison finished lamely. She fought the urge to tumble.

"Come with me." Columbus pulled her on to the back porch so they could have a private moment for themselves. "I want to be able to talk to you without everyone interrupting and hearing us."

"Thank you," Addison said. Her heart was in her throat, unsure of how this was going to go.

"Here's the thing: I like you. I really do," Columbus reached for both of her hands, and Addison waited on the inevitable drop. "But I'm getting ready to go to college, and you are about to throw yourself back into gymnastics. I just don't know how it can work."

"Columbus," Addison sighed. "I like you too."

"It sucks, I know." He pulled her into a tight hug. "You are talented, brilliant, and beautiful. But I also would never want to do anything to jeopardize your relationship with Catesby, especially since I know she's going to be headed to Georgia next fall. I want you to enjoy senior year together, your relationship with her is too important."

"Why is this so hard?" Addison put her forehead against his chest. "I know it doesn't make sense for us to date, but I really do like you." She looked up at the first guy she had been able to have a crush on, her best friend's brother, and took a deep breath as she stepped out of his embrace. "We're still friends, though, right?"

"You're not getting rid of me that easily," Columbus laughed. "Besides, you promised to come watch some of my baseball games."

"I can't wait to see you play college baseball," Addison grinned.

"And I can't wait to see where gymnastics takes you next—Worlds, Seoul, and everywhere in between." He kissed her forehead. "You are going to Seoul, aren't you?" For some reason, at his question, the memory of Tate's attempted comeback played through her mind.

* * * * *

Addison: Age 12

"Come on, Tate," Addison whispered through her fingers, which were covering her face. Tate had just fallen off the beam. It was her signature event.

"She's finishing," Julie said. Addison braved another look at her cousin, who was climbing back onto the beam.

"I guess that means she's hanging out with us during the Olympics?" Davis looked at his aunt.

"More than likely." Julie let out a long sigh.

"Come on, Tate," Addison said again, trying to block them out and focus on the end of Tate's routine. Full spin with no wobble, ring leap, back tuck, choreography to the end of the beam, deep breath, back handspring, back handspring into a double twisting layout with a deep bend but no fall. Addison jumped up and cheered loudly; Tate had finished strong.

A few minutes later, Tate waited for her turn on floor. "I can't believe this is it," she said as she waited.

"Give them a show," Ray grinned, his eyes twinkling. Tate hugged him and then Ashley before rushing up the steps. She received the start signal and left everything out on the floor. She knew this was going to be her last time competing. She nailed her routine; in fact, it was one of the best Addison could remember her doing. When she finished, she received the sendoff of a standing ovation that shut down competition for a couple minutes. But no one cheered louder than Addison, who had never been prouder. When the Olympic team was named at the end of the night, no one was surprised when Tate's name was not called.

* * * * *

"Oh, I'm going to Seoul," Addison insisted, crossing her arms and pursing her lips. Columbus laughed and let her head back inside. Now that she knew where things stood between the two of them, she could let herself focus on her future again.

Tate's comeback hadn't gone the way she had hoped. But Addison wasn't Tate, and her experience would be different. Addison had no intention of pausing her gymnastics career—not when she was just getting started. She had accomplished so much in her short seventeen years on the planet, but there was still so much more to accomplish: Worlds medals and another Olympic team to make in four years. Dreams had come true, but there were always more dreams waiting around the corner, and for Addison, the dreams were always Olympic.

GLOSSARY

I realize that not everyone is what is known in the gymnastics community as a "gym nerd." Since you might not know all the different gymnastics terms, I'm including this glossary for you. But there is also one on my website if you are someone who needs visuals. You can find it at ruthannecrews.com/gymnastics. I want you to be able to know what's going on, so here we go:

Let's start with some questions you might be asking:

- ***What is elite gymnastics?*** *Elite gymnasts are those who complete at the highest levels of international competition. In the US, to be considered an elite, a gymnast must go through the numbered levels that end in 10 and pass an elite compulsory test to show that they can compete the necessary skills.*
- ***Is there a difference between junior and senior athletes?*** *The only difference is age. For women, most junior elites are between 12 and 15, but every now and then, an 11-year-old will sneak through. To be considered a senior elite gymnast and be eligible to compete at major international competitions like the Olympics and Worlds, you have to be turning 16 sometime that year. In the US, most of the men who make up the senior team are at least 18, but they can be as young as 16.*
- ***What does it mean to petition?*** *Gymnastics is a sport that, by nature, has a lot of injuries. When a gymnast is unable to compete in a qualifying competition, they can petition to be allowed to compete in the next qualifier for the event they are trying for, like Nationals or Olympics Trials, based on their previous scores.*
- ***How is gymnastics scored?*** *There are two parts that make up an elite score: the D score and the E Score. The D score is the difficulty score, and it is calculated based on the elements that a gymnast puts into his or her routine. The E Score is the execution score, which is out of ten. It is calculated based on how well a gymnast executes or performs the elements in the routine. Currently, a high score is in the 14s or 15s, and a low score is in the 11s or 12s.*

- ***What's the deal with going pro?*** *Gymnastics is weird sport where the female athletes have traditionally competed the highest levels before they go to college. This means that, instead of going to college and then going pro, many gymnasts have chosen to turn professional first, which requires giving up their eligibility to compete at the collegiate level. Going pro for a gymnast simply means that they can take the cash prizes that come at some of the events and have endorsement deals. The Name, Image, Likeness (NIL) Deal has provided a way for some gymnasts to compete in college while profiting off themselves without having to go fully pro.*
- ***What is with all the chalk?*** *Chalk is a way that gymnasts combat the sweat and friction that comes from competing at the highest levels. The chalk absorbs some of the sweat so they can have a better grip on the apparatuses and combats the friction so they can glide more smoothly on events like bars and beam.*
- ***What is an inquiry?*** *An inquiry is an appeal submitted by the coaches when an athlete's score comes back lower than expected. It is essentially asking the judges to re-score the routine in hopes of a higher score. Typically, an inquiry comes when, like in Addison's case, the coach thinks the judges missed an important element in the routine, and they want their athlete to get credit for the full difficulty of the routine. It must be done quickly and requires $200 in cash to get it done.*

Women's Artistic Gymnastics is made up four events or apparatuses. Here they are in Olympic Order:

Vault: Where a gymnast runs full speed towards the vault table, hits a springboard before the vault table, and then launches off the table onto the mat. Here are some of the terms that have to do with vault:

- Yurchencko - most common type of vault; a backwards entry to the table before flipping off of it
- Double Twisting Yurchencko or Yurchencko Double Full - a vault where you twist your body around twice before landing on the mat.
- Amanar - a vault that requires you twist your body around two and half times between pushing off the table and landing on the mat.
- Cheng - a vault where you go onto the table facing forward and twist

one and half times before landing on the mat.
- Rudi - a handspring vault where you twist one and half times.

Uneven Bars: Two bars set at different heights. The high bar is about eight feet high, and the low bar is about five and a half feet high. The gymnast must use both bars. In many countries, including the US, gymnasts use grips on bars to help them stay on better. Here are some of the terms that have to do with bars:
- Giant - a straight-body full lap around the bar, typically used to gain momentum for bigger releases or the dismount.
- In-Bar Stalder - circles around the bar around with legs in a straddle position
- Pak - a transition to the low bar from the high bar where the gymnast flips and grabs the low bar
- Tkathev - a release move that goes over the bar in a straddled position before having to grab the bar again.
- Gienger - a release that starts as giant with a back flip with a half twist
- Jaeger - basically the opposite of Gienger; instead going backwards, the gymnast goes forward.
- Shaposh half - a transition from the low to high bar where the gymnast circles around the low bar before swinging back up to the high bar with a half twist so she lands facing the outside of the bar.

Balance Beam: A ten-centimeter-wide beam covered in suede on which a gymnast has to spin, leap, and tumble in multiple directions. A beam routine is 90 seconds long, and there is a warning bell that sounds when there are ten seconds left. Most gymnasts typically begin their dismount when they hear the warning bell. Here are some of the terms that have to with beam:
- Candle Mount - when a gymnast dives backward over the beam and lands with their arms wrapped about the beam & their legs straight up in the air.
- Acro Series - in elite gymnastics, there is a requirement to have three acrobatic elements—tumbling moves, like things you could see in a floor routine—in a row
- Back Handspring Layout Stepout Layout Stepout - a very common

acro series where gymnasts do a back handspring and then two more back flips landing one foot at a time.
- Side Sumi - a sideways aerial where the gymnast grabs her leg and lands facing sideways
- Arabian - a back flip with a half-twist into a front flip
- Sheep Jump - a gymnast kicks her legs up at the knees and throws her head backwards
- Ring Leap - split leap in which the gymnast's back leg comes up and her head is thrown back so that she makes a ring with her head and leg
- Sissonne - a split jump where the gymnast lands on one foot
- Wolf Turn - a full turn done were a gymnast crouches down with one leg out and turns around the squatted leg; can be a single, a double, or a triple turn.
- Double Y Turn - two full turns with one leg lifted into the air so that the body and leg make a Y shape.
- Flourishes - arm movements made to help choreography

Floor Exercise: A routine set to instrumental music typically with four tumbling passes in it. Many of the terms that go with Balance Beam can also be done on the floor.

Men's Artistic Gymnastics is made up of six events or apparatuses. Here they are in Olympic Order:
- Floor Exercise: Basically the same as women, except with no music
- Pommel Horse: A horse with two handles on which the men turn and scissor around and around
- Still Rings: straight and precise body positions while holding on to the rings
- Vault: the same as the women
- Parallel Bars: two side by side bars that they flip through and handstand above
- Horizontal (High) Bar: The single bar that they swing around and do releases above

ACKNOWLEDGEMENTS

Megan Lawrence, my fearless editor, thank you for continuing to shape my writing and make it the best it can be!

Chase and Jordan Parker, thank you for the fabulous headshot. You know how to make a girl look good!

Megan Stroud, Becca, and Mary Sanders, my fearless cover designers. I can't thank you enough for your vision in helping me have the best cover possible! And Mary Claire, for truly capturing my vision and helping me with this process!

The Gymcastic Podcast, for being my one-stop-shop for all my gymnastics research or at least pointing me to the places for my research.

Kerry Bair, for all your help with making sure that I talked about gymnasts and food properly. I know it's a sensitive topic but I also know that athletes have to fuel their bodies properly.

Dr Jordan Knoefler, I cannot thank you enough for looking at the Achilles tear and helping me make sure I was accurate with healing time and recovery!

Katie Schmeltzer, Did you ever think that when you were editing all those papers in high school that one day you would be editing my book? Thank you for lending your expertise for the final polish.

Anna Schaeffer, I genuinely can't thank you enough for all the help, support, and encouragement you have given me through this process. I couldn't ask for a better writing buddy, critique partner, and overall cheerleader. I can't wait until the next one, whoever's book it might be!

To everyone who read a version of this book, I cannot thank you enough. You were a vital part of this process.

Meredith Toering, who named the Chinese gymnasts for me. Thank you, Mei, for giving me Xiao Mei.

Victoria Swilling, who even though she decided not to be a doctor, was gracious enough to allow me to use her name for Addison's doctor and answered my medical questions.

Bethany Cromie, who named so many of the other characters in this book. Thanks for putting up with me through this whole journey.

Mary Margaret Watt, the queen of the questions. I could not have interviewed Addi without your help.

Anna Claire Jones, thanks for always listening to my "gym nerd" rants and being willing to watch any gymnastics meet with me

Elizabeth Cook, for reading the very rough first draft of this book--I couldn't have done it without you.

Camryn Kile and Maddie Britt, my teenage fan club who have Roses more times that I could and read an early version of this story. I'm thankful to have you to write to!

Mama and Jim, I don't have words to express all the things I need to say but I'll settle for thank you. I couldn't do this without your support, wisdom, and encouragement.

Daddy and Piper, Thank you for everything! I'm so grateful for your support and encouragement.

Joshua, Cammie, Charlie, John, and Sarah, while the boys might read this one either, I know that you both will, so tell them thank you for me. I can't tell you how much your support means to me. Thanks for being the best sibling crew there ever was.

Gram, when I was deciding on character names, the easiest one was her coach who I knew had to be named after Paw Paw. I hope you see him on the pages of this book like I tried to do. Your love and support mean everything to me, here's another book for you to share with your friends!

Mimi, Book 2! Here's another one for you to add your collection and share with all your people. I could not have done this without your support, moral and financial. Thank you for all words of wisdom and encouragement, I know I always have you in my corner.

KK, I'm so very grateful for your support and love. Thank you for all your encouragement!

Travis, you have jumped in and helped with things that you never expected to and I'm genuinely grateful for your support and guidance… even if it's just offering your opinion.

The rest of my family (Addi, Shanna, Curt, Jason, Kasey, Annabelle, Luke, Susan, Nathan, Collins, Clara, Ty, Uncle Charlie, Aunt Kelly, Uncle Brooks, Aunt Jolee, Uncle Richie, Aunt Amy, Mallory, Erika, Susannah, Jacob, Jake, Charlie, Julia, Matt, Mabel, Jackson, Brooke, Tori, Hunter, Beckett, Carter), I couldn't do this without you cheering me on!

Natalie Dixon, Susan Sanders, Beccy Clark, Phyllis Rogers, Wendy McLeod, Leah Glow, Carol Charles, Cath Lynn Lanier, Mitzi Adkinson, Lesli Todd, and the rest of my mom's friend group: My second moms who have spent time praying over this book, I cannot express how thankful I am to have you in my life and in my corner.

My Students, who fell in love with Columbus and helped me describe the characters, I'm so grateful for all your help, support, and love. I hope you enjoy the final product!

My Roof Lizard Fam (Lauren, Davis, Hoyed, Griffin, Shepard, Steve, Dana, Natalie, Haley, Jaycee, Tommy, Lisette, Rachel, Kim, Hugh, Owen, Jay, Ivy, Anna, Olivia, Megan, Clay, Beau, Hart, Chase, Jordan) You are the true definition of community and I'm so thankful for your prayers and support!

Byne Christian School and Greenbriar Church, thank you for helping me find community back in Albany and supporting me in all my devours. It's because of you that I know I'm in the place I'm supposed to be doing the thing that I'm supposed to be doing.

Mr. David and Mrs. Cathy Lynn, Working at Plantation Gallery has been the biggest unexpected blessing and I'm so thankful to have both of you in my corner, cheering me on.

The NC Crew, I miss you all so very much and I'm grateful for your continued support. There is a reason that I chose to make her gym in North Carolina. I can't wait for you to read this one!

Cynthia Merrill, Kath Richards, Rebecca Caz, and the rest of The Writing Team members, I'm so very grateful for each one of you and how you have helped me learn about myself, my writing process, and strengthened my craft.

My Readers, I write for you. It means the world to me that you would pick up a copy of my book when you have so many options. I don't take for granted your time and imagination that you spent on me. Please keep reading and supporting authors like me!

"Now to Him who is able to do immeasurably more than all we ask or imagine, according to His power that is at work within us, to Him be glory in the church and in Christ Jesus throughout all generations, for ever and ever! Amen" (Ephesians 3:20-21, NIV)

AUTHOR BIO

Ruth Anne Crews is an upper elementary school teacher who wants to inspire a love of reading in her students and everyone else in her life so she writes the stories for them. When she's not teaching her students about how much God loves them, you can find her listening to a podcast or Taylor Swift. She loves all things pop culture and superheroes. She lives in her hometown in South Georgia surrounded by family. Follow along with all her adventures on Instagram @ruthannecrews and on her website, ruthannecrews.com

www.ingramcontent.com/pod-product-compliance
Lightning Source LLC
Chambersburg PA
CBHW010345220726
48290CB00016B/2641